THE COLUMBINE EFFECT

How five teen pastimes got caught in the crossfire
And why teens are taking them back

THE COLUMBINE EFFECT

**How five teen pastimes got caught in the crossfire
And why teens are taking them back**

Beth Winegarner

Table of Contents

Introduction

During his teenage years, David was miserable. He felt bored and powerless. He watched as his classmates turned to drugs, shoplifting, and other illegal activities to escape their boredom. Instead, he played video games, particularly horror games and first-person shooters such as *Diablo II* and *Counter-Strike*.

In video games, all players start out in the same place: level one. Through hard work and hours of dedication, they rise through the ranks. Their characters become more capable and powerful. Sure, the challenges mount, but practice has earned them plenty of skill.

Through games, David's self-esteem flourished. In online games, he discovered that players didn't judge him by his appearance; they couldn't see what he looked like. Because so many online games are team-based, he was able to make friends and accomplish tasks with them. They shared victory as well as disappointment.

However, during hard times David disappeared into gaming. His grades suffered. "I stopped talking to friends who weren't gamers. My parents were mad as hell," he said. "They did everything they could think of to try and stop me, but I always found a way to game."

His parents' efforts were not only fruitless, they built a wall between David and his family. The gaming world became his only source of solace and support.

Then, one day, he got a car, and things began to turn around. David could leave the house and go visit friends. Sure, he visited the friends with whom he played online games, but it was a chance to socialize face-to-face rather than behind the screen.

"Things consistently improved from that point. I worked

hard in college, and loved it. Then I got jobs that I enjoy even more," he said. Still, he loves and defends the games that provided him so much relief.

"I always get angry when game addiction is blamed as the cause of suicide, divorce, and school violence, because I am certain that the game addiction is a reaction to misery, not the cause. It is possible that the gaming addiction ultimately makes the problem worse, but it's not the original cause. And people who choose to end their lives, or attack others are more likely deeply disturbed in many aspects of their lives. Gaming may be their last retreat."

Bonnie* was a teenager when her mom told her she was evil and kicked her out of the house. It wasn't because Bonnie was misbehaving, mistreating her family, or doing anything illegal. It was because she had discovered a new faith.

Growing up, Bonnie's family was Catholic. They didn't attend church regularly, but her parents' beliefs informed the family's day-to-day lives. At first, her mom seemed open-minded about spirituality. "[She] strongly believed in never forcing a religion on anyone, including her daughter. I believe that I am especially lucky for that, because it gave me time to realize and research religions in an open manner," she said.

However, there were limits to that open-mindedness. When Bonnie discovered Wicca, a nature-based pagan religion that teaches members to do no harm, her mother balked. Tension mounted between them, and Bonnie's mother kicked her out more than once because they disagreed over issues of faith.

Each time, she was allowed return: "I have nowhere else to go." However, at home, her mother doesn't allow the most basic tools of Bonnie's religion, including books and pentacles. "It upsets me, because I don't look down upon her beliefs," she said.

Despite these tensions, Bonnie feels Wicca is the right path for her—"my true calling." It encapsulates the peace-loving feelings she has fostered her whole life. For her, Wicca feels like coming home.

---

*   Not her real name.

Tara was 17 when she and her boyfriend—both longtime heavy-metal fans—scored tickets to see Ozzfest heavy metal festival in Atlanta, a few hours away from her home in Tennessee. She told her mom where she was going, packed a bag, and traveled south to rock out. When she returned, with her long-haired boyfriend standing beside her, her mom told her to leave and not come back.

The couple stayed with friends for as long as they could hold out, but Tara returned home when she ran out of options. Her mom let her in, but the two never discussed the incident—or any of the tensions between them. That tension only fueled Tara's love of heavy-metal music.

"The words are very easy to decipher when you are a lost and angry teenager: perseverance, not stepping down, dealing with love you can't have or have lost," she said.

Tara's behavior got worse. She drank frequently and ran away from home several times, ultimately moving out during her senior year of high school. Before long, she had checked herself into rehab to try to clean up her life. "I couldn't feel anything but anger and regret," she said.

She got pregnant toward the end of her teens, giving birth to a baby girl. As a mom and metalhead, there are times she regrets that her mother didn't show more interest in her life —particularly her interest in the music that comforted her most. "You want your child to feel like you care, and a lot of times they express feelings of angst through music," she said.

I'm Not a Juvenile Delinquent

"Teenager" is a relatively new concept: psychologist G. Stanley Hall first recognized adolescence as a separate period of human development in 1904. But teenagers didn't really came into their own until the 1950s, when the first baby boomers reached that precarious age. They were the first generation of teens to have cultural options to call their own, including rock and roll and comic books.

With the rise of teenage culture came the rise of parental worrying over that culture. Many rock songs—

particularly those performed by black artists—were blacklisted from radio stations. The United States Senate held hearings to explore the relationship between comic books and juvenile delinquency, a move that would be echoed by the Parents Music Resource Center 30 years later. Despite these roadblocks, comics and rock music became increasingly popular among 1950s teens, birthing the tension between parents and kids now known as the generation gap.

For each subsequent generation, teen culture has grown a little wilder, a little more transgressive. Music, films, books, and games explore ever-darker topics. There are many reasons for this. For starters, society itself is increasingly complex, and teens are asked to face troubling topics, from street violence to HIV, at earlier and earlier ages. In addition, teens are always looking for something to set themselves apart from their parents. Something that will shock and offend. If adolescence is about nothing else, it's about striking out on your own. It's about creating a self that is independent from parents and the culture that came before. Many teens do this, either accidentally or intentionally, by finding interests that surprise and anger their parents.

And yet, many adults seem to forget they did these same things. They look at teens and wonder what is going on. Why is the music so loud? Why are the games so violent? Why are the songs so graphic? They think these influences can't possibly be safe or healthy. And so they clamp down. Newspapers link these influences to juvenile crimes without evidence, cementing adults' fears. Over time, adults not only mistrust the influences, they begin to mistrust teens themselves.

In each of the stories that opened this chapter, a teenager had found something—music, spirituality, gaming—that provided comfort. A lifeline. A way of connecting with him- or herself, and at times, connecting with like-minded peers. And in each case, adults acted in precisely the wrong way.

Of course, the mistrust between adults and teens works both ways. Yes, teens often go out of their way to hide their lives from their parents. They refuse to talk, and they get surly when pressed. That's part of growing up. That means it's often up to parents to do the tough work of staying engaged—even when they're being thwarted at every turn—and studying up on what their kids are doing. It's also up to parents to react with an open mind (and not believe everything they read in the papers) when their teen shows interest in something offbeat.

Our culture is rife with situations in which teens were publicly misrepresented—with dire consequences. These stories have fueled the fears and misunderstandings that underlie many adult-teen relationships to this day.

Problem Child

In March of 1987, four Bergenfield, New Jersey, teenagers parked a Chevy Camaro in a vacant garage beneath the Foster Village apartments. The garage had recently become a hangout where local teens could drink, smoke pot, and listen to music without parents or police interfering. On this night, they closed the garage door, opened the windows, and left the car idling. Six months after a drunken friend of theirs had plunged off a 200-foot cliff to his death, these teens made good on a suicide pact. Their deaths left locals wondering when the copycat suicides would begin—and eyeing local misfit teens, the "burnouts," with unease.

In Bergenfield, there seemed to be a fine line between adult concern and criminal suspicion. It didn't help that the teens in question had already written off older generations as uncaring adults who couldn't and wouldn't understand. When the suicides came, the burnouts dug in their heels, refusing to talk. Donna Gaines, author of *Teenage Wasteland*, spent months working essentially undercover with these kids, hoping to learn anything that might shed light on their culture.

"Kids who realize they are marginal fear reprisals," Gaines wrote. "Like any other alienated youth since the conceptualization of 'youth' as a social category, they don't like to talk to adults. About anything. After the suicide pact a few 'burnouts' told reporters they were reluctant to confide in school guidance counselors because the counselors might tell their parents and 'they'd be punished or even sent to a psychiatric hospital.'"

That wasn't the only reason Bergenfield teens were

reluctant to speak up. After the suicides, adolescents were encouraged to suppress their thoughts on day-to-day reality, Gaines wrote. Getting through the day, for many of these kids, meant disassociating from their feelings—and sticking close with friends, otherwise they feared they might start believing adults' version of the "truth."

Like so many other teenagers, Bergenfield's youth sought refuge from this impossible situation in music: Ozzy Osbourne, Iron Maiden, Mötley Crüe. Some of them explored the occult or even called themselves Satanists, sometimes to scare or impress people. The teens who committed suicide were found next to an AC/DC album with song titles such as "Hell Ain't a Bad Place to Be," "Problem Child," and "Rock N' Roll Damnation." Some adults in Bergenfield came away with the idea that there were heavy-metal influenced cults among the town's teens, according to Gaines.

Because neither side opened up, parents often remained in the dark—both before and after the suicides. The burnouts perceived adults as uncaring and clueless. One told Gaines, "Parents don't give a shit, they don't want to face problems until things blow up. Then, when shit happens, they panic, they think you're nuts. But they still won't help you out."

There are many adults who do care, and who do the work necessary to connect with kids under just about any circumstance. Unfortunately, parents and adults who miss the mark are also pretty common. Recent history is filled with examples of this. By misunderstanding what teens are about, why they're behaving the way they do, and why they're listening to, reading, playing, and exploring the things they are, society has turned against some of its most vulnerable adolescents.

Am I Evil?

In West Memphis, adults utterly failed to make sense of boys like Damien Echols and Jason Baldwin.

Damien was a misfit teen in the small Arkansas town. He lived in a two-bedroom trailer with his mother, stepfather, grandmother, and sister. He grew up poor and abused (one social worker described his family's problems as "severe"), and suffered from depression. At least one psychiatrist thought he might be bipolar. He dropped out of school and was a bit aimless, and had been accused of both threatening his ex-girlfriend and of forming a suicide pact with her. He developed a reputation among local teens, partly because he dressed so differently from them, wearing the black clothes he preferred. He hung out primarily with his friend Jason.

"Others didn't like us. They'd been accusing me of being a Satanist since the sixth grade. It was because I had long hair and wore concert t-shirts, with bands like Metallica and Guns N' Roses, and Ozzy Osbourne and U2," Jason said. "Even though Damien and I dressed differently to each other, we were also different from everybody else. And the music we liked was different from whatever they were listening to, too."

Music was one of the only comforts in Damien's world, particularly before meeting Jason. "The worst part wasn't the poverty, the heat, the cold, or even the humiliation of living in such circumstances; it was the absolute and utter loneliness," he said. "I didn't have a friend in the world ... If not for my small battery-powered radio, I would have died inside."

Damien dropped out of high school. When his girlfriend broke up with him, he showed up at her door. The girlfriend's mother told police that Damien had threatened the girl. Damien wound up in juvenile hall.

Poor. Abused. Depressed. In trouble with the law. Each of Damien's circumstances alone was enough to raise red flags for adults. However, those red flags indicate a kid who needs help and support—not suspicion, as he earned from one adult who seemed to be paying attention, juvenile officer Jerry Driver. Even when Damien did begin to open up, such as when he told a counselor he was interested in nature-based Wicca, adults didn't take what he said at face value. Driver, in particular, claimed repeatedly that Damien was Satanic.

"[Damien] expressed considerable displeasure with Mr. Driver in making such assertions," according to the counselor's notes. "Damien acknowledges he is a witch, and indicates this is his religious preference. He also distinguishes his religious beliefs from Satanism, indicated he believes in a series of gods and goddesses, and he sees this as his religious preference, which should not be of concern to state authorities."

Word got out among fellow juvenile inmates, where rumors circulated that Damien and his girlfriend planned to conceive a child who would be sacrificed in a Satanic ritual. Driver bought the rumor hook, line, and sinker. Months later, when Christopher Byers, Michael Moore, and Stevie Branch were murdered on the night of a full moon, police began working with the theory that the killings were cult-motivated. That got Driver thinking of Damien.

Despite the assurances of Damien's doctors that the teen was harmless, Driver continued to dog him. "He thought Damien was looking for power," Mara Leveritt wrote in *Devil's Knot*. "He felt that the teenager's unusual appearance, his unconventional religious beliefs, and the Satanic rituals that Damien denied—but that Driver was convinced that he had conducted—were the attempts of a social outcast to acquire some form of control."

Driver's perception of Damien became crucial both to the investigation leading to his (and Baldwin's) arrest in conjunction with the murders, and to the trial that followed. In 1994, when Damien was 19 and Jason was 17, they were found guilty of the murders. Damien was sentenced to death. Jason, along with acquaintance Jessie Miskelley, who was also convicted in the case, was sentenced to life in prison.

By the end of the trial, Driver wasn't the only one convinced that Damien's different look and tastes indicated something much more sinister than run-of-the-mill teen rebellion. When he was arrested, newspapers blared headlines such as, "One Suspect Was 'Scary,' Talked of Worshiping the Devil" and "Worship of Evil Debated as Motive in Killings." Some articles claimed Damien carried around a cat skull, and that Jason was "into that Devil stuff." Soon, the whole community was persuaded that these different-looking boys were evil killers.

As it turns out, the media is quite good at circulating such non-truths, particularly where teens are concerned. Five years later, one of the biggest stories of teen violence would contain so many faulty facts that a whole generation of teens would come under suspicion from the adults they knew and trusted.

Bullets, Bombs & Bigotry

Eric Harris and Dylan Klebold, two 15-year-old boys with wildly different backgrounds, became friends in suburban Colorado. Neither fit in with the mainstream crowd. Both were skinny, a little gangly, a little awkward. Together, they discovered a fondness for violent ideas. They played plenty of rounds of *Doom* online; Harris even developed modifications for the game, ones that other players could download and use.

Within two years, however, their activities turned criminal. They broke into a locked van and stole computer equipment, earning them a trip to juvenile hall. Eric showed signs of antisocial personality disorder and was ordered to attend anger-management counseling. He began taking an antidepressant, Luvox. Eric and Dylan were released from juvenile hall early for good behavior. They were good at acting polite and charming, which helped obscure the fact that they were experimenting with building pipe bombs and storing the materials in their bedrooms.

"I feel like God. I am higher than almost anyone in the fucking world in terms of universal intelligence," Eric wrote in his journal. A little later he asked, "Ever wonder why we go to school? It's not too obvious to most of you stupid fucks but for those who think a little more and deeper, you should realize it is society's way of turning the young people into good little robots."

In their senior year, the pair made a video for a school project called *Hitmen for Hire*. In it, they used fake weapons to shoot students in the hallways on campus. Violent themes also surfaced in their creative-writing assignments.

The pair began talking about going on a killing spree. A friend over 18 helped them gather weapons, including two shotguns, a TEC-DC9 pistol, and a Hi-point carbine. One April morning, after months of meticulous planning, Eric and Dylan brought their guns and bombs to high school and began shooting. They killed 13 students and teachers and injured 24 others before turning their guns on themselves.

In the hours and days after the Columbine High School shootings on April 20, 1999, reporters flocked to Littleton, Colorado, vying for their chance to tell the story of the great American high-school tragedy. Competition was fierce, particularly for any unique angle, source, or nugget of information that would make a news outlet stand out. In the wake of major tragedies, journalists fight to grab—and maintain—the attention of the audience.

Students told reporters the boys were goths, members of a group called the Trenchcoat Mafia, and fans of Marilyn Manson. Most of these students didn't know the boys personally, but reporters ran with the details, giving readers the impression that cultural influences—not mental health issues coupled with alienation—led these boys to kill.

"The coverage of the shooting and its aftermath was grotesque, even outrageous. Journalism, including its most serious practitioners, accepted and transmitted the idea that two students turned to mass murder because they played nasty computer games, associated with the gloomy (but nonviolent) goths, or had access to Internet bomb-making sites," Jon Katz wrote in *Brill's Content*. "Dumb and demonstrably false as it is, this idea was so widely disseminated and discussed by journalists that most Americans actually came to believe it."

CBS's *60 Minutes* ran a segment called, "Are Video Games Turning Kids Into Killers?" and *TIME* ran photos of the killers while calling them "The Monsters Next Door." Hundreds of other articles and news programs ran stories linking computer games, goths, and the World Wide Web to "aberrant" behavior and even mass murder. The coverage did its job. A week after the Columbine High School shootings, a Gallup poll revealed that more than 80 percent of Americans thought the Internet was at least partly responsible for the incident.

Not only is there no evidence that video games, music, goth culture, or the Internet cause kids to go on shooting rampages, Eric and Dylan weren't goths—and didn't listen to Marilyn Manson, as some sources claimed. How did this story get so far before fact-checking and reason were able to halt it?

Reporters from *USA Today* and the *Philadelphia Inquirer* were among the first to the scene. They talked to a number of students, including one who called himself Mike Smith, Jessica Seigel wrote in *Brill's Content*. Smith told them he was a point guard for the Columbine basketball team, and that he knew the killers. He shared vivid stories about how the boys were part of a goth group called the "Trenchcoat Mafia." Smith went on to say that school officials had ignored ongoing tensions between the goths and jocks, who called the boys "gays" and "inbreeds." The *Drudge Report* and *Rivera Live* then repeated Smith's quotes.

It wasn't until after the earliest reports were published that Richard Jones, national correspondent for the *Philadelphia Inquirer*, discovered that Mike Smith did not play point guard for Columbine. In fact, nobody named Mike Smith was enrolled at the high school. "It was your worst nightmare," Jones told Seigel. "The story had the ring of truth. You don't think someone would lie to see their name in the paper."

One of the most error-riddled pieces that aired after the Columbine shootings was a *20/20* special focusing on the attacks. During the segment, anchor Diane Sawyer claimed, "the boys may have been part of a dark, underground national phenomenon known as the gothic movement and some of these goths may have killed before." Sawyer couldn't have gotten it more wrong. In fact, goths are generally so peaceful that many will not defend themselves even when attacked.

Despite the facts, the concept of a dark, gothic influence or a group with a catchy name like the Trenchcoat Mafia gave reporters something on which to hang their stories. "The Trenchcoat Mafia was mythologized because it was colorful, memorable, and fit the existing myth of the school shooter as an outcast loner," Dave Cullen wrote in *Columbine*. "We remember Columbine as a pair of outcast goths from the Trenchcoat Mafia snapping and tearing through their high school hunting down jocks to settle a long-running feud. Almost none of that happened."

While most reporters blame the post-shooting chaos for the inaccuracy of their stories, at least one of the first news outlets to the scene managed to get it right, according to Cullen. The first print story covering the massacre ran in the *Rocky Mountain News*, and it went to press before Eric and Dylan's bodies were found in the school library. The story "was gripping, empathetic, and astonishingly accurate. It nailed the details and the big picture of two ruthless killers picking off students indiscriminately," Cullen wrote. That means it was possible, in the height of deadline fever, to be faithful to the facts. Many journalists at the scene chose other avenues.

Fortunately, at least some reporters appeared to learn from their mistakes. One year later, when 13-year-old Mitchell Johnson and 11-year-old Andrew Golden shot five people at their middle school in Jonesboro, Arkansas, CNN chairman Tom Johnson explicitly told reporters not to stake out students' front lawns or force microphones into the faces of grieving families, according to Seigel.

Years later, as Cullen and others uncovered Eric and Dylan's journals, it became obvious that mental-health issues, not music and video games, drove the two to murder. Dylan suffered from depression—and identified with characters who seemed on the brink of suicide. Eric showed classic signs of psychopathic behavior, from committing crimes without remorse to hiding his exploits behind a veneer of charisma. But those details were slow to emerge—too slow for the fast, competitive pace of the journalism world. The information that is revealed first is often the information that sticks. The world moved on, continuing to believe that goths, games, and Marilyn Manson had something to do with it.

Interestingly, there is no "profile" of an American school shooter. The teens who have committed these crimes had very little in common in terms of cultural influences. Only 25 percent were interested in violent movies, and less than that played video games—below the average for teenage boys, according to Cullen. The one thing they did have in common is that 98 percent had suffered a loss or failure they perceived as serious. Taking such failures overly seriously is also a common symptom of depression.

However, the media's approach to Columbine—and the misinformation that spread across the nation—launched a wave of discrimination against American teens, particularly those who identified as goths, or who played video games such as *Doom*. In "Voices from the Hellmouth," a piece on *Slashdot* that ran about a week after the shootings, teens chimed in about the sudden distrust and hatred they faced.

"It was horrible, definitely," e-mailed Bandy from New York City. "I'm a *Quake* freak, I play it day and night. I'm really into it. I play *Doom* a lot too, though not so much anymore. I'm up till 3 a.m. every night. I really love it. But after Colorado, things got horrible. People were actually talking to me like I could come in and kill them. It wasn't like they were really afraid of me—they just seemed to think it was okay to hate me even more. People asked me if I had guns at home. This is a whole new level of exclusion, another excuse for the preppies of the universe to put down and isolate people like me."

Anika78, who lived in suburban Chicago, said she was stopped at the door of her high school because she was wearing a trench coat. "I was given a choice—go home and ditch the coat, or go to the principal. I refused to go home. I have never been a member of any group or trench coat mob or any hate thing, online or any other, so why should they tell me what coat to wear?"

Other teens, gamers in particular, objected to the media's implication that video games were to blame for Eric and Dylan's killing spree. "Sometimes I think the games keep me from shooting anybody, not the other way around," said Zbird in New Jersey. "Something much deeper was wrong with these kids in Colorado. To shoot all those people? Make bombs? You have to be sick, and the question they should be asking isn't what games do they play, but how come all these high-paid administrators, parents, teachers and so-called professional people, how come none of them noticed how wacked [sic] they were?"

Another gamer, an anonymous Slashdot reader, took the argument even further. "These games are not only not evil, they are great. They are good. They are challenging and stimulating. They help millions of kids who have nowhere else to go, because the whole world is set up to take care of different kinds of kids, kids who fit in, who do what they're told, who are popular. I've made more friends online on Gamespot.com than I have in three years of high school."

While magazines such as *TIME* and *Newsweek*

continued to tout the risks of video games, and scientists hunted for links between gaming and aggressive behavior, some media outlets did what they could to clear up post-Columbine misconceptions. It wasn't enough. In the months and years that followed, teens—boys in particular—were regarded with persistent mistrust. If the message of Columbine was that any boy, at any time, was an unpredictable time bomb waiting to go off, then it made sense to treat all of them as explosive. Unfortunately, nobody thought about what that would do to the boys in question.

"It's a bad time to be a boy in America. As the new millennium begins ... the defining event for boys is the shooting at Columbine High," Christina Hoff Sommers wrote in *The War Against Boys*. Taking two killers, such as Eric and Dylan, as representative of the "nature of boyhood" is both misguided and disrespectful of boys, she added.

"It has become fashionable to attribute pathology to millions of healthy male children. ... We are turning against boys and forgetting a simple truth: that the energy, competitiveness, and corporal daring of normal, decent males is responsible for much of what is right in the world," Sommers wrote. Meanwhile, other authors and supposed experts on teens, such as William Pollack, author of *Real Boys* and *Real Boys' Voices*, claimed that the Littleton shooters were "the tip of the iceberg, and the iceberg is all boys."

And so, within 50 years, adolescents have gone from being a newly recognized (and occasionally mistrusted) segment of the population to being practically the enemy. Pinpointing the causes of teen violence is messy work, fraught with complications such as mental-health diagnoses and hard questions about whether parents, teachers, or other mentors may have influenced a wayward teen. As a result, adults often grasp at straws.

News article after news article and expert after expert have told parents that a variety of media influences are dangerous for children. They've claimed that these influences simultaneously desensitize teens to violence and fill them with such intense emotions that they can't help but act out. Many of these claims are based on correlative data: it's true that many killers listened to heavy metal, or played violent games, or explored an alternative religion. It's true that many teens who commit suicide do these things, or play role-playing games or participate in goth culture.

Far from being the cause of teen violence or self-harm, these influences are most often a form of solace. They provide comfort, a chance for teens to imagine themselves as heroes, an opportunity for adolescents to feel like they have some control over their lives, and a sense of tribe, of *belonging*, when interests lead adolescents to find others who share those interests. These aspects are powerful enough for everyday kids. But for those who don't fit in, who exist on the margins of society, who have been abused or bullied, they can be a lifeline.

Experts have recommended taking these things away from teens. I can't imagine a worse idea. On the contrary— adolescents should be encouraged to explore the media, cultures, and spiritualities that call to them. Parents should absolutely be involved in that process.

That's what *The Columbine Effect* is for. It provides a detailed look at every major teen interest, subculture, and spiritual path that has been condemned by reporters and "experts" as causing violence or suicide. It reveals where our misconceptions come from and why they're wrong. It also shows why each of these appeals strongly to adolescents—and why it's good for them.

Fear, including fear of teens themselves, has robbed many parents and teens of the potential to relate to each other, to grow close when things are most difficult. Bonnie, David, and Tara didn't need to suffer such separations from their parents— or from the interests that meant so much to them. There are many stories like these. That can change.

In *Bowling for Columbine*, Michael Moore asked Marilyn Manson what he'd say to the kids at Columbine High School, or to the people in their community. Manson responded, "I wouldn't say a single word to them. I would listen to what they have to say, and that's what no one did."

Kids have been saying for years that they need this music, these games, these faiths, these cultures. It's time we started listening.

Darkness as Armor

Black dresses, black boots, high heels, spiked collars, capes, and trench coats were all staples of Stephanie's wardrobe when she was 14. She discovered gothic culture and fashion growing up in the small California town of Napa. Goth clothing matched her love of industrial music and gave her the chance to stand out at school.

Stephanie's best friend began dressing goth around the same time, along with others in their social circle. Their fondness for the same clothes and music created a powerful bond between them that felt like a shield from the stresses of high school and teen life.

"Wearing black instantly made me feel safer. I felt more empowered because it took a lot to dress differently than everyone else," she recalls. "Some people treated me with respect thinking that I was doing something amazing, but some called me bruja (witch) and insisted I did curses." Partly as a result of those accusations, Stephanie taught herself more about metaphysics, and discovered a spiritual path that stuck with her.

Stephanie was in high school when Eric Harris and Dylan Klebold opened fire on their classmates at Columbine High School, killing 13 students and teachers. In the weeks following those shootings, there was a nationwide backlash against "different" kids, particularly goths. Many school leaders feared—mistakenly—that goths were violent and dangerous. Kids in black experienced a wave of discrimination and unfair treatment unlike anything they'd seen before.

"[Columbine] was one of the most important things to happen in my life," Stephanie recalls. "They all thought I was going to go off the deep end, especially my principal. I had to sit through therapy lessons and people trying to make sure I didn't need to be expelled or monitored. I had known most of these people most of my life, and the sudden change was inexplicable. Suddenly people I had known my entire school career wouldn't let me wear spiked collars or trenchcoats."

After many parent-teacher conferences, Stephanie and school leaders agreed she could keep wearing black if she left the long coats and collars at home. Later, the school banned students from donning black clothes at some events, giving goths fewer options.

Years later, Stephanie still considers herself a "goth at heart." She wears black when she can. She looks back at her early goth years fondly, and says they permanently changed her for the better. "I got used to sticking up to myself, explaining weird concepts, vocabulary and metaphysical ideas to everyone. I got used to being patient when explaining to people what things meant, and for some reason, a lot of people got used to coming to me for life's answers."

Devil in my Lunchbox

It wasn't long after Adam Lanza killed 20 young children and six staff at Sandy Hook Elementary School in Newtown, Connecticut, before the press began playing up the "goth" angle. The UK's *Mirror* and *Daily Mail* newspapers—notorious for their sensationalized, histrionic writing—ran articles about Lanza with headlines like, "He was a nerd, genius, Goth: Profile of gun killer Adam Lanza" and quotes such as, "he was very thin, very remote and was one of the goths." The single source for this "goth" description seems to be the mother of a boy who knew Lanza. It doesn't sound like she ever met him herself, or that she knows what a goth is.

The same thing happened when police identified 17-year-old Austin Reed Sigg as a suspect in the murder of 10-year-old Colorado girl Jessica Ridgeway. Predicably, the *Daily Mail* was among the first publications to pile on the "goth" bandwagon, running a headline that read, "CSI student, 17, who 'murdered and dismembered Jessica Ridgeway was a Goth, wore black and was infatuated with death.'" Sigg's fellow students are the ones who apparently identified him as a goth, though at least one sounds suspiciously like she's responding to the question, "would you describe him as a goth?": "'He was very quiet, shy and to himself. I would say he was gothic," she said. Another student, quoted in an *Associated Press* article, claimed "he used to hang out with a lot of us in what we called the goth corner (of the school cafeteria), where all the metalheads were." Perhaps these reporters were only trying to create a picture of Sigg's personality, but they mostly wind up creating the impression that goths are gruesome, violent people.

The "goth" description has developed an aura of mystery and danger, played up again and again in news reports about violent young people. Thomas "TJ" Lane, who shot and killed three fellow students at his Ohio high school, was described by a fellow student as going through "a gothic phase." After 13-year-old Casey-Lynne Kearney was stabbed to death in a park in Doncaster, England, her suspected killer, 26-year-old Hannah Bonser, was described by neighbors as "having the look of a goth."

Why does this term hold such power? Since the Columbine High School shootings, goths have held an undeserved reputation as a violent, even murderous group. It all started with teenagers telling lies to scoop-hungry reporters at the scene. One or more students claimed to journalists that Harris and Klebold were members of a group called the "Trench Coat Mafia," and that this group was goth-based. However, these students likely didn't even know Harris and Klebold—and they certainly didn't know goth culture.

Nevertheless, the media ran with it. ABC's news magazine, *20/20*, aired an hourlong special on goths one day after the shootings. "The boys may have been part of a dark, underground national phenomenon known as the gothic movement and some of these goths may have killed before," said *20/20* anchor Diane Sawyer. Her correspondent, Brian Ross, said, "It's what's known as the gothic movement, violent and black." Their statements weren't true, but they frightened many adults, kicking off the discrimination and profiling Stephanie and many others endured.

20/20 and the *Associated Press* both relied on interviews with Denver Police Sergeant Dave Williams, a supposed expert on goth culture, for information. Among other things, he claimed that goths were a violent cult led by musician Marilyn Manson. He also told the *Associated Press* that many goths play *Vampire: The Masquerade* and that players "assume the personas of vampires and act out attacks. ... There are people who I have seen who lose touch, who think the gaming system and mythos are real. They have gone off and done some very strange things." He also told *AP* that trench coats are the modern, goth equivalent of vampire capes.

"[Harris and Klebold are] basically outcasts, Gothic people. They're into anarchy. They're white supremacists, and they're into Nostradamus stuff and Doomsday," Columbine High School junior Peter Maher told reporters. According to the *AP* story, "Several students said the shooters were deeply into death—talking, reading and dreaming about it. They said the Trench Coat Mafia members wore their trench coats every day, no matter the weather, even in class."

This confused jumble of statements may sound like sense to someone who isn't familiar with goth culture. It might sound that way especially to someone who is frightened of a teenager who dresses in dark clothes and acts flamboyant and different. Many journalists didn't know any better. They didn't know that goths are generally peaceful, or that not everyone who wears a trench coat is goth. They didn't know that not all goths play role-playing games—or that RPGs are harmless. They definitely didn't know that Marilyn Manson is not a gothic band, or that Harris and Klebold weren't fans. And they didn't talk to any goths who could have set them straight. Fortunately, other reporters have done the legwork. It has taken many years to untangle this mess of information—and clearly not everyone has gotten the message.

One of the worst offenders is David J. Stewart, author of an online essay called "Goth Will Destroy Your Child." In it, he claims, "Goth glorifies things that are sick, nasty, improper, freakish, and downright demonic. ... Goth causes teenage girls to become whores, depresses kids to the point of cutting themselves, and turns otherwise normal kids into Columbine shooters. The Goth culture is obsessed with death and the darker side of life, which is clearly evidenced in Goth music.

Goth is of the Devil."

He makes a number of mistakes in his writeup. For starters, he lumps all kids who wear black into one big "goth" category, rather than acknowledging the vast range of black-clad subcultures. He also cites a number of violent cases supposedly involving goths, when in fact very few of them do. He even goes so far to associate goth culture with "sexual immorality" and pedophilia. None of his claims are backed by real evidence.

Fortunately, some media outlets gave goths a voice in their post-Columbine coverage. They helped set the record straight about what goth culture is and isn't. And others saw the spotlight on goths as a plus, despite the misinformation. "The massacre of students at Columbine High School in ... Colorado, in April 1999, was among other things the catalyst for a positive retrieval of goth identity. Young goths would come to be distinguished from the more nihilistic, proviolent 'Trench Coat Mafia,'" Ken Gelder wrote in "The (Un)Australian Goth: Notes toward a Dislocated National Subject."

"Violence is not what goth is about," Karen, a 14-year-old Berkeley goth, told Neva Chonin of the *San Francisco Chronicle*.

"Just because someone dresses in black doesn't mean that they're goths—or that they want to murder people. The media goes crazy about this stuff because it makes good reading," 16-year-old Jessie said.

Even teens outside the culture agreed that it was wrong to represent goths as violent. Roxane, a 16-year-old hip-hop fan, told Chonin, "Goths are not people who want to fight. They're wimps who dress scary because they have no other way to defend themselves."

Columbine wasn't the only crime in which a violent teen was painted as goth. On October 15, 2005, 16-year-old Scott Dyleski killed his neighbor, Pamela Vitale, at her home in Lafayette, California. Vitale was found just inside the door, bludgeoned to death. A few days later, Dyleski was arrested on murder charges.

Investigators believe Dyleski and a friend were using Vitale's credit cards illegally to purchase pot-growing supplies.

After Dyleski mistakenly gave Vitale's address on an order, one of the companies suspected fraud and refused to deliver the supplies. Dyleski may have feared that Vitale would discover the activity. He went into her home to investigate and possibly steal items, and was surprised when she returned to the house. He hit her on the head numerous times, killing her.

Newspaper reports depicted Dyleski as a dark, disturbed teen who dressed in a goth manner. Although his family said he had abandoned his goth phase by the time of Vitale's death, Harold Jewett, the prosecutor in Dyleski's trial, said the teen identified with goth culture—and also that he carved occult symbols into Vitale's back. Dyleski's spiritual or cultural affiliations didn't have anything to do with the crime, but they were spotlighted in news reports and the trial nonetheless.

The goths I interviewed said that post-Columbine reporting was a major source of misinformation about the culture, but by no means the only source. Jenn, 39, grew up in Salt Late City, Utah, and discovered goth culture when she was 15. She said that adults and outsiders take one look at goths in their elaborate makeup and black clothing and make assumptions. "[They think] that goth kids are stupid, depressed, miserable, drug-using losers," she said. "I was a straight-A honors student through high school and college."

Similarly, Nicky was bothered by the popular idea that goths are mean, crazy, insane, or "miscreants of society." She said mainstream culture has a hard time accepting outsiders, such as goths.

Many think goth culture has something to do with paganism, or with depression. Stephanie said it's a mistake to assume that goths are into witchcraft and Satanism, or that they're overly emotional. Many people believe that goths' black clothing represents gloom and despair. "Not necessarily for most of us," she said.

In the UK, the media—music journalists in particular—have been major purveyors of negative information, according to Cobweb, a British goth. "People think we're annoying and depressing," he said. "The thing that amuses me most is that they think we're doing it to annoy them, or that it's a phase or something and we'll get better."

Goths do dress to set themselves apart from the norm. But there's a difference between wanting to be noticed and wanting to be *judged*, especially in a negative way. Like anyone else, goths want to be understood as individuals and weighed on their personalities and achievements. To some, the off-putting exterior might be intended as a challenge: "I dare you to get to know me." Many wear black clothes and elaborate makeup as a kind of armor to protect themselves from harm, since so many are sensitive and opposed to violence and conflict.

Go Away White

As a reporter, I once attended a meeting in a town where gang activity had expanded dramatically, leading to 13 homicides (including the deaths of several teen gang members) in a single summer. During the meeting, police explained some of the characteristics of gang members: they tend to wear the same colors, and they tend to hang out in groups of three or more. One woman stood up and asked, "What about those kids who dress in black and hang out behind the Safeway? Are they a gang?"

"No, ma'am," one officer responded. "Those are goths. They're harmless."

Goth is much more than wearing black, but that's a starting point—a key one, since it's a color that shocks and worries many parents. In our culture, black means death. That's an important association for goths. Many romanticize aspects of death and dying, though in a much less literal way than you'd think. And, while adults may fear that the color is affiliated with violence, goths tend to be among the least violent teens.

The term "goth" or "gothic" might bring to mind the Visigoths—the East Germanic barbarians who interfered with the late Roman Empire. In this case, "goth" refers to gothic literature of the 18th and 19th centuries, including works by Edgar Allan Poe, Lord Byron, Mary Shelley, Emily and Charlotte Brontë, and Sheridan Le Fanu. "The Raven," *Frankenstein, Wuthering Heights,* and others laid the groundwork for the dark, romantic leanings of goth culture.

28

Goth first appeared in Britain in the early 1980s. It was born out of the British punk scene, but in many ways, it presented a polar opposite to that scene. Punk was aggressive and political, while goth was more peaceful and had no political core. Goth fused a variety of disparate elements, including punk, glam, and the burgeoning New Romantic movement. Goths wore a predominantly black uniform, though it could be almost anything: cowboy goth with long duster coats, black jeans, stetson hats and boots, or Victorian goth with corsets, ruffles, and lace. Goths of both genders frequently dye their hair black—and sometimes other bright colors as well. Many men and women also wear heavily stylized makeup, featuring very pale or white foundation with dark, dramatic paint on the eyes and lips.

Goths often want to stand apart from the rest of the crowd. Their look is distinctive, eye-catching, and theatrical. Many who are drawn to this culture feel different from the norm. Goth style gives them a way of both expressing and celebrating that feeling with others who live on the margins.

When Jenn discovered goth culture, it was the mid-1980s. Her favorite music—the New Romantics, including Duran Duran and Tears for Fears—was dying out. Goth music cropped up as a replacement, and she embraced it wholeheartedly, both the music and the look. She began listening to Bauhaus, Tones on Tail, Dead Can Dance, The Cure, Ministry, Gene Loves Jezebel, Christian Death, the Cocteau Twins, and many others from the classic goth catalog.

She wore mostly black, with sapphire, deep red, and dark purple touches. "The colors were only there as accents for the black," she recalls. "My makeup was a very pale foundation, strong red, purple or black lips and rich colored eyeshadow. Black eyeliner was used to both line heavily the eyes—especially as the Eye of Ra—or draw curlicues, vines or teardrops as well."

Becoming goth wasn't a huge leap, Jenn recalled. "I already existed outside cultural norms. I enjoyed being an iconoclast and challenging others' perceptions. I actually relished being different."

Cobweb was 15 when he stumbled upon the gothic look and music scene in northern England, predominantly by discovering albums and clothing in local stores that he liked. None of his friends were into the culture or the music. For him, it was about emulating a style and feeling he had seen in town.

"What first hit me [about goth] was the beauty. The people I'd seen when I was younger had been strange, stunning, and other-worldly. I felt like that on the inside, and wondered why everyone didn't want to look like that," he said. "I'd fall in love with the costumes and makeup I'd see in films or pop videos."

Many goths say that wearing all black makes them feel safe; it acts as a kind of armor. Some people wear black to hide or blend in, but not goths. Most dress in a way that makes them stand out. So how does this protect them? If you've seen goths in full regalia—mohawks, chains, piercings—you might think twice about approaching them. That's one way the style works as armor. Black clothes also make it more difficult to spot someone in the shadows of a dark club or on the street at night, two of goths' favorite hangouts. Others have argued that black clothing represents a protest against the norms of fashion. Most people wear a little black, but it's mixed in with neutrals and colors. For goths, dressing entirely in black can mean a rejection of mainstream standards of beauty.

This also explains the unusual, dramatic makeup some goths wear. If a teen feels unattractive, elaborate face paint can create a kind of beauty. Sure, it's a different flavor of beauty than what's recognized by everyday society; that's part of the point. By creating its own norms, goth offers misfits and teens with low self-esteem the chance to feel beautiful.

The first goth was probably Siouxsie Sioux, a British scenester who followed the Sex Pistols as a teen. While in France with the band, she was beaten up for wearing a black armband bearing a swastika. She claimed she wore the armband only to shock people, not because she liked Nazi culture. However, soon she abandoned the Nazi-themed clothing, as well as the glam and fetish wear she wore to discos. Instead, she began back-combing her hair, which made it stand up. She used heavy, dark makeup with feline touches around the eyes—a look that would be imitated by goths worldwide for decades, according to author Paul Hodkinson. Sioux formed a band with the Banshees, playing a pastiche of punk, glam, pop, hip-hop, and rock.

Sioux wasn't goth's only muse. The unique goth sound emerged from other directions, including the "androgynous glamour and deep-voiced vocals of David Bowie" and the "depressing angst of Joy Division," Hodkinson wrote in *Goth: Identity, Style, and Subculture*. Although gothic culture is deeply about look and style, it is also about music. Early goth bands employed a variety of motifs that set them apart, such as deep, morose vocals; minor keys; slow, tense melodies; and a spacious atmosphere. Many early goth bands, including Bauhaus, The Birthday Party, Alien Sex Fiend, Sex Gang Children, and the Virgin Prunes adopted this style. Others, such as the Cure and the Southern Death Cult, infused their music with more rock and pop elements.

The birth of this eerie, atmospheric sound was a natural progression from the music created by the Doors, the Velvet Underground, and others, Michael Bibby wrote in "Atrocity Exhibitions: Joy Division, Factory Records, and Goth." According to Steve Severin of Siouxsie and the Banshees, "We didn't tell John [McKay, The Banshees' original guitarist], 'Oh, you have to play an A-sharp minor there, and it'll be really spooky.' We'd say, 'Make it a cross between the Velvet Underground and the scene from *Psycho*.'"

New technology helped bands create a sense of space and distance. On the 1978 Siouxsie and the Banshees single "Pure," McKay used long, sustained single notes on his guitar, which he played through an echo effect. Sioux's vocals were mixed into the background, making her sound as though she were far away, according to Bibby. Many bands, including the Banshees, Bauhaus, and Joy Division, used various sounds to create a sense of dread.

The early goth sound was sometimes paired with references to historical atrocities, especially the Holocaust. This was especially true of Joy Division, which recorded for a Manchester label called Factory. The band's fondness for such symbols caused many people to assume they were racist or Nazis. Instead, the concept was meant as an allegory for human misery.

"Such icons for Joy Division and the Factory style took on a stronger sense of nihilism—they signified that all life is atrocity, the concentration camp is the paradigm of existence, and history compels us to failure, demise, and apocalypse," Bibby wrote. One Joy Division lyric shows how "mass murder is, however repulsive such a reductionism might be, metaphoric of personal suffering." Goth appeals to teens and adults who feel separated from mainstream culture, often against their will. Being marginalized can hurt, so it's no wonder this particular symbolism appeals.

Many say Bauhaus' song "Bela Lugosi's Dead" is the quintessential early goth song. Inspired by the famous *Dracula* actor, the song opened another famous vampire film, *The Hunger*, starring David Bowie, Catherine Deneuve, and Susan Sarandon. The song, framed with anxious drumbeats and guitars that sound like something out of a horror soundtrack, is performed in a highly theatrical manner. The spare lyrics tell the story of Lugosi's imagined funeral and imply that he may yet rise from the grave. It provides the ideal mood for getting "gothed up" for the evening, or—even better—dancing.

A second wave of goth culture emerged in the mid-1980s, inspired by early goth music and   traditional rock elements. The look was more straightforward: dark hair, tight black jeans, pointy black boots, and sunglasses. The bands who fostered this second wave were much more radio-friendly and accessible, including the Sisters of Mercy, the Mission, Fields of the Nephilim, All About Eve, and The Cult (formerly the Southern Death Cult). These bands brought British goth into the limelight and made it an international phenomenon, putting goth style and music within the reach of American audiences. Disaffected American kids ate it up. By the end of the 1980s, Nine Inch Nails had fused gothic music with angry, electronic-infused sounds, catapulting the entire scene into the pop charts.

Goth music and style basked in the cultural limelight through the late 1980s and into the 1990s, influencing mainstream music and fashion. However, by the mid-1990s, the mainstream moved on—to bubblegum pop—and goth returned to its former underground status. A new generation of bands carried the torch, relying on word-of-mouth, the club scene, and independent labels and media for promotion. One branch of goth music melded with electronic dance, launching bands such as VNV Nation, Apoptygma Berzerk, and Covenant. The scene retains a healthy following today, thanks to plenty of support from old and new generations of fans, who share resources on the Internet and gather at local clubs as well as major goth festivals, such as the Whitby Gothic Weekend in northern England and the Wave Gotik Treffen festival in Germany.

However, aspects of goth have held strong in the mainstream, due in part to the survival of stores such as Hot Topic. Hot Topic sells clothing and accessories in a goth-pop style: faux black-leather pants with "bondage" buckles on them, studded collars and belts, t-shirts with popular goth bands on them, jewelry, corsets and bodices, short frilly skirts, leather boots and shoes, and so on. Original goths regard those inspired by the Hot Topic phenomenon as "baby goths" who are "barely scratching the surface of the scene," according to Hodkinson. One goth told him, "You go to [a club] and there's all these fifteen-year-olds jumping about with their Marilyn Manson t-shirts." Another said, "they've got short hair, and they've just got a little bit of eye-liner, a little bit of lipstick and they think, 'Oh, I'm a goth.'" Similarly, the Columbine High School shootings returned goth to the public eye—though in a less-than-accurate way.

There are a number of subcultures sometimes confused with goth, including emo and rivet culture. Rivetheads are fans of industrial music—harder, brasher sounds that are a more direct and electronic descendent of punk. Like goths, they typically dress in all black, but with a harder, less romantic edge. Some rivetheads wear military-inspired outfits, some resembling armor or factory attire. Cargo pants and steel-toed boots are the norm, particularly for men. Emo also emerged from the punk world, but features melodic guitars and intensely emotional lyrics, hence the name. Emo fashion is strikingly different from goth: skinny jeans, often in bright colors, tight t-shirts, studded belts, and black wristbands are common. Many emo kids dye their hair black cur it and asymmetrically so that it hangs fully over one eye. Emos have a reputation for being shy, sensitive, and angst-ridden, though as with any culture, people's moods and temperaments are all over the map.

Some goths have branched out into a style called steampunk, which—like goth itself—emerged from literature. In this case, it's inspired by steam-powered machinery reminiscent of the Wild West, Victorian England, and the early industrial period, and the science-fiction works of authors such as China Mieville and Philip Pullman. Steampunk fashion and design is often based in browns and copper or brass colors, leather, gears and clocks, aviator goggles. It features clothing drawn from the late Victorian era, including corsets and formal dresses and long coats for women, and suits with waistcoats or vests for men. Parasols and pocket watches are common accessories, but so are fake rayguns and eyepieces that look almost robotic or Borg-like. There are steampunk games, books, and bands; there's even steampunk furniture, home design and computers.

Goth culture is known for romanticizing death and the macabre as metaphors, but goths themselves reject the idea that it is about "being miserable and dull," Hodkinson wrote. As one told him, it's about "rejoicing in a high-spirited view of the darker side of life, pushing the frontiers of style and sound."

Indeed, the nature of the goth identity is "fraught with contradictions," Rebecca Schraffenberger wrote in "This Modern Goth (Explains Herself)." "[Goths] use negativity in a very positive way," she explained. To be a goth, "one must be a romantic idealist—naïve and vulnerable enough to attract the predatory impulses of other teens. One must be introspective, analytical, intellectually curious, and generally thoughtful. Also, in goths you'll find a deep-rooted attraction to anything mysterious and supernatural. A goth generally feels a lot of anger, mostly directed at the past, and at the injustices and absurdities of the present. ... A goth sees beauty in what is dreadful or forbidding. All this is bound up within a creative personality and an acute aesthetic sense."

Parents may not know what to do with a teenager who is suddenly dressing in black, wearing elaborate makeup, and flirting with these kinds of contradictions. Some handle it better than others. "My mother wasn't too pleased, and demanded that I never dye my hair black or she would jokingly 'kill me,'" Nicky said. Still, her mom seemed to recognize the underlying harmlessness of her daughter's new identity. "She knew better than to reject what made me feel so much happier, since she knew I had never fit in with my peers and classmates ... My choice never strongly affected my relationship with my mom, thankfully."

If the denizens of the goth world enter that world because they feel like outsiders in the mainstream, it's understandable that they resonate with ideas of death and the macabre. Being an outsider can make you feel ugly, alienated, and alone—thrown away. Seeing beauty in death and decay is a way of reclaiming one's own personal beauty. Through that lens, many goths find a way to feel good about themselves, and discover a self-confidence they may not have otherwise had. It takes courage to intentionally stand out as many goths do.

Although the look and the music are what make goths distinctive, the defining characteristic of the culture is its social aspects. Goths often discover the scene through friends who are either already part of it, or are getting involved. Once they're part of goth culture, many stick with it well beyond adolescence —in spirit, even if they do not dress the part in adulthood. Goth style and sound create a way for teens to separate themselves from mainstream culture and identify themselves as outsiders. Sharing goth culture with others helps cement that feeling of otherness.

"I just don't remember much of my life before I became gothic," Nicky told me. "I think that I was lost until I found my own niche. I know that by finding others like me I felt that I belonged somewhere and that there were people just like me and I wasn't alone."

"Goth is a tribe. ... it's just a group of people that get together and say ... 'we have something in common—we have how we dress, how we look, how we feel and the kind of people we're interested in or music we're interested in, in common," one told Hodkinson.

One of the primary ways for goths to socialize is at events—clubs, concerts, and anyplace where folks can get dressed up, gather, and dance. Some bigger cities will have clubs devoted to goth music and style. Others get by with having a "goth night" once a week in venues where other nights are set aside for metal, country, pop, and so on. The evening often starts at the home of one friend, where everyone gathers to dress up and put on makeup. Many goths dress in a distinctive style throughout the day, but they go all out for a night out with friends.

Jenn primarily socialized with other goths at Salt Lake City clubs such as the Ritz and Palladium, as well as at live shows when goth bands came to town. When those options weren't available, "We also took over whole sections of 24-hour diners like Dee's and Denny's," she recalled.

For many years, Cobweb socialized exclusively with goths. Over the years, his social circle has widened to include people who "tend to be sympathetic to goth and we share interests which fit well within the umbrella of goth," he said. In goth's heyday, he would attend shows or clubs three or four nights a week. Now that the scene has tapered off, he goes out a handful of times a year and primarily socializes with friends at their homes.

This kind of socialization helps bolster the culture from within. "[Being goth has surrounded] me with people who share my philosophies, which has probably strengthened and reinforced what was already there and protected me, to a certain extent, from compromise," Cobweb said.

Hodkinson noted that these kinds of events helped solidify the identities of goths who participated in them, and encourage further participation in the scene. Clubs often help set the stage for this by offering a dark, smoky atmosphere, loud music, and posters with "goth" themes. When people dance, they have to dance in particular styles—"headbanging" and other non-goth manners of movement are frowned upon, even shamed. Newcomers to the scene might be shunned, but if they are persistent—and if they adopt the styles properly—they are often welcomed enthusiastically.

"Goth club experiences involved something of a displacement of everyday inhibitions, a degree of 'losing oneself' while dancing, with or without drugs, and for some a degree of escape from more stressful elements of life," he wrote.

Although goth offers an alternate standard of beauty, goths are not protected from scrutiny among their peers. As with many social scenes, goths are apt to judge one another, just as they are likely to create an "us and them" mentality when comparing themselves with folks in the mainstream. Many, especially those who have been loyal to the goth scene for decades, are guilty of "gother-than-thou" syndrome— thinking that others are less legitimate, or somehow doing it wrong.

Many told Hodkinson they joined the goth world because it gave them the freedom to behave and dress in any way that they wanted. It also let them show how different their style is from anyone else's. However, those who strayed too far from the style "rules" wound up on the outs. The only ones who could get away with significant deviations from dark clothing, stylized makeup, and so forth, were those who had become well-known and respected in their scene. They had been part of the goth world so long, they knew which breaches would be acceptable.

Cobweb has gotten away with such exploration and experimentation. Instead of black, he has gone through periods of wearing predominantly beige or brown clothes, which are more to his taste. "I've never really been able to settle down into a 'look' for long," he said. "I'm very 'pick and mix' and tend to steal from a multitude of styles, absorbing and altering them as seems fitting. ... In the '90s when goth began to solidify and define itself properly, I was never keen on staying within the boundaries we were erecting for ourselves."

Such discussions of what is or isn't "goth" abound. They are inspired by the desire of those within the culture to remain authentic, Lauren Goodlad and Michael Bibby wrote in *Goth: Undead Subculture*. By focusing on such distinctions, goths help protect the culture from outside influences.

Another way to keep goth culture intact is to only date other goths. Goths rarely date outside the scene. Whether that's because a non-goth romantic partner wouldn't be acceptable, or because they don't tend to socialize with non-goths, is not entirely clear.

Goth culture provides a special refuge for boys. In most subcultures, boys and men are pushed to dress and act in a "manly," even aggressive fashion. In the goth world, slender, androgynous men are celebrated. Many men will wear their hair long, remove any visible traces of body hair, and wear makeup. Others wear feminine clothing, including skirts and corsets—particularly at clubs. Men in the scene more openly hold hands or show affection, even if they are heterosexual. The men's room at a goth club is as likely to have as many guys touching up their makeup as women in the ladies' room. Hodkinson argues that the emotional content of goth lyrics allows men in the scene to recognize and display their feelings more readily, offering an alternative to the steely exterior encouraged by mainstream culture. The culture embraces a variety of sexual perspectives, including bisexuality, homosexuality, and sexual fetishes, according to many goths.

"Men are drawn to the subculture by its rich opportunities to display sensitivity, emotion, theatricality, and artiness—behaviors that, in today's hypermasculine culture, are not only associated with women, but often invidiously relegated to them. Likewise, goth women seek out the subculture partly to enjoy the companionship of such like-minded men," according to Goodlad and Bibby.

The fact that goths exist outside the mainstream may contribute to the idea that androgynous male goths are all gay— another category of people who are stigmatized in American society, Joshua Gunn wrote in "Dark Admissions: Gothic Subculture and the Ambivalence of Misogyny and Resistance." Gunn agrees that creating space for men to explore traditionally feminine clothing styles and expression is good for both genders: "[It] affords women a comfortable space in which to be intelligent and artistic as well—sometimes also 'feminist' or sexually 'aggressive.'"

Parents may be unsettled by aspects of goth culture, including the fascination with death, the macabre, vampires, and so on. Such films as Francis Coppola's *Bram Stoker's Dracula*, Joel Schumacher's *The Lost Boys*, and Neil Jordan's "*nterview with the Vampire* (based on the popular vampire novels by Anne Rice) resonated with goths primarily because they identify with "the vampire's extreme alienation," according to Goodlad and Bibby. Goth aesthetics were also expressed in films such as Tim Burton's *Edward Scissorhands*, Allan Moyle's *Pump Up The Volume,* and Michael Lehmann's *Heathers.*

In these latter films, "goth style is integral to articulating a desire for—and the possibility of—alternatives to the suburban status quo," Goodlad and Bibby wrote. At the same time, they created an association in mainstream minds between goths and deviance, which may explain why so many believed goth culture could have been behind the Columbine shootings.

The preoccupation with vampires does enhance the "death chic" popularized in the goth scene, according to Gunn. Goths of both genders strive for a pale, deathly pallor and thin, even emaciated bodies. While the former can be achieved with makeup, the latter is out of reach for many people without extreme dieting. There are many goths in the healthy and plus-size ranges—and they are welcomed into the scene—but they are not always considered the ideal.

Although goths are very serious about the styles that define them, it's important for outsiders, including parents, to understand the sense of humor involved, according to Gunn. "Gothic style is consciously flamboyant and playful; it is a mindful, performative gesture in which liberation is thought to be achieved through a display of ironic indifference." In other words, goths are trying very hard to classify themselves as non-mainstream. At the same time, they act as though they don't care whether they are non-mainstream. Goths go to great lengths to insist their "look" doesn't mean anything special, and yet it's designed to provoke fear and anger in those who don't "get it," Gunn wrote.

The androgynous look popular among goths can also trouble parents, especially if they fear the idea of their child identifying as homosexual. "I think my dad was worried I was gay early on. He was traumatized by my first frilly velvet shirt," Cobweb said. "I had a very gothic wedding and I think that was the first time he saw me in full makeup and realized that, for me, looking pretty had nothing to do with my sexuality."

Another aspect of goth culture that may confuse outsiders is the use of religious and spiritual imagery. Many goths wear crosses (sometimes upside-down) or ankhs, the cross of Egyptian history. Others wear pentagrams and other images from paganism. For some, this is a reflection of their personal spirituality. For others, it is just part of the look and doesn't hold deeper meaning.

"Many goths can be characterized as religious nonbelievers who, nonetheless, derive pleasure from inventive and often ironic play with religious signifiers—a practice that may sometimes involve spiritual effects," Anna Powell wrote in "God's Own Medicine: Religion and Parareligion in UK Goth Culture."

By the same token, there are Christian goths—though for them, religion comes first and goth culture comes second. Oher goths have broken away from the Christianity of their upbringing. Those who did said it was important for them to be spiritually autonomous and self-determined, according to Powell. Some of those remained nonreligious, while others experimented with paganism: witchcraft and Wicca, earth mysteries, chaos magic, and occultism, as well as paranormal activity, mysticism and divination. Exploring spirituality is a healthy part of adolescence, especially if a teen finds something to call home. The goth world is particularly welcoming of such experimentation, and there is plenty of overlap between the goth and pagan worlds.

For some teens, goth is a phase, albeit an important one. For others, it becomes a life-long style. Adult goths often "dress down" for work by sticking to darker colors—and then break out the fancy clothes and makeup for evenings and weekends. Those who leave the scene do so for a variety of reasons.

Jenn's mother died suddenly when Jenn was in college, away from home in Texas. She already felt alienated at school, but her mother's death sent her into a months-long depression during which she didn't go out and socialize. "There wasn't any reason to get gothed up to stay at home," she recalled. Soon after, her father was diagnosed with terminal cancer, and died 18 months later. Jenn moved to California to be near her step-mother. It was then that she realized her goth period was over.

"I basically outgrew it," she said.

Angel With the Scabbed Wings

Sophie Lancaster, 20, and her 21-year-old boyfriend, Robert Maltby, were walking through a popular Lancashire park just after 1 a.m. on August 11, 2007. They were mobbed by a group of teens, who assaulted Maltby without any apparent provocation. When Maltby fell unconscious, Lancaster cradled him in her arms, hoping to protect him from further harm. The youths turned on her, kicking her in the head repeatedly as witnesses called police for help. Both Lancaster and Maltby were taken, unconscious, to a local hospital. Maltby survived with brain damage, but Lancaster never woke up. She died of her injuries on August 24, 2007. Police said that Lancaster's and Maltby's goth appearance may have motivated the attacks. Two of their attackers were later convicted of murder, while three others were convicted of grievous bodily harm.

Unfortunately, goths' distinctive look—as well as their reputation for being peace-loving—has a downside. Many of them have been the targets of bullying and assault. When the goth world shared a place in mainstream culture, goths were much more accepted, according to Cobweb. But when it returned to the underground in the mid-1990s, things changed. "These days, being a goth can get you killed. ... Being a minority, especially a distinctive one, will always lead to trouble." He has been assaulted numerous times, even though he does not fully "dress up" for day-to-day ventures out of the house.

One early autumn day in the mid-1990s, Cobweb woke up and prepared for the day. He teased up his hair and put on a little makeup—eyeliner but no eyeshadow or lipstick—as well as boots, black jeans and a simple band t-shirt. Dressed this way, he went into town to buy groceries.

A couple of hours later, carrying sacks of food in both hands and another on his back, Cobweb trudged home. As he walked along the sidewalk, he heard someone shouting over the sound of traffic. He didn't think anything of it until he heard the word "goth." Just as he considered turning around to look toward the shouting, an empty soda can hit him on the back of the head. That got his attention.

Cobweb turned and saw five young men in a red Beetle with the top down. They looked like students. From their accents he could tell they weren't local. Although it was obvious they were shouting at him, Cobweb attempted to ignore them. He kept walking. However, traffic was moving slowly—slowly enough that the Beetle was keeping pace with him.

"They were obnoxious but I wasn't frightened. I assumed they were harmless. They didn't look like thugs or anything," he said. When their car stopped at the next red light, the boys jumped from the car and knocked Cobweb to the ground, kicking him. Then, just as quickly, they returned to their car and drove away. "I wasn't badly hurt. I'd been curled up into a ball and was protected by the kit bag I'd had on my back. I got a black eye, a bloody nose, and some pretty impressive bruises on my shoulder."

To make matters worse, as Cobweb gathered up his groceries and got ready to go home, a woman came up and said, "'I saw what happened. You deserved that!' I've still no idea if she'd mistaken the situation or was genuinely evil, but that probably had more effect on me that the attack," he said.

In 2011, Melody McDermott—who frequently sports dark clothing, dramatically dyed hair and facial piercings—was a tram with her boyfriend in greater Manchester when she was attacked by two men, one of whom kicked her to the floor and stomped her face, leaving her with a broken eye socket and permanent facial paralysis that prevents her from smiling fully. Her attacker was sentenced to less than seven years in jail, while his accomplice received a sentence of a little more than two years. Gena Willenberg, an American living in Scotland, was beaten by teens in 2012 after they accused her of being "goth." She was left with a broken nose and severe bruising on her chest.

In Iraq, government admonishments against goth and emo culture led to several youth being stoned to death in 2012. After the Iraq Interior Ministry released a statement that condemned the "phenomenon of emo" as Satanic, and described emo fashions — such as dark clothes, skull-print T-shirts and nose rings — are "emblems of the devil," the stonings began. Locals estimated that anywhere between 15 and 60 youths were killed in the attacks, while many others were wounded, apparently as "warnings." In Uzbekistan, gothic-looking youth were frequently harassed by police, while Russian state television claimed that goths engage in cannibalism.

In the months following Lancaster's death, Ade Varney and others petitioned the British prime minister to include such attacks under the definition of "hate crimes." Goths "get verbal assaults every day, and not just from young people. But now younger teenagers have the mentality of hardened criminals and I definitely sense this violent aspect getting worse," Varney wrote in the petition. In most places, hate-crime laws have not been rewritten, but in April 2013, the greater Manchester region of England announced that it would begin treating attacks on goths as hate crimes.

It's hard to say precisely why such vitriol and violence is directed at gothic youth. Granted, goths make a point of dressing flamboyantly so they will stand out. Goth men often look quite effeminate, which might make others believe they're gay. People who look different, and people who are assumed to be gay, are often targets of abuse.

Madeline Burtenshaw, a goth woman and Christian who keeps a blog, wrote "an open letter to the Church of England" in 2012 after repeatedly being shunned at her local church. When she came to evening services straight from work, still dressed in her professional clothes, she was welcomed. But other times, wearing "long black and purple skirts, eyeliner and ornate cross necklaces," she was met with "whispering, pointing, and people generally wondering how I dared to come into their church." After one such visit, she shook hands with a welcoming-committee member who then then turned to a neighbor and asked, "we won't get more like that, will we?" She told the church how frustrated she is that such places are meant to be welcoming, when her experience was anything but.

"Maybe it would be better for such churches to have a dress code," she said, "although if long black dresses and silver crosses are to be banned, it may prevent some of the clergy from entering the building."

Instead of being violent, goths tend toward pacifism. A security guard and DJ who works at one of San Francisco's goth clubs said his clientele in general will not fight, even when provoked. If a teen is involved with goth culture—or even if he or she wears pretty black clothes and a little eyeliner—it would be a good idea to talk about bullying and abuse. Discuss safe routes home from school and evening activities, or perhaps covering up if that's not possible. Be creative. A teen may not want to hide his or her own identity, and may feel such attacks "shouldn't happen." But it's important to be realistic as well. There are ways to keep safe without compromising the look too much.

After all the negative press, when a teen adopts an all-black uniform—particularly if that uniform is frilly and flamboyant—it can be unsettling. Add black hair, white face makeup, and black eyeliner and lipstick, and "unsettled" might turn to "frightened." After all, your fresh-faced child now looks like someone from another planet. You can't see his or her features under all that paint. And you've heard that goths can be violent killers. What if your teenager looks this way because he or she is feeling violent, too?

Conversations are good, and time spent listening to gothic music together can be even better. Try to put it all into context: is he or she doing as well in school as before? Are drugs and drinking a factor? Is this newly minted goth getting in trouble with school officials or police? Some goths do get into trouble, but overall they're a reasonably well-behaved bunch.

Even so, some parents set guidelines for their kids' appearance. Nicky, a 25-year-old who grew up in Napa, said her mom did just that when she was a teen. So did Stephanie's. "My parents set strong boundaries," Stephanie said. "My mom would let me dress goth, but I couldn't go to school dressed 'inappropriately,' meaning anything too revealing. I was not allowed to do anything permanent, such as tattoos or hair dying. I was allowed to get extra ear piercings."

Just making an effort to understand the changes—which may be the start of a lifelong love affair with goth—can go a long way. "Both of my parents tried very hard to understand what it was all about," said Cobweb. "I'm not sure they ever really understood, but they tried."

A Hero's Quest

Vanessa* was a typical teenager. She grew up in New South Wales, Australia, and her parents were her major source of stress. At the age of 14, she dipped her toe into the world of video games for the first time with *Puzzle Bobble*, an addictive Japanese puzzle game. She soon discovered that games provided a "time out" from the troubles of everyday life.

Soon, Vanessa developed a taste for fighting games, including *Tekken* and the *Virtua Fighter* series. Characters in these games brawl in hand-to-hand combat, using trick moves and the occasional sword or spear, until one wins. Vanessa was one of the few females playing such games, and her skills were a source of self-confidence: "I loved that guys would challenge me, as I'm a girl, and I could whip their asses and usually continue on to finish the entire game." After all, physical size or strength doesn't matter when you're playing a virtual character on a screen.

In the *Virtua Fighter* games, Vanessa could play against the computer. It would catch on to her favorite moves and counteract them, making it harder for Vanessa to beat the console. This forced her to hone her fighting skills.

She also developed a fondness for certain role-playing video games, particularly *Baldur's Gate 2*. After a player finishes the game, the character Drizzt Do'Urden, a dark elf from *Dungeons & Dragons* lore, is unveiled. Vanessa loved playing the game a second time as Drizzt. "He's ambidextrous and wields two scimitars—how very cool."

Video games provided a vacation from everyday stress— and more. Vanessa said the in-game aggression was healthy. "Electronically killing stuff is always good for releasing tension.

---

* Not her real name.

I think being in another 'realm' or 'fantasy' land also allows you to disassociate from reality and ensure that you don't bring violence into real life."

Pitfall

Almost every time a teenager or young adult brings a gun into a school and kills other kids, the national conversation turns to violent video games. That was never more true than after the shooting at Sandy Hook Elementary School in Newtown, Conn., on Dec. 14, 2012, which left 20 young children and six teachers and other staff members dead. The shooter, 20-year-old Adam Lanza, probably played video games; most young men do. (A plumber who worked for Lanza's family told news tabloids that Adam played *Call of Duty* for hours at a time; not the most reliable source.)

Whether or not Adam played video games—or violent video games in particular—almost seemed beside the point. America was swept up by the idea of a connection between them; it gave people something they thought they could fix. In the two months following the massacre, there were more than 11,000 news articles that included the phrases "Sandy Hook" and "video games." A month after the shootings, President Barack Obama asked Congress to give $10 million to the Centers for Disease Control to study the "the relationship between video games, media images and violence." Other politicians went further: onetime presidential candidate Ralph Nader called video games "electronic child molesters" that turn children into monsters.

When teens commit horrific violence, we often look to outside sources, such as video games, for a potential motive. Even adults who commit mass shootings are not entirely immune from this kind of scrutiny. The day after Aaron Alexis shot and killed 12 people at a navy yard in Washington, D.C., on September 16, 2013, news outlets jumped on his friends' reports that he had played *Call of Duty* as much as 16 hours a day. Those same friends, however, also reported that Alexis had been hearing voices and that he believed he was being influenced by low-frequency electromagnetic waves.

Similarly, when Anders Breivik, then 32, went on a bombing and shooting spree in Norway in July 2011, he killed 77 people in Oslo and nearby Utøya. Beforehand, Breivik wrote a manifesto in which he claimed he used *Call of Duty: Modern Warfare* as a training simulator. Some believe he played *World of Warcraft* to unwind. However, his manifesto instructs readers who are planning similar attacks to *claim* they have taken up *WoW* in order to explain why they're spending so much time indoors and away from social contact: "This 'new project' can justify isolation and people will understand somewhat why you are not answering your phone over long periods. Tell them that you are completely hooked on the game ... You will be amazed on how much you can do undetected while blaming this game."

Although it's clear that Breivik's massacre was motivated by his personal politics—and not by too many hours playing video games—that didn't stop leaders in Europe from acting on the supposed link between gaming and real-life violence. Two weeks after the events in Norway, game retailers in the country suspended sales of the *Call of Duty* franchise, among others. Almost a year later, British MP Keith Vaz said the events in and near Oslo called for "closer scrutiny of aggressive first-person shooter video games." The move gained little support and was later tabled.

The temptation to link violent video games with school shootings goes at least as far back as the Columbine High School massacre in 1999. It's true that Eric Harris and Dylan Klebold played *Doom*; Harris even wrote a handful of add-ons for the game. But authors and psychologists who have examined the Columbine High School shooting—as well as other school shootings—have not found games responsible for sparking these awful crimes. In fact, data from 2000 suggested that the young men who committed school shootings were *less* interested in video games than other boys their age, though that figure has likely changed as games have become more mainstream. Instead, many who study teen shooters have found found that their emotional backgrounds and access to guns were likelier culprits.

But that hasn't stopped university researchers from

trying to nail down a connection between violent video games and juvenile violent crime, conducting numerous studies on how these games affect young people. For years, the majority of those studies suggested a link between violent games and aggressive behavior. However, those studies show correlation, not causation, and there's a big difference between the two. Many of those studies are deeply flawed, either because their sample size is small or non-representative (the participants are often college students, who are a little older than the violent teens in question), or because test subjects are asked to play games they don't ordinarily play or enjoy, a situation that's bound to make anyone feel frustrated and surly.

For example, one study asked 91 women to play either *Street Fighter II* or *Oh No! More Lemmings*. The former is a fighting game similar to *Tekken*. The latter asks the player to place cute little lemmings around a screen to prevent the other lemmings from walking into danger. Researchers found that the women who played *Street Fighter* for 20 minutes were more likely to show aggressive behavior after playing, in the form of blasting a loud noise at someone. However, the women were only tested for a short time after gameplay; researchers didn't test whether those feelings lingered. In addition, there's no information that suggests whether the women were familiar with the games they played, or whether they enjoyed them.

In recent years, researchers have moved beyond simple studies where they bring in 100 college students to play video games and then test them for aggressive feelings. In early 2011, longtime video-game researcher Douglas Gentile published a study with the American Academy of Pediatrics in which he looked at 3,000 students over a two-year period in Singapore, finding that one in 10 of them was "addicted" to video games, and that there was some connection between "excessive" gaming and depression, saying, "although children who are depressed may retreat into gaming, the gaming increases the depression, and vice versa." While even seasoned journalists at Reuters reported this to mean that the hours spent gaming *caused* the depression, Gentile, in a separate study, cautioned readers from taking away any kind of causal link between intense gaming and behavioral issues: "it is equally likely that children who have trouble at school seek to play games to experience feelings of mastery, or that attention problems cause both poor school performance and an attraction to games."

In another longitudinal study of 5,000 teens over four years, a cadre of researchers at Dartmouth College led by Jay G. Hull investigated whether there were any links between video games that "glorify reckless driving" and actual reckless driving among teenagers. The problems with this study were many, including the fact that teens were being asked to self-report their driving habits, and teens have been known to brag about, or at least exaggerate, their reckless behavior. Meanwhile, the American Automobile Association calls teens, particularly male teens, the most aggressive drivers on the road—video games or no. Even if there is a connection between teens who like to take risks behind the wheel and teens who like to play *Grand Theft Auto* or *Burnout*, it's also possible the link goes the other way: adolescents who drive a little recklessly might enjoy a video game where they're allowed to do that. And, ultimately, the in-game version is much safer.

In another, more nuanced study, Brock University researchers Paul Adachi and Teena Willoughby looked at whether it was games' levels of competitiveness—not their levels of violence—that might be linked to aggressive behavior. They ran two trials, one in which students played two competitive games for 12 minutes; one was violent, one wasn't. Then, the students made up a cup of hot sauce for a "taster" who supposedly didn't like spicy food, and found that the gamers made equally spicy brews, suggesting that violent content alone was not a factor in aggressive action. In the second trial, 60 students were asked to play one of four different games, some competitive, some not. The competitive gamers made the hot-sauce cups hotter than the non-competitive gamers.

In this case, there are a number of unanswered questions, such as whether providing someone a hot-sauce drink constitutes aggression. Even though they were told the taster didn't like spicy food, many people think they're doing someone a favor—not attacking them—when they serve them food that's outside their comfort zone. In addition, this study, as with almost every study on gaming and aggression, doesn't show whether the behavior lasts beyond the few minutes following a game, or whether someone who's willing to give a cup of hot sauce to a stranger would be willing to do something more overtly aggressive or violent in everyday life.

There's another problem with experiments that have focused on video games: almost all of them have given subjects license to behave aggressively or even told them to be aggressive. Having permission to be aggressive can encourage people to act that way, both in a study setting and in the real world, Jonathan Freedman wrote in *Media Violence and its Effect on Aggression*.

In 1999, Dr. Stuart Fischoff, founder of the Media Psychology Lab at the California State University in Los Angeles, gave an address to the American Psychological Association—an address whose message still hasn't reached the general public or the legislative world.

"'There is no unity of expert opinion on the effects of entertainment violence," Fischoff said. "Whether we cite 100, 1,000 or 10,000 research studies which conclude that exposure to violent media produces violent behavior, 10,000 is no more persuasive or credible than 100 if the designs of the research are flawed and/or the generalizations to an external population of behaviors are patently unjustified."

Likewise, in 2011, when the Swedish Media Council undertook a survey of more than 100 studies on kids, violent video games and aggression, they found a statistically significant link between violent video games and aggressive behavior. But their interpretation of this finding was the opposite of what we've come to expect in the United States. Among other things, they said, "Many of the studies use different methods to measure aggression, many of which lack a clear connection to violent behaviour." They also found that the research didn't provide enough evidence to suggest a causal relationship between gaming and aggression, and that "The few studies that have attempted to examine other causes of aggression found that factors, such as poor physical health or family problems, can explain both violent behaviour and a propensity to play violent computer games." However, plenty of perfectly healthy and happy kids also play violent video games.

Even Leland Yee, the California senator who authored legislation that would have made it illegal to sell "M" rated games to minors, agreed that there are no valid studies proving a link between video-game violent and real-life violence. "There's never been a true cause-and-effect study that shows that if you watch these games you're going to commit greater violence. That kind of study can't happen in a free society," Yee told me. "In order to [study] the cause and effect, you have to get a random group and place [subjects] in one group or another. If you don't want your kid to play violent video games, and we put them randomly into that group, you might not want us to do that."

And yet, Yee is convinced that these games are dangerous for kids. He argued that "ultraviolent" games, as he calls them, are very different from other forms of media and have the potential to twist kids' minds. "Number one, it's interactive. This is about participating in an active way in the commission of a particular heinous behavior," he said. "The second quality is the overlearning that goes on. This is not about watching that scene one or maybe two times. This is seeing something tens of thousands of times. This is where we get reports of kids practicing this behavior during the day [in games] and then acting it out at night." He said the Columbine High School massacre was an example of this second point.

Yee isn't alone in believing that games influence some teens' long-term behavior, despite no scientific evidence that they do. Game companies—particularly Rockstar, the company that has produced the *Grand Theft Auto* franchise—have been sued numerous times for allegedly causing teens to commit crimes. In October 2003, the families of Aaron Hamel and Kimberly Bede sued Rockstar after the teens were shot by William and Josh Buckner. The lawsuit alleged that *Grand Theft Auto III* created "psychological effects" in the Buckners, prompting the shooting. After the case failed to move forward, both sides moved for dismissal.

In February 2005, 17-year-old Devin Moore sued Rockstar. He blamed the *Grand Theft Auto* series for causing him to shoot and kill three Alabama policeman after they arrested him for stealing a car. A year later, the case was dismissed. In September 2006, the families of Delbert Paul Posey, Tryone Schmid, and Marlea Schmid sued Rockstar after Posey's son, Cody, played *Grand Theft Auto* obsessively before killing the trio. A judge threw out the case in December 2007.

In all three lawsuits, the attorney representing the plaintiffs was Jack Thompson, a Miami lawyer who has since been disbarred—and fined more than $43,000 by the Florida Bar Association—for his conduct in these and other cases.

Rockstar faced legal action for another game, the brutally graphic *Manhunt* (which is so graphic, most gamers don't like it). In Febrary 2004, Warren LeBlanc, 17, killed his 14-year-old friend, Stefan Pakeerah. LeBlanc pleaded guilty to the murder in court, where Pakeerah's mother claimed the killer had been "obsessed" with the video game. However, police denied any link between the game and the killing, saying that LeBlanc was motivated by other criminal activity. Still, the media played up the link between the game and the murder, causing some shops to pull *Manhunt* from their shelves.

Despite the legal firestorm launched against game companies (the Guinness Book of World Records called *Grand Theft Auto* the most controversial video game in history), those cases haven't validated a link between gaming and violence. In each case, there were many other motivating factors that led a teenager to commit those crimes. "Children want to have exciting fantasies, but they usually don't want to suffer injuries, get in serious trouble, or alienate the rest of the world. Consequently, the media can inspire them to play violent games —but not even a constant diet of the most exciting media violence will induce them to be violent in reality," Gerard Jones wrote in *Killing Monsters: Why Children Need Fantasy, Super Heroes and Make-Believe Violence*. In fact, some research suggests that playing violent games with a friend—whether the friends are cooperating or competing—can reduce the level of aggression in children's play, according to Patricia Marks Greenfield's *Mind and Media*.

Jones studied the relationship between youth violence and violent entertainment in depth in *Killing Monsters*. For the most part, teenage boys who were likely to bring guns to school with murderous intent did not care much for video games, according to Jones. Many of them enjoyed target shooting with real guns. In fact, easy access to guns was a much more common predictor of violent behavior than kids' media interests.

"Studies reveal that the vast majority of kids who take up guns in adolescence have grown up in households where guns are used or in immediate environs where guns have become part of everyday youth culture, such as gang-controlled neighborhoods," Jones wrote.

Reporters have focused intensely on school shootings since the 1990s. This increased focus suggested that teens were committing more violence than ever. Legislators and parents connected this "trend" with the rise in popularity of violent entertainment, including video games. However, when looking at the actual data, many researchers found that the opposite was true. As violent entertainment became more popular, violence among teens actually dropped.

By contrast, kids raised during the 1970s—when entertainment media went out of its way to decrease its representations of violence in young people's entertainment—engaged in more crime. "The kids who spent their formative years in that pop-cultural milieu became the teenagers of the mid-1980s, when juvenile crime rates rose again. The kids who spent their formative years in the 1980s, on the other hand, when action-packed movies, TV shows, video games and combat toys seemed to be taking over kid culture, became the teenagers of the late 1990s, when those rates plummeted," according to Jones.

The relationship between real violence and fantasy violence is much more complex. The entertainment industry goes in waves, offering violent games and films, and then pulling back. Peaks in violent media typically come after a period of intense violent crime on city streets, according to Jones. And, once youth make use of that entertainment—violent video games in particular—youth crime rates drop, including those involving guns. But games keep getting blamed, in part, because adults don't know much about them.

"Many forces have been shown to contribute to

aggression: religious fervor, patriotic fervor, sports rivalry, romantic rivalry, hot summer nights," Jones wrote. "Entertainment has inspired some people to violence, but so have the Bible, the Constitution, the Beatles, books about Hitler, and obsessions with TV actresses. We don't usually condemn those influences as harmful, because we understand them better, we understand why people like them and the benefits most of us draw from them. What's lacking is an understanding of aggressive fantasies and the entertainment that speaks to them."

Jones did find a link between aggression-prone teens and those who are attracted to the goriest games. These teens' temperaments drive them to seek compelling alternatives to real-life aggression. Brutal games help them make sense of their aggressive feelings, which are not socially acceptable, Jones wrote. Among this group, the ones who spent the most hours with violent entertainment committed far fewer serious crimes.

Among wayward teens, the biggest culprit is free time, according to Jones. "Unemployed boys who aren't great academic achievers are more likely to amuse themselves with video games; unemployed boys who aren't great academic achievers are also more likely to misbehave," he wrote. Teens who have jobs, or who are doing plenty of homework, playing sports, or performing volunteer work not only don't have enough time to play hours of video games, they also have less time to get into trouble.

A much better predictor of whether a teen will become violent is his family background, according to Maggie Cutler's essay "Research on the Effects of Media Violence is Inconclusive." Boys who watch *Fight Club* are likely to wind up in their school's film club; boys whose fathers are behind bars are more likely to wind up in jail. Santana High School's shooter, Charles Andrew Williams, was probably motivated by the anniversary of the Columbine High School shootings—not the fact that he watched *The Mummy*, Cutler wrote.

Experts also claim that violent video games cause players to become desensitized to violence. They say this is especially true for "impressionable" teenagers whose sense of morality is perceived as not fully formed. Some gamers have admitted to feeling a certain numbness playing violent games, such as first-person shooters. However, they said that feeling is usually produced by games that are poorly written—ones that that do not tell a complex, evocative story.

"I do not mind being asked to kill in the shooter: Killing is part of the contract. What I do mind is not feeling anything in particular—not even numbness—after having killed in such numbers," Tom Bissell wrote in *Extra Lives: Why Video Games Matter*. "Many shooters ask the gamer to use violence against pure, unambiguous evil: monsters, Nazis, corporate goons, aliens of Ottoman territorial ambition. Yet these shooters typically have nothing to say about evil and violence, other than that evil is evil and violence is violent."

Jim Rossignol, author of *This Gaming Life*, asked teen gamers whether shooter-style games made them want to pick up real guns. Many of them found the idea absurd. They saw little connection between on-screen shooting and real-life gunfire, it didn't even make them want to join the military to defeat enemies. Most of Rossignol's subjects, who grew up in suburban England, had never even seen a real gun in their lives.

Some believe that first-person shooters can serve as military-training tools, including for target practice. *Battlezone* was modified by the United States Army to train soldiers how to fight in armored vehicles. *Counter Strike* was used by the Chinese government to test antiterrorist tactics used by the People's Armed Police. "Whether these games enhance actual fighting experience is doubtful, but there is no question that shooters train those who play them to absorb and react to incomprehensible amounts of incoming information under great (though simulated) duress," Bissell wrote. When he was embedded with the Marine Corps in the summer of 2005, Bissell learned that most of the Marines he talked to were avid shooter-game fans who brought their came consoles with them when they were deployed.

However, those games could not equip soldiers for the reality of taking another human life. Rossignol cites Evan Wright's book *Generation Kill*: "Wright, who rode with the elite First Recon unit in Iraq, describes how the soldiers discovered the true depths of their innocence as they shot real people. He describes how the men broke down when they saw the consequences of gunfire, and he speaks with frightening clarity of how there was no way that gaming, no matter how violent, could have ever prepared them for those experiences. These soldiers might have killed thousands on their PlayStation, but death up close was a completely different and unbearable experience, well beyond their coping mechanisms. Simulated death is not death."

Sean, an Ohio resident who started playing games when he was 5, agreed that playing a shooter was not the same as real-life shooting lessons. "I have been playing shooters for years, and the couple of chances I've had to pick up a real gun, I couldn't shoot for the life of me. Moving and clicking a mouse, or using a controller does not equate to holding, aiming, and firing a real gun. If there were a zombie apocalypse, I'd probably be the first to go."

There's also the issue of whether video games allow players to "blow off steam," to release anger and anxiety from real-world experiences. Many players do find games cathartic, or at the very least a vacation from day-to-day worries. Others said that playing games for this purpose didn't work—it only made them feel worse. "I sometimes try to use games as a distraction from unpleasant real things, or to lift my spirits when I'm feeling sad or angry. Usually it works out to the opposite effect, with my mood ruining the playing experience," said a 15-year-old California gamer who started playing before he was 7.

A 14-year-old from northern California put it even more simply: "When I'm angry, I tend to suck at a game, and when I'm sucking, it only makes me angry."

The gamers I interviewed said that adults frequently get the wrong idea about video games. One said many make the mistake of thinking that games are "just toys," and no more. Instead, he—and many like him—find video games a vehicle for understanding other aspects of life. "I have personally found them as a means of contemplation or observing ideas I haven't thought of before, which I then integrate into my imagination," said the 21-year-old, who started playing video games when he was 4. "When not playing video games, I tend to pretend about being a hero or anti-hero, since my imagination is my most faithful and ever-present companion."

Why is it so hard to convince people that video games are a legitimate form of art and entertainment—one that teaches more than it harms? Well, just look at where resistance to gaming comes from, according to Henry Jenkins, professor of communication, journalism and cinematic arts at the University of Southern California—and a game fan.

"[Resistance] is coming from the partisans of other arts. It comes from the film critics who are worried that their preferred medium is going to be superseded. It is coming from literary critics who are concerned that young people are playing games rather than reading books. It comes from those whose notion of art is so narrow that few works qualify. ... It comes from gamers who worry that calling games art means that they are going to become too obscure and pretentious," Jenkins said.

Dream Chronicles

The first video game, invented in 1947, allowed players to simulate firing a missile at a target. But the first coin-operated video-game machines and home consoles didn't appear until the early 1970s. It was another decade before they took off commercially, with classic games such as *Space Invaders, Asteroids,* and *Pac-Man.* Since then, video games have become hugely popular. By the mid-2000s, roughly 70 percent of households had video games in their homes, according to *Play the Game: The Parent's Guide to Video Games* by Jeannie Novak and Luis Levy. The average player is 35 years old. Males play an average of 7.6 hours per week, while females play 7.4 hours per week.

Video games are serious business. Computer and video game software sales topped $25 billion in 2011, which included $16.6 billion in software sales, according to the NPD Group. Action and strategy games are by far the most popular.

The average game buyer is 30 years old. Forty-seven percent of players are women, and more adult women (30 percent) play video games than juvenile boys (18 percent).

Ninety percent of juvenile gamers said their parents are present when they purchase or rent games, while 66 percent of parents believe games stimulate their kids' minds, according to the ESA. Sixteen percent of games sold in 2009 were rated "M" (mature). However, 7 of the 10 top-selling games in February 2010 were rated "M."

The Entertainment Software Ratings Board rates games based on whether their content is suitable for a given age range. The ratings have nothing to do with how challenging games are to play, as some parents believe. Most people are already familiar with the ESRB's rating system, but here's a quick rundown just in case: "EC" is for early childhood, "E" is for everyone, "E10+" is for everyone over the age of 10, "T" is for teen, "M" is for mature (over 17), "AO" is for adults only, and "RP" is for rating pending. Early-childhood games are aimed at kids age 3-10 and are usually educational, while "E" games are suitable for all ages and contain either no violence or only "cartoon violence," where cartoon characters fight and defeat each other in non-gory ways. "E10+" games might feature slight violence, while "T" can contain stronger language, crude humor, and some blood but no gore. "M" games can contain gore, as well as profanity and sexuality. "AO" games are only for those over 18, and can contain nudity and graphic sex, as well as extreme violence and gore.

Some have accused the ESRB of not rating games accurately, or of giving some very intense games an "M" rating rather than an "AO" rating so that they can make money. Many retailers will not sell "AO" games at all. In one case, *Grand Theft Auto: San Andreas* received an "M" rating, but gamers later discovered—by way of a software patch written by a fan—a hidden segment of the game featuring graphic sexual content. The game was re-rated "AO," after which the game's publisher, Rockstar, allowed consumers to exchange their "AO" version for a modified "M" version with the sexual material removed.

The rating system is meant to provide information to buyers. Although younger gamers are discouraged from purchasing "M" rated games, it is not against the law for them to do so. In California, Yee authored legislation that would have made it a crime for stores to sell these games to minors.

California's legislature approved the bill, which was signed into law by Gov. Arnold Schwarzenegger in 2005. The Electronic Software Associated sued, defeating the law in California. California appealed to the United States Supreme Court, which struck down the case in 2011.

"Psychological studies purporting to show a connection between exposure to violent video games and harmful effects on children do not prove that such exposure causes minors to act aggressively," Supreme Court Justice Antonin Scalia wrote in the majority ruling.

A former child psychologist, Yee agreed that no scientific studies have definitely linked violent games to adolescent behavior, but he doesn't want to take chances with young minds. "There will be individuals who will play the most horrible games, committing the most horrible scenes, and will have enough internal controls to understand this is fantasy and make-believe," Yee said. "But there are many other youngsters who don't have those kind of internal controls. Some are able to handle it and some can't handle it. For kids, let's not take that chance and put them in that situation."

Still, teens have a harder time buying "M" rated games than seeing an "R" rated movie, buying an "R" rated DVD, or buying an album with a parental-advisory sticker, according to the Federal Trade Commission. Even though teens are legally allowed to buy "M" rated games (and it's illegal for them to see or purchase "R" rated movies), sellers are generally complying with the guidelines.

What, exactly, is a "violent" video game? It's true that many video games feature some "violence," in which the character shoots, knocks down, or otherwise defeats enemies in the course of gameplay. In some games this is "cartoon" violence. There's no blood. Cute characters might squash each other, or even blow up enemies, but it's not the same. When we talk about violent video games, we're mostly talking about ones in which considerable blood and gore is shown, and ones in which the gameplay is more fast-paced, aggressive, stressful, and combative. These are the ones that have been blamed for teen aggression and violence.

When video games first became popular in the 1970s

and 1980s, their technology was relatively primitive. Even though the most violent games showed some blood, the video quality was poor enough that it just didn't look that realistic. In the 1990s and beyond, as video quality improved, games became more sophisticated. It's much easier to depict a World War II battle scene, for example, if the imagery is lifelike enough to evoke 1940s Europe and make the player believe he or she is on the battlefield. That's one reason the "M" ratings— along with the rest of the rating system—didn't really emerge until the 1990s; before then, gore was almost undepictable. But with modern computers and consoles, that has changed.

While realistic games are more evocative, there is a limit to how realistic they can be. Researchers have found that if a replica of a human being—a robot, or an animated person in a film or video game—is *too* realistic, but not perfectly realistic, viewers are weirded out. (This phenomenon is called the "uncanny valley.") There are many theories about why this happens: It's possible that the combination of human features and less-than-lifelike behaviors remind us of our own mortality, or that those "dead" traits may kick off hardwired feelings related to mate selection, germ avoidance, or discomfort over violating social norms. In any case, it means that overly authentic games usually make players uncomfortable and unwilling to play. Games can maintain a level of realism that is enough to immerse the player, but not so much that the player forgets it's fiction.

Games are very different from film and TV. For starters, players become one of the characters in the story. Often, players don't get any choice about which character they play. But there are plenty of times when they can customize their character, either to look like themselves or to look like someone (or something) entirely different. In a stand-alone game— rather than an online game—chances are good that the other characters are operated by the computer, and will behave in a number of pre-scripted ways. In online games, most, if not all, of the other characters are controlled by another player.

In many of the more violent games, enemies are not human. They're demons, zombies, monsters—something the player would certainly want to defeat, if the situation were real.

In a few games, particularly the *Grand Theft Auto* franchise, the computer-controlled characters are humans, and players can hurt or kill them. Sometimes, players *have* to kill them in order to move forward. To some critics, it makes a huge difference whether you're asked to kill monsters or humans in video games. Yee's law specifically targeted games where the violence is aimed at "human figures."

Many games feature relatively large "worlds"— environments that can take many hours to explore. In some cases, players can travel through these worlds without following the storyline for a while. That makes games much, much bigger than films or television. Games "contain more than most gamers can ever hope to see, and the person deciding where to point the camera is, in many cases, you—and you might never see the 'best part.' The best part of looking up at a night sky, after all, is not any one star but the infinite possibility of what is between stars. Games often provide an approximation of this feeling, with the difference that you can find out what is out there," Bissell wrote.

Much of the concern about violent video games has focused on first-person shooters, largely because the player is issued a powerful (if virtual) firearm and moves through the game as though they're walking from place to place, firing at enemies. A few shooter games are set in "shooting galleries." Most take place in real-world settings, or historic, fantasy, or dark horror worlds.

In *Doom*, one of the earliest and most popular first-person shooters, the player portrays a space marine posted on Mars. He discovers he is the last man alive among evil demons ready to attack Earth. In the final levels of the game, the player winds up in Hell. Thanks to the reasonably sophisticated graphics available in the 1990s, *Doom* offered plenty of blood and gore—though gamers of today look back at the early *Doom* games and realize the gore isn't as realistic as it used to seem. Despite its themes, the game drew many new players into video games. Some 10 million people played Doom in its first years, and then moved on to other games, arguably spawning the gaming subculture.

The best-selling first-person shooters of all time come

from the *Grand Theft Auto* series. Part driving game, part action-adventure, part shooter, it's awash in parodies of American culture. The open-world setting lets the player do whatever he or she wants: drive around aimlessly, crash into things, carjack ambulances and rescue other characters, explore fictional cities, pretend to be a sniper, blow up dozens of cars. The possibilities aren't endless, but they are extensive and imaginative. Here, players get the chance to try a number of experiences they could probably never have in reality (and likely wouldn't want to have).

The *Grand Theft Auto* series launched in 1997, but it didn't really take off until *Grand Theft Auto III*, the first 3D game, emerged in 2001. In each of the games, you play a criminal, often working your way through a variety of rival organized-crime rings until some ultimate face-off with a crime boss. The series has faced plenty of criticism for the possibilities it offers—such as the ability to kill any of the thousands of computer-controlled characters in the game, including drivers, pedestrians, police, and prostitutes. You can also steal people's money once they're dead. (For what it's worth, most of them have very little money; players earn much more for completing missions, such as driving a taxi and taking fares to their destinations, taking injured characters to the hospital in an ambulance, or putting out fires with a fire truck.)

Grand Theft Auto makes no apology for being violent, even graphically violent. But it's worth noting that the violence has almost a comic-book atmosphere. *Grand Theft Auto* doesn't feel realistic; it feels like make-believe. At the same time, the freedom afforded by the game sparks the imagination and mischief. It invites players to ask, "I wonder what would happen if I ..." and then gives them the chance to find out. Frequently, there are consequences for wrongdoing. Run over too many pedestrians or blow up too many cars and the police will come after you, first in cars, then in helicopters and tanks. Drivers pick fights with you if you try to carjack them. Still, players don't forget this is a simulation—one that can be turned off it it becomes too much.

The whole game is laced with humor. Radio stations feature call-in shows and advertisements that parody what you'd hear on your way to work in the morning. It's this potent combination of humor, fantasy, darkness, and the temptation to explore criminal behavior that has made *Grand Theft Auto* so popular.

In the realm of top-selling shooters, *Call of Duty* gives *Grand Theft Auto* some serious competition. The series of first- and third-person shooters is set in wartimes from World War II to the modern day. The first game, released in 2003 for the PC, puts you right in the midst of World War II fighting. Your soldier is supported by a range computer-controlled soldiers, from two infantrymen to a large regiment of tanks. You're outfitted with an array of historically accurate weapons, and you experience shell shock—complete with muffled hearing and ringing ears—when things go wrong. Missions take you to America, Britain, and the Soviet Union.

In other *Call of Duty* games, you may serve with the Red Army, the British Army, the French Resistance and Polish Army. Or you may be deployed to a fictional near-future setting where a radical leader has just executed a Middle Eastern president. The *Modern Warfare* series has faced plenty of criticism and scrutiny for re-creating modern-day terrorism scenes, such as a bomb attack on a London subway, or simply for putting players into everyday settings and asking them to fight enemies.

"It felt almost surreal watching soldiers move through residential neighborhoods, clearing homes of foreign soldiers and finding shelter in a fast food restaurant as enemies pinned them down. The unease heightens as players venture inside a Washington D.C. consumed by fire," Brett Molina wrote for *USA Today*. "Some of these unsettling feelings stem from just how incredibly realistic the game looks. The visuals are astounding, and each environment—from snowy mountains in eastern Europe to the favelas of Brazil and a war-torn Washington D.C.—is captured with intricate detail."

Because these games are so realistic, some fear that young gamers might not be able to discern between the game and reality—although most kids are clear about where that boundary lies. But the realism is also part of the appeal: *Call of Duty* offers a taste of modern-day warfare without having to join the military or travel to dangerous parts of the world. Some of the games teach military and defense history, while others offer a chance to explore current conflicts.

Along with open-world shooters such as *Grand Theft Auto* or military-style shooters such as *Call of Duty*, survival-horror games are another popular branch of the violent-game tree.

Imagine a post-apocalyptic world filled with demons, zombies or monsters. Now imagine you're one of the only survivors. That's the premise of many survival-horror games, which are the video-game counterparts of horror films and books. Because of the setting, resources—from food to ammunition—are scarce. This forces players to fight and shoot less, and find more imaginative ways to bypass enemies.

Although fighting is less common here than in other action video games, it does happen. Given the nature of the enemies, it can be fairly graphic and scary. At the end of most survival horror games, the player must defeat a supreme, monstrous "boss" who is often the leader of the other enemies in the game. Defeating this primary villain frequently returns the game world to a more peaceful state. Survival-horror characters are often less heroic, more everyday, and more vulnerable, which makes winning feel that much more triumphant.

There are a number of popular survival-horror series, including *Left 4 Dead* and *Silent Hill,* but the most popular of all is the *Resident Evil* series, which pits human survivors against virulent, violent zombies. The series kicked off with the first game in 1996, in which a series of strange murders have rocked the fictional town of Raccoon City. You play an investigator, either Chris Redfield or Jill Valentine, sent in to find out why another recon team has gone missing. Somehow your team becomes trapped in a zombie-filled mission, and it's your job to break them out by solving the house's puzzles and riddles. There's a limited amount of ammunition, so you must find other ways past the zombies.

The original *Resident Evil* game was edited considerably before its release in the United States, but still carries an "M" rating. In Japan, where it's known as *Biohazard*, the game includes extra scenes and more gore. Some of that material was included in *Resident Evil: Director's Cut.*

In subsequent games, the player returns to Raccoon City, taking on different roles to fight zombies, to cure viruses that turn people into zombies, or—in one of the most recent games—to travel to Africa to discover the root of the zombie virus.

Many see the *Resident Evil* series as groundbreaking, and several of the games have received high ratings from critics. They're popular in part because, while violent, the games encourage experimentation, according to Bissell.

"The violence of *Resident Evil* was surprisingly occasional but unbelievably brutal. It was also clinical, which encouraged a certain wicked tendency to experiment," he wrote. "As you found and used new weapons, it turned out that zombies reacted to them in various ways. A shotgun could blow the legs out from under a zombie, and the well-placed round of a .38 could take its head right off. I do not claim to be a historian of video-game dismemberment, but I am fairly sure that no game before *Resident Evil* allowed such violence to be done to specific limbs. It provided gamers with one of the video-game form's first laboratories of virtual sadism, and I would be lying if I did not admit that it was, in its way, exhilarating. (They were *zombies*. You were doing them a *favor*.)"

Oddworld

Evan Jones was three when he picked up a video-game controller for the first time. His earliest games included the demon-riddled *Diablo II* and classic first-person shooters *Quake* and *Counter-Strike*. To this day, *Diablo II* remains one of his favorite video games for its addictive role-playing style.

"It may not have stunning visuals, but the gameplay is superb and it has a unique leveling system for its time," he says. This exemplifies what many players—teen or adult—look for in a game: story and craft, not top-notch graphics or over-the-top gore. It also offers standalone or cooperative options, which satisfy a range of moods, Evan says: playing alone is a thrilling challenge, but playing with friends "can make even the hardest bosses easy."

Despite his early introduction to violent video games, they aren't the only games Evan, who was 16 when I interviewed him, likes to play. He's also fond of *Garry's Mod* with its seemingly endless possibilities; *Starcraft II*, an intricately detailed game requiring on-the-fly strategy, and *Portal 2* for its elaborate puzzles. He's also taken with *Killing Floor*, a gory first-person shooter set during a mutant outbreak in London, which he likes for the fun, team-based gameplay and its dark wit.

Although Evan hasn't encountered many games that were too intense or violent for him, he did stop playing *Doom 3* soon after he started, "because it was scary ... and I was nine," he says.

Evan is surrounded by gamers, including his dad and stepdad, both of whom are familiar with the range of video games on the market. His parents buy him the video games he asks for, and they haven't discussed the level of violence in games with him. That hasn't prevented the teen from reflecting on the games or recognizing them for what they are: fiction.

"I see violent video games as an outlet to aggression and stress in teens and adults," Evan says. "[Games] never have shaped my feelings towards real-life violence, as I have never liked violence at all."

Video games—including violent games—can put you right in the thick of a life-or-death story that can teach you a whole lot about yourself and, frequently, your ability to cooperate with others when the stakes are high. It's not that the violence itself is a draw, but rather that the violence often reflects the reality of a conflict-riddled puzzle that's yours to solve. That's what draws many gamers in and keeps them coming back for more.

Infectious, violent zombies were bearing down on Bissell and three friends. He and his team were racing to a safe house, where the zombies couldn't hurt them. His friends were attacked on the way. Only Bissell made it inside.

Through the window, he could see his teammates bleeding out. In another minute or two, they would be dead.

"All it would take to end the round would be a Hunter [zombie] or a Smoker [zombie] incapacitating me. So I stayed put. Better one of us than none of us. My downed friends failed to see it that way. Over my headphones, they vigorously questioned my courage, my manhood, the ability of the lone female survivor to repopulate the human world on her own, and my understanding of deontological ethics."

One of his teammates died. Bissell tried something risky: he shot one of the zombies through the closed door, killing it. He stepped outside and quickly killed two more. Buoyed by his success, he dashed over to help one of his surviving teammates up. Together they got the other survivor to his feet. The trio made it inside the safe house and shut the door.

"At great personal risk, and out of real shame, I had rescued two of my three friends and in the process outfaced against all odds one of the best *Left 4 Dead* teams I had and have ever played against," he wrote. "The people I saved that night still talk about my heroic action—and yes, it was, it did feel, heroic—whenever we play together. ... all the emotions I felt during those few moments—fear, doubt, resolve, and finally courage—were as intensely vivid as any I have felt while reading a novel or watching a film or listening to a piece of music."

Bissell's story highlights many of the things players love about video games. They allow players to insert themselves into interesting situations that would never happen in real life. They force players to solve high-stakes problems quickly. They bring up a wide range of emotions (many of them positive). They allow players to triumph over difficult odds and become a hero or witness another person's heroism. They permit the kind of aggressive play that many crave but that isn't socially acceptable. In many cases, they provide a social framework. Not every game provides all of these experiences, but many games— even the most grisly—offer a few, and some of the best allow for most of them.

Games, like other arts, feed our deepest intellectual, emotional, and sensual needs, according to Rossignol. He argues that gamers purchase games because they provide significant emotional and physical practice. "For hard-core gamers, video games have done more than distract or entertain us. They're vital experiences in which we've uncovered something useful, something vital in our lives," he wrote.

There's no way to describe the "average" game fan. Gamers come in all shapes and sizes, from all ages and backgrounds. "There are people who like games, and there are people who haven't found the games they like yet," said game designer Morgan Jaffit. "When you consider that things like bridge, baseball, *Farmville*, *Call of Duty*, Lotto, crosswords, and more are all games of one kind or another ... it's really hard to find anyone who 'doesn't care for games.'"

In many games, the player enters the game world as one of its main characters. Sometimes, the character is pre-assigned. In *Crysis 2*, it's a marine code-named Alcatraz who battles aliens in a post-apocalyptic New York City. In *Red Dead Redemption*, it's former outlaw John Marston. Government officials kidnap his family, then order Marston to help them track down his bad-guy ex-friends. In other games, players choose from a handful of characters of different sizes, genders, and qualities. Each one will have strengths and weaknesses that make the game play slightly different.

The majority of these characters are human, Greg Short, the co-founder of Electronic Entertainment Design and Research, told Bissell. Not only that, but most of them are between the ages of 18 and 34. "People like playing as people, and ... they like playing as people that almost precisely resemble themselves," Bissell summarized.

Many roleplaying-style video games allow for a lot more character customization. Players can create a character that is human, elf, dwarf, orc, or a variety of others—not to mention male or female, with unique clothing, hair, and other stylistic qualities. Some gamers, such as BioWare employee Drew Karpyshyn, have trouble identifying with a predetermined character, so being able to customize their on-screen persona is attractive. "When I make a character—even if I don't make the character look like me—that is the character I'm inhabiting through the game. Even if it's a female character or not even a human character—it doesn't matter. I feel connected," Karpyshyn told Bissell.

Whether playing a pre-assigned or custom character, players may be portraying someone quite similar to themselves. However, it's just as likely that they're trying on a new personality. Many men will opt to portray a female character, which lets them experiment with what it's like to be perceived as female. It also makes it easier to befriend women players. Teenagers, in particular, may find it psychologically useful to experiment with different personas in games, just as they are working out their personalities in real life. When players are allowed to customize their characters, they are engaging their imagination, according to video-game scholar Patricia Marks Greenfield.

The freedom to choose one's character helps make players equal. Almost anyone can play a video game, and many can succeed, regardless of how they look or how strong they are. "If you were a jock or a nerd, the keyboard still responded the same. [Games] leveled the playing field in a way that made it fun for everyone to play while being anonymous," a gamer from Toronto, Ontario, Canada, who started playing games when he was 10 told me. "You could be your character, and as long as you could perform on-par with the others, it didn't matter how big or how small you were, or what color you were, or if you were a boy or a girl."

Video games offer a variety of "worlds" to choose from, whether it's a fictional version of mob-controlled New York City or a cluster of Milky Way planets thousands of years in the future. Games are so broad and varied that players can replicate almost any kind of experience. Like books and films, when games are well-written they can be incredibly immersive, supplying the player with a variety of experiences he or she wouldn't be able to have—or, often, want to have—in reality. "For most players, video game violence enables them to break rules in a safe setting, to engage in antisocial behavior they would never actually commit in real life," Karen Sternheimer wrote in *It's Not the Media*.

Many players enjoy video games precisely because it allows them to "try on" these kinds of scenarios. "The best part about them is you can do anything you want in a video game without consequences," a 14-year-old gamer from Gualala,

California, told me. "You can be in the army without dying, feeling pain, or being yelled at by a crazy sergeant. You can travel to strange worlds and fight aliens without the risk of the earth being destroyed."

The ability to explore these experiences was especially enticing to Bissell as a young gamer. "Sometimes I think I hate [games] because of how purely they bring me back to childhood, when I could only imagine what I would do if I were single-handedly fighting off an alien army or driving down the street in a very fast car while the police try to shoot out my tires or told I was the ancestral inheritor of some primeval sword and my destiny was to rid the realm of evil. These are very intriguing scenarios if you are twelve years old," he wrote.

Sometimes, these fictional explorations can help players reflect on concepts that carry over into day-to-day life. "I was a very shy, sheltered kid," said a resident of Sacramento, California, who started playing games when he was 9. "Games, among other things, were a social learning experience, showing me situations from other perspectives and allowing me to examine concepts of good and evil without suffering real-world consequences."

Children—even young children—unanimously preferred video games to television when polled by academics, according to Greenfield. The reason? Games gave them active control of the story. "One nine-year-old girl said, 'In TV, if you want to make someone die, you can't. In Pac-Man, if you want to run into a ghost [and kill it], you can.'"

Many gamers said the combination of escapism and control made video games particularly rewarding. "I find that taking part in the story makes it affect you a lot more than it would if you were simply observing the story from the outside like with other media," Sean said. "I don't mean as far as making you violent from playing a violent game. What I mean is, the death of a character can seem more personal, can seem more sad. When the bad guy does something particularly bad, you can feel more anger as well."

Getting to know one's character is just the beginning. In most video games, players have to solve problems and puzzles to get ahead. As they play, the challenges become more and more difficult. At the end of each level there is frequently a "boss," a major villain that must be defeated. With each new predicament, players use the skills they learned in previous levels. Most games end with a major showdown between the player's character and the primary villain. Defeating this villain often means winning the game after many hours of hard work, trial and error, and frustration.

These achievements can really feel good—even in violent games. One teen I interviewed, the 15-year-old Californian who began playing games when he was less than 7, said his favorite game was *God of War.* "It features reasonably realistic, graphic depictions of various swordplay, and sometimes even amputation and decapitation. The most gruesome part of the game in my opinion is an animation in which the player-character rips a zombie's arm off, then proceeds to beat the zombie to (re-)death with that same arm." Rather than finding this unnerving, it's all part of the fun of the game: "As with most games, I enjoy the challenge—both in combative reflexes and the mental challenge of intricate puzzles—and the sense of accomplishment that comes afterward," he said.

Although many are quick to point out that video games teach excellent hand-eye coordination, they offer much more than that. Gamers learn to infer a game's rules by observation, to be fast and to time moves effectively, and to process multiple sets of information at the same time. They also develop their spacial skills, according to Greenfield. The Federation of American Scientists released a report in 2006 showing that video games help players pick up the kinds of thinking, planning, learning, and technical aptitude required in the modern job market. The FAS also found that educators failed to understand the kinds of abilities kids learn in games.

Video games are able to sneak in these lessons while players are having fun. "To succeed in even the simplest platform game, children have to lock their problem-solving into a tight cycle of observe, question, hypothesize, test. Curiously, this exactly matches the scientific method that education has been trying to embed in young scientists since the birth of science," Stephen Johnson wrote in *Everything That's Bad Is Good For You.*

Educational games aren't the only ones that allow these abilities to develop; just about any video game requires problem-solving. In fact, for some kids, arcade-style games are the most educational. Studies of learning-disabled children found that they were more likely to pick up skills and education from video games than from the classroom, because they shied away from traditional instruction and education. "Some children who refused to concentrate on conventional learning tasks concentrated very well on arcade-style games, showing perseverance and making a great deal of progress from trial to trial," Greenfield wrote.

Violent, stressful video games teach something extra: how to resolve difficult situations while under pressure. And, as some in the industry point out, games are becoming more challenging. "The first and last thing that should be said about the experience of playing today's video games, the thing you almost never hear in mainstream coverage, is that games are fiendishly, sometimes maddeningly, hard," Johnson wrote.

However, gamers don't just give up when games become difficult. "Games present us with unusual, often intractable, problems. We do not sit back in our armchairs and passively digest them—we puzzle over them, wrestle with them, and defeat them," Rossignol wrote.

In fact, facing off against a difficult game—or a game in which glitches occur, freezing the game or even crashing it entirely—teaches players to control their frustration. This happens even in violent games, where players must behave aggressively within the game, but be quiet and calm so that they can play deftly, Laurie Taylor wrote in "The Positive Features of Video Games." Through this, players learn to cope with massive levels of frustration, and resolve problems without throwing in the towel. And, as players grow bored with a game they've mastered, they move on to a new one, seeking new experiences and challenges, according to Greenfield.

Researchers at the University of Rochester found that gamers who play fast-paced, violent games actually develop a heightened sensitivity to the world around them. This benefits them not only within the game, but also while driving, multitasking, reading small print, and keeping track of friends in a crowd. Young adults who played 50 hours of *Call of Duty* or *Unreal Tournament* were more likely to develop these abilities than those who played 50 hours of *The Sims*. Up to 25 percent more likely, according to the scientists.

One reason games are able to teach new skills is that they stimulate the reward centers in players' brains. In an experiment described by Po Bronson and Ashley Merryman in *NurtureShock,* Dr. Adriana Galvan watched the brains of children, teens, and adults on an fMRI scanner while they played a pirate video game. As players succeeded, they would win some gold. Young kids found any amount of gold thrilling—they were just happy to win something. Adults' brains lit up in response to the size of the reward: a little bit for a single coin, or a lot for a big pile of booty. Teen brains only lit up when the pile of gold was huge—and seemed to dip a little bit with smaller rewards, as though they were disappointed. However, the big jolts of pleasure were really big among teens, enticing them to seek those super-sized rewards as they played.

Some games ply the brain's reward systems by boosting the player's adrenaline level, Josh Quittner wrote in *Time.* A game developer told him anonymously that the easiest way to trigger adrenaline is to make someone think they're going to die, even if it's just fiction. If a game is really engaging, it can have this effect. It can also lower the rate at which someone blinks. This further draws the player in, and produces more dopamine (the brain's reward chemical) as a result. "I find [playing violent games] relaxing, almost meditative ... they work out my twitchy reflexes. ... Statistics indicate I'm pretty normal," Quittner wrote.

But games are more than just relaxing. "I feel intense emotional experiences [when I play]," a Stanford, California, resident told me. "*Silent Hill* gives me nightmares—real, visceral, adrenaline-rush nightmares, which I think is amazing. *Ghostbusters*, on the other hand, gives me a giddy, silly thrill whenever I successfully trap a ghost and then look at how much damage I caused to the lobby of a posh hotel in the process. *Ico* fills me with a sweet, melancholy sense of wonder, much like a Miyazaki movie. The only common idea or theme is that each game evokes an immersive emotional response of some sort."

Sean said his all-time favorite game is *Gabriel Knight: Sins of the Fathers* because of its rich storytelling, which "combined to help me form a real hatred for the main antagonist and a need for revenge. ... I've never felt such complicated emotions like that, at least, not as powerfully, with any other media."

Parents may wonder how much attention game designers pay to their audience. When creating games with lots of bloodshed, or intense, aggressive action, are designers thinking about how they will affect players? The ones I asked said that they spend plenty, if not most, of their time focusing on the player's experience, but in a more holistic manner. They hope to welcome gamers into an all-encompassing world and engage them in an emotional, psychological, and—hopefully—fun way.

It's certainly no accident that games spark such intense feelings, according to Don Daglow, designer and producer of dozens of games, including *Neverwinter Nights* and *Tony La Russa Baseball*. Designers, like other entertainment writers, are doing their best to capture the audience's interest—and to move them. "When a play, or a movie, or a good game are over, you want the audience to be thinking differently about some aspect of their lives based on the experience. For all those reasons, tremendous attention is paid to how we make the audience feel," Daglow said.

For many designers, including Jaffit, the ability to create those feelings within the player, and to invent a world that other people can interact with, is everything. "Games involve a conversation between the player and the designer in a way no other medium does," Jaffit said. "Games are for makers, and dreamers, and weavers of magic and story. That's the most exciting thing I can imagine being allowed to do."

Jaffit called game designers the "guardians of the player experience." Their job is to create an environment that supports a specific experience for the player. Not every designer handles that responsibility in the same way—and some are more considerate of specific psychological effects than others. "I personally find myself spending more time concerning myself with successfully setting up a specific scene, tone, and environment for the player than I do 'worrying' that it may all go hideously wrong," Jaffit said.

Because video games are so good at engaging players' brains and emotions, they can be powerful vehicles for emotional release and transformation. Darker, more violent games do this especially well when the on-screen play matches the level of emotion or anxiety the player is experiencing in everyday life.

A teenager may be very angry and unable to express himself, but after a half-hour of gaming, he's calm enough to discuss his feelings. "By ACTING on his anger (instead of just watching violent TV), the kid releases the tension he has gathered inside," Jennie Novak and Luis Levy wrote in *Playing the Game.* "What have you observed? Do your kids calm down after some frantic onscreen action? Or do they try to replicate what they see? More often, the catharsis theory stands correct."

The emotional experiences in video games, even violent games, can provide relief for the player. In *Resident Evil,* characters fight to survive against an advancing horde of zombies. However, storytelling in even the scariest game can provide solace. In *Resident Evil,* "brothers and sisters work together to protect themselves from monsters and to survive in unbearable situations. This common element offers comfort by showing that the child playing is not alone and that she can succeed despite her conditions," according to Novak and Levy.

Violent and horror-based games, like horror films, help people explore unacknowledged fears and conflicts. By doing so, they reveal that many share these fears, Quentin Schulze and others wrote in *Dancing in the Dark.* A boy named Jonathan sought refuge in scary games after the terrorist attacks on New York and Washington on Sept. 11, 2001. "The only time that he wasn't scared was when he was playing scary games—then he felt okay. Killing games gave Jonathan control over events where he and others felt none and, perhaps even more important, they gave him control over his own feelings," Lynn Ponton wrote in the introduction to Jones' *Killing Monsters.*

Jones found young people almost universally use fantasies of combat—including combat in video games—to access their emotions, control their anxieties, feel stronger, and calm themselves down in the face of real violence. In-game fighting allowed them to fight their way through emotional challenges. "I've seen young people turn every form of imaginary aggression into sources of emotional nourishment and developmental support," Jones wrote.

Adults are often baffled by young boys' seemingly insatiable need for aggressive play. Boys pretend to shoot, stab, and dismember one another every day, according to a survey of kindergarten teachers. Even if parents and teachers attempt to redirect the play, it evolves into something new and just as rough, Wynne Parry wrote in *LiveScience*. Interestingly, if teachers told the kids they could play, but that nobody could portray a villain, boys were much less enthusiastic; something about the interaction between "good" and "bad" roles sparks their imagination and energy.

Some researchers found that aggressive play began overwhelming teachers in the 1980s. They linked this to an increase in ads pitching superhero action figures to kids. Suddenly, kids wanted to act out those superhero roles at recess, much to the chagrin of disciplinarians. But Michael Thompson, author of *Raising Cain: The Emotional Life of Boys*, doesn't think television is to blame.

"The media has provided boys with particular superheroes to believe in and to attach their fantasies to, but the impulse to be a superhero is innate," according to Thompson. Many argue that boys are more likely than girls to engage in superhero fantasies. But in the world of video games, at least, girls and women are just as likely to want to play the hero's role. Plenty of them play epic, heroic games—including the most violent games on the market.

Many kids engage in and require forms of aggressive play in order to maintain psychological health, according to Jones. Daily life, even for kids in the happiest of families, includes moments that scare and hold power over them. Violent, gory games and rough play allow kids to experiment with those feelings in a safe way. "Young people find it soothing to immerse themselves in familiar or predictable portrayals of unreal people going through an exaggerated version of what troubles them," he wrote. "Children crave fantasy violence for many reasons, but one reason they so often crave it raw, loud and angry is that they need it to be strong enough to match and master their anxiety and anger. Entertainment violence has become far more intense and explicitly gory over the past forty years because the reality with which we confront young people has become so much more intensely and explicitly violent."

It's possible that if children and teens grew up in a culture less preoccupied with violence, they might crave less violence in their entertainment, according to Jones. But we don't live in that kind of culture. It's not fair to ask kids to be satisfied with fiction and fantasy that is more sanitized than reality, he wrote.

For a variety of reasons, adults and children process these violent fictions differently. Adults, parents in particular, can fall prey to the idea that children will act out what they see in entertainment, according to Jones. But kids know games allow them to pretend they're something they'll never be in reality. Being able to explore these concepts in a safe, controlled environment is a valuable way to reduce the power of ideas and identities that are forbidden.

There are times, however, when such stories leave kids without understanding or closure. "Young people often haven't learned how to see their anger from the outside even as they experience it. ... That's where the adult ability to put emotions and fantasy into perspective can serve them well. The simplest displays of adult empathy can open the door for kids to engage with us," Jones wrote.

Some parents have told me that they notice their kids behaving differently—rowdier, talking back more—following a gaming session. Sometimes, a video game leaves the player immersed in the game world after shutting off the machine. Moviegoers often feel the same way after they leave the theater. Bissell is a big fan of first-person-shooter games, but sometimes finds it difficult to clear his head after a long period of play. "I often feel agitated, as though a drill instructor has been shouting in my ear for five hours. Reflection and thought seem like distant, alien luxuries. I step outside to clear my head, but the information-sifting machine I became while playing the shooter does not always power down. Every window is a potential sniper's nest; every intersection is waiting for a wounded straggler to limp across it," he wrote.

Other writers described similar after-effects from playing first-person-shooters. "You find yourself stealing up on street corners as if preparing to strafe the adjoining block; you seem to see a crosshair traced across the bodies of passersby," Wagner James Au wrote on *Salon.com*. "For the overwhelming majority of us, with well-adjusted social lives and a diverse range of interests, the grid recedes."

Some video-game studies have shown that levels of norepinephrine—part of the brain's fight-or-flight response—remain elevated in young people after they've played violent video games, according to Jones. However, that also happens when people play tennis or go for a run. With time, brain-chemical levels return to normal and players relax. Just like two hours watching British comedies might leave you speaking with a touch of an English accent for a while, the after-effect is there, but it fades away.

After years of researchers attempting to show even tenuous links between violent video games and aggression, a handful of academics are now working on the opposite end of the spectrum: looking for quantitative evidence that violent games are actually good for players. Michael Ward, in the University of Texas at Arlington's department of economics, studied juvenile crime rates in cities which had more or fewer video-game stores, and discovered that when teens had easier access to video games, their violent-crime rates were lower.

This was for one very simple reason: "Video games not only cost money, but they also cost time. It takes a lot of time to beat the game, and so all those hours you're playing the game are hours that you're not getting into trouble," he said.

Jayne Gackenbach, a researcher at Grant MacEwan University in Canada, has spent the past few years examining how certain violent video games can help post-war soldiers reduce their incidence of combat-related nightmares. She studied 86 American and Canadian soldiers, 64 who were "hard-core gamers," according to the *Wall Street Journal*, and 22 who played less often. Both groups had similar levels of combat experience, and neither reported post-traumatic stress disorder or other mental imbalance.

The gamers and non-gamers were told to describe two dreams: the most recent they could recall, and a dream about military life that stuck with them. For the latter, they filled out an extensive questionnaire, which Gackenbach's team coded. The researchers discovered that the military dreams of frequent gamers were much less frightening than the dreams experienced by casual gamers or non-gamers.

This is a very small study of a very specific group, but it's possible that video games could help other gamers, who are dealing with overwhelming stress or trauma, avoid terrible nightmares.

At Ryerson University, Holly Bowen and Jessica Spaniol tested the long-held theory that violent games somehow desensitize players to real-life violence—something many people believe, despite plenty of evidence to the contrary. They gathered 122 subjects, male and female, and divided them into two groups: those who had played some video games within the prior six months, and those who hadn't. The gamers had played a variety of genres, from sports games to first-person shooters.

Bowen and Spaniol's subjects were shown 150 images representing negative, positive and neutral scenes. An hour later, the students saw those same images again, as well as a new set of 150 "distractor" images, all of which were shown in random order. After each image, subjects reported whether they had seen it before. At the end, they were tested regarding their emotional state. Although the researchers were sure the gamers would turn out to be less sensitive to negative images, they found no differences in the emotional states of gamers and non-gamers who'd seen those images.

Instead of making gamers go numb, games often inspire such passion that gamers start giving back. Some gamers design their own simple games, though this was much easier when games were less sophisticated. Others enjoy what's called modding, or creating modifications to existing video games. This is done by writing small bits of computer code that add additional levels, characters, and monsters; fix game-design flaws; or allow a player to move through a game more quickly.

In fast-paced shooter and other aggressive games, being able to run and transition quickly, shoot faster and more accurately, and see things more clearly can make the difference between success and failure.

Some games, such as *LittleBigPlanet,* have built-in features that allow players to design their own levels that other players can then explore. Most of the time, modding is done by players themselves, who upload their creations to online sites where others can download and use them.

Among the most popular mods in fall 2010, to take a random example, included one that repaired menu and interface issues in *Elder Scrolls IV*, another that added 12 new generals to *Command & Conquer: Generals Zero Hour,* and one that changed the lighting in *Crysis* to make the game world look more realistic. Again, all of these are dreamed up and written by players, not game designers. Each one requires imagination, creativity, programming skills, goal-setting and follow-through in order to come to life.

"Browsing through modding archives is like visiting a library of rewritten classics," according to Rossignol. "It's as if someone were able to edit Shakespeare with pulp fiction tropes or rewrite Conrad to beef up the metaphors. There are mods that turn traditional point-and-shoot gun games into John Woo-inspired acrobatic gun jiggling; others turn gung-ho combat games into hide-and-seek."

In some cases, mods are what make a game as popular as it is. In other cases, dedicated modders become hirable talent for game companies, according to Rossignol. This is one way in which passion for a particular hobby, even one that parents might find unsavory, can turn into a viable career.

Online games provide many other opportunities for creativity. In games where thousands or millions are playing simultaneously, players can create projects or jobs within the game world. This might involve running a business or helping other players learn how to get around the game. Or maybe players will assemble a coalition of villains and overthrow a major player. In any case, these experiences build skills that can translate into real-world ability, opportunity, and confidence.

"Finding a project for yourself within a game world could be much like finding out what you want to do in life generally: experimentation, exploration, coping with both social and physical situations. Games are providing gamers with a lexicon in which many different kinds of creativity are possible," Rossignol wrote. These skills will only become more important as games evolve: "The future of games, say the big companies, is in new and accessible versions of the sandbox games: the places where gamers use games as sculptural, expressive media."

In online games, players often form close friendships—either with people they already know, or with new groups. Although there are plenty of benefits to the player who plays a stand-alone video game in solitude, the social benefits provided by massively multiplayer online games are more widely recognized. "The simple fact that so many people have been brought together because of hours spent at a screen and keyboard is fast becoming recognized as one of the most significant positive effects that games are having on society," according to Rossignol.

In multiplayer games, the range of players is almost unthinkably diverse, and this has its own set of consequences. It's not always clear who is trustworthy; this is one aspect that leads players to form alliances with folks they've played with before. However, there are times when total strangers will work together—such as to defeat a common enemy—in ways that would not happen in real life, Rossignol wrote.

In order for such teamwork to succeed, players must communicate well and work together toward a common goal—the exact kinds of skills required in most workplaces, particularly tech-based offices. It also teaches a degree of loyalty. Frequently, these teams or guilds become tight units that stick together as they switch to new games. These bonds can last for years, even decades. And they can be especially important to gamers, who frequently are nerdy kids who don't easily make friends.

"I have been impressed by the camaraderie among gamers," a video gamer from Illinois, who started playing when he was 13, told me. "I have become friends with quite a few people I interact with through games and through game communities. Those who have played a game have shared an experience, similar to those who used to share watching newscasts with Walter Cronkite or Peter Jennings or watching 'must-see' television sitcoms. Gaming has become part of popular culture rather than just a nerd's domain."

Because video games are vital to so many, in 2011 Ashly Burch created a website where gamers can share their stories, called *How Video Games Saved My Life*. Since the site's creation, hundreds of gamers have chimed in. Their stories involve the full range of video games, from block-building *Minecraft* to post-apocalyptic *Fallout 3*, and the full range of human experiences, such as rebuilding relationships with family and kicking drug addictions.

"I [created the site] because games aren't taken seriously as a medium, and they need to be. There's this stigma that's just clinging on for dear life that games are adolescent, violent, dangerous, et cetera," Burch told *Ars Technica*. "*How Games Saved My Life* as a title is a sort of deliberate exaggeration—the aim of the blog is more to capture any way in which games have positively affected the player. But some people's lives have literally been saved by games, as a few submissions have shown. It's remarkable, and wonderful."

Call of Duty

Tim Berglund's son, Zach, was born into a world where video games are commonplace. By the time he was four, he was playing some of the *Mario* games designed for kids. Although Tim himself is not an avid gamer, he grew up with the *Mario* and *Legend of Zelda* titles and knew his way around a video game. So when Zach approached his teen years, Tim and his wife decided—based on reading parenting magazines, an approach he admits isn't all that scientific—that their son wouldn't be allowed to play first-person shooters until he was 14.

"I made a judgment about approximately how old he had to be before the formative influence of spending your recreational hours aiming and shooting at human figures was small enough to be outweighed by the highly positive utility of how dang fun shooters are," Berglund recalls.

When I interviewed the pair, Zach was 16 and Tim was 38. By that time, a handful of popular first-person shooters were among Zach's favorites, including *Halo: Reach* and the *Call of Duty* series. Because so many of these games allow participants to play with friends—either side-by-side at the console, or over the network—they were also an opportunity for Zach to socialize. In fact, Tim thinks it's likely that his son played these games before he turned 14, simply because he visited with friends whose parents are more lenient about violent video games.

"Our priority was not so much total abstinence from shooters, but rather abstinence from the habit. We kept them out of the house so they wouldn't get played in volume until we were ready," he says.

When I asked Tim whether violent video games seemed to make his son more aggressive, he said he and his wife definitely notice an "attitude change" when Zach overdoes it with games, but he didn't think the games' level of violence had anything to do with it. In fact, when Zach plays with friends, seems to emerge from a gaming session feeling calmer and more relaxed. But there are other times when he's less cooperative and prone to testing boundaries after playing. Tim believes that has less to do with content and more to do with the vast differences between the game world—which is entirely based on goals, achievements and rewards—and the real world, which is only like that some of the time.

"I think the problem is that siblings, parents, and school work are really awful things in comparison to the very achievable pleasures of video game success," Tim said. "Train yourself in the short-time-constant world of video game rewards, and everything else is a drag. A relatively immature young person resolves the conflict by having a bad attitude."

Every parent weighs these factors differently, and every parent reaches different conclusions about what they will let their kids play, if they choose to establish boundaries. Even some professional video-game designers are uncomfortable with the content of certain games.

"When the Mortal Kombat game had fighters tearing out the spines and hearts of their enemies, our sons asked for the game for Christmas and we did not buy it for them due to the content," Daglow said. "Frankly, I don't believe that playing the game would have changed any long-term behavior of our sons. But parents make powerful statements to their kids by saying what is and is not acceptable in the home, and to us that was unacceptable with our younger son at his age."

However, teens who want to play these games will usually find a way to do so, like Zach probably did. "There's clearly no technical way to keep adult-rated games out of people's hands," Jaffit said. "If there were, we'd be able to stop games being pirated before they're released, and we can't manage that."

Many parents wind up deciding to let their kids play games with "mature" content, but play cooperatively with their kids. Parents who do this may be in for a surprise—a much more pleasant one than they imagine. Cooperative gameplay can lead kids to open up to their parents, because the context of the game makes it feel safer to do so. In *Play the Game: The Parent's Guide to Video Games*, Jeannie Novak and Luis Levy provided an example of this from a younger gamer, but the same can happen with older kids as well:

"Let's say you have a young boy who is afraid of the dark. While you are both playing Super Mario Bros., your kid might one day, out of nowhere (and without a single question from you), say exactly how he feels while trying to progress through Bowser's Lair. The dark and scary, dungeon-like castle will bring his fear afloat, and because your kid feels comfortable playing, he might blurt it out in the same breath as he says, 'I hate this boss!' This is a very basic example of how games can 'unlock' your kids!"

Even if a parent-teen gaming session doesn't deliver any major revelations, it's still worth trying. Daglow pointed out that because many of today's parents played video games as kids, chatting with teens about them can bridge the generational divide and create common ground. "Getting the kids talking from spontaneous passion, without feeling that they're being micro-evaluated and analyzed, will teach us far more as parents about what interests and motivates our children."

One teen, a 15-year-old from California, said he loved talking games and playing with his dad. "I was able get my father to play *Halo: Combat Evolved* with me on many occasions. He was never very good at it but I still enjoyed the experience more simply from it being a shared experience. There is also a game my father frequently plays by himself, *Age of Empires,* which we have played together on a few rare occasions and enjoyed each time."

Daglow seconded the idea that playing together can be a good way to bridge the gap. Parents might feel silly learning a new video game, particularly in front of a teenager who has spent hours mastering it. However, in doing so, parents provide a potent example that it's important to overcome the fear of looking bad while learning something new, Daglow said.

Time journalist Joshua Quittner, also a gamer, suggested that parents simply use their eyes and their instincts, and intervene only when something is influencing their teen's emotional well-being over the long term. He also quoted psychologist Michael Thompson, who said, "Is the violence that a boy is enacting on Nintendo translating into his daily life? ... Then you have to put limits on him. But if it isn't affecting his behavior, if it stays in the realm of fantasy, that's a sign of health."

Because violent video games get so much negative attention, adults may worry about how the games will influence young players, whom are presumed to be open, undiscerning or even gullible to games' license to be aggressive, to explore criminal behavior, or even to kill within their fictional worlds. However, most of the gamers I interviewed knew their own limits when it came to playing scary or gory games. A few said there was no such thing as a game that was too frightening or too gruesome, while others found certain games challenging for these reasons and only played them in short bursts. But most played these games a few times and then stayed away, protecting themselves from scenes that made them uncomfortable. It's clear that kids are thinking about these issues as they play, and recognizing when something is too much.

"*Doom 3* scared the crap out of me at times. It was just so immersive," said a gamer in Melbourne, Australia, who began playing at age 10. "*Silent Hill* was pretty creepy too. I never stopped playing them because they were scary, though."

Another teen gamer from California agreed on *Doom 3's* fright factor. "I found walking down dark passageways, and the fear of a monster suddenly appearing in front of me, unpleasant. ... Being scared was a contributing factor in quitting prematurely."

Others named survival-horror games, including *Resident Evil* and *Left 4 Dead*, among the most frightening. "I had nightmares the first few times I played *Left 4 Dead*, which is essentially an interactive horror film about zombies," said an Illinois gamer who started playing at 13. "The game *Call of Cthulu: Dark Corners of the Earth* was also frightening in how it played out madness in a first-person format, using accelerating heartbeats, flashes of gruesome images and motion blur."

Even when gamers are disturbed by something in a video game, they're often impressed at how effective it is in evoking those emotions. "There are some that were too scary for me to keep playing, the primary one being *System Shock 2*," Sean said. "The atmosphere and tension in that game are just so well done that I couldn't bring myself to play it after a while." Others agreed *System Shock 2* was ultimately too much for them.

The rewards of violent video games—skills, emotional resonance, safe exploration, social connection, and the chance to learn one's limits—are frequently unrecognized by parents and educators. I had one parent tell me that she saw no benefit whatsoever to teens playing violent video games. The gamers, however, see it rather differently.

"What have games given me? Experiences," Bissell wrote. "Not surrogate experiences, but actual experiences, many of which are as important to me as any real memories."

The Search for Meaning

Elise[*] was 15 years old when friends introduced her to a nature-based religion called Wicca. She was raised in the Catholic Church, but her experiences with religion had left her feeling bitter about spirituality. "I felt there had to be a better explanation than 'God created Earth, end of story.' There are too many wondrous things on this planet for it all to be the idea of one being."

In the beginning, Elise was as skeptical of Wicca as she'd been of Catholicism. She read books on Wicca, but never followed the teachings and rituals they contained. Instead, they inspired her to create her own spirituality.

One of her first spells was meant to make her eyes turn green. She blessed a glass of water using a ritual she wrote herself, then dropped the water into her eyes. It didn't work.

Water didn't always fail her. On vacation with her dad and stepmother, she had a profound experience on the beach in Maui.

"I went for a walk alone, and found a spot to sit in front of the moon. It was just so powerful. I sat and watched the waves move in and out, before realizing that they were moving in the motions I wanted them to. That feeling of finally being in control of something in life put me at ease, if only for a moment. As I asked the water to move to and fro at differing intervals, it obliged.

I realized then that casting [spells] was about friendship and comfort, not control. Whenever I tried to command something to happen, it never would. But even today, if I ask nicely for something, it almost always comes. I found a friend in water, and more specifically, in the ocean."

---

*   Not her real name.

Magick Without Tears

On December 9, 2007, Matthew Murray brought guns to the Youth With a Mission training center and the New Life Church in Colorado. He killed two people before being wounded by a security guard and then taking his own life. In online postings before the attack, Murray allegedly wrote, "You Christians brought this on yourselves ... All I want to do is kill and injure as many of you as I can, especially Christians, who are to blame for most of the problems in the world."

He went on: "All I found in Christianity was hate, abuse (sexual, physical, psychological, and emotional), hypocrisy, and lies. ... I'm going out to make a stand for the weak and the defenseless. This is for all those young people still caught in the Nightmare of Christianity, for all those people who've been abused and mistreated and taken advantage of by this evil sick religion."

Murray was homeschooled in a heavily Christian household, and had trained for a while at Youth With A Mission before being expelled, according to news articles. After his expulsion, he descended into anti-Christian sentiment, ending with the shootings. If those online posts were indeed from Murray, it's clear that he was enraged—and felt he had found appropriate targets in the New Life Church and the Youth With a Mission training center.

In the news coverage that followed, reporters played up Murray's involvement in the Ad Astra Oasis. The AAO is an offshoot of the Ordo Templi Orientis, once led by famed occultist Aleister Crowley. A minister who runs the Good Fight Web site received an email he believed was from Murray, claiming the shooter studied Crowley's teachings as well as the Qabalah. However, Murray had been asked to leave the AAO because group leaders felt he "wasn't fitting in," so it's not clear how the group could be associated with his actions.

It's even less clear what was going on with Murray psychologically. His ouster from both the Youth With A Mission center and the AAO suggests that there was something about him that didn't jell with either organization. It's unlikely that those expulsions, on their own, drove him to kill. Plenty of people suffer setbacks without resorting to homicide. It's more likely that Murray's emotional instability is what led leaders in both religious groups to ask him to leave. It's also likely that those expulsions further cracked his mental state.

Instead, at least one news article focused on Murray's occult interests as a potential motive for the attack. It cited Crowley's reputation as "the most evil man in the world," and called Murray a follower. The article played up Crowley's occult escapades and mentioned that one of Crowley's "compatriots reportedly died from drinking the blood of a cat during one ceremonial episode, according to documents on Crowley's life." It even suggested that Crowley inspired modern Satanism—but Murray wasn't a Satanist (and neither was Crowley).

If this was your only source of information about Murray's rampage, you would be left with the impression that his occult interests sparked his violent actions. You might also believe that occultists, and specifically Satanists, are more prone to murder.

In the wake of violence, we long to understand why someone would do such a thing, especially when the killer has died and cannot speak for himself. Journalists attempt to explain the attack in a way that draws the reader in, even if that explanation isn't well-informed. However, because occult faiths do not by themselves sanction or encourage violence, the explanation is a dangerous one. It was unlikely that Murray's occult interests drove him to kill, so it's irrelevant for reporters to mention those interests in their articles.

This kind of journalism works, in part, because Americans love a good scare. We seek it in our fiction—video games, horror movies and mystery novels—and in our nonfiction, from true-crime books to the nightly news. Average Americans know very little about paganism, Satanism, or divination, so it's easy to scare them with what they don't understand. Some teens who explore these things are *hoping* it will scare their parents.

"Since the unknown is feared, and therefore since the occult is feared ... there is a tendency for us to give power to those things we fear and make them appear even when they are not relevant," journalist Margot Adler, author of *Drawing Down the Moon,* told me in an interview. "We have a terror about the occult, so if there is the slightest possibility that there is an occult connection, even if it is just someone is dressing goth, or wearing black, or even a trenchcoat, or Heaven forbid using a pentagram, suddenly all sorts of ideas are collected around the crime or incident."

The media is at least partly responsible for playing up these fears, according to Adler. Journalists tend to misrepresent occult groups in two different ways. In one approach, they are portrayed as evil, frightening, criminal, and immoral—what Adler calls the "Exorcist-Rosemary's Baby" view. "It is nourished by the media because it sells ... and encourages a fear of the unknown that blunts most people's curiosity and adventurousness," she wrote in *Drawing Down the Moon*. In the other approach, occultists are painted as "trivial, escapist, anti-intellectual, antipolitical, narcissistic, amoral, and decadent." Neither one is true. In fact, Adler argues that if the pagan and occult movements were recognized as the intellectual and artistic cultures they are, academics would jump at the chance to study them.

Cultural fears of pagan and occult practices are longstanding—and they haven't died down with the advent of more and better information, or broader cultural acceptance of pagans. When audiences began devouring the *Harry Potter* books and films, many feared that young readers, engrossed by the wizard's coming-of-age story, would want to become wizards and magicians themselves. However, once the tale had been out for several years, and it was clear that kids' souls were not being threatened by the popular story, some religious leaders had a change of heart. In its review of the final film in the series, *Harry Potter and the Deathly Hallows 2*, the Vatican newspaper, *L'Osservatore Romano*, reported, "evil is never presented as fascinating or attractive in the saga, but the values of friendship and of sacrifice are highlighted." Another critic noted, "the saga champion[s] values that Christians and non-Christians share."

However, after the worries about Harry Potter died down, fears about the popular *The Hunger Games* series took over. The series was number three on the list of most-challenged books, according to the American Library

Association, in part because they were considered "occult/Satanic," possibly for their suggestion of child sacrifice, which is neither occult nor Satanic. Even the Internet itself, with its wealth of information about every belief and practice under the sun, is distrusted by some religious conservatives, who claim that using the Internet makes teens more vulnerable to "demonic influences," including possession. It's worth noting that some of the leaders who have suggested this—Catholic Father Gary Thomas, for example—are exorcists, whose life's work is helping people rid themselves of possession. When you have a hammer, everything looks like a nail.

Many of the pagan teens interviewed for this book were frustrated by the ideas others have about their beliefs. One, a 19-year-old from Northern California who became interested in the occult at age 10, said lots of people think that the occult is evil—or a passing rebellious interest that the teen will outgrow. Others think occultists are "flaky hippies who just want peace and love," he said. Instead, "Most occultists are normal people."

Many don't just fear the occult itself—they're also afraid of learning anything about it, according to a Georgian whose occult interest sparked at 10. "The majority of society ... has literally no education regarding that subject matter and is furthermore conditioned to fear it. Not just fear the path itself, but fear the education about that path. A lot of people are afraid to even know, as if that will somehow taint them."

These fears, combined with misunderstanding, can build walls between parents and teens. A child may have stumbled onto a spirituality that feels right—or a set of tools that are helping him or her build self-confidence—but fear may lead parents or others to disparage their discovery. Knowing more about these beliefs, and where those fears come from, can help.

Murray's story is not the first time the public has been frightened into believing that pagans are dangerous. During the Middle Ages, and later the Salem Witch Trials, women (and some men) were persecuted, tortured, and killed for supposedly practicing witchcraft. They were blamed for all kinds of problems, from sour milk to bad weather. In each case, a small group of influential people managed to sell the idea that their neighbors either possessed supernatural powers, were under the thrall of the Devil, or both. Once the public bought the story, they urged torture and public execution of the accused. One author, Brian Levack, estimated that as many as 60,000 people died during the witch hunts of the 14th through 17th centuries.

Author and professor Richard Ofshe knows these kinds of panics well. In such situations, the public becomes brainwashed by people who circulate false ideas. This creates a kind of temporary hysteria, according to Ofshe, who spent much of the 1980s debunking claims of Satanic ritual abuse. In many of those cases, the supposed victims were children. Under the guidance of psychologists or similar professionals, these kids "revealed" stories of molestation, violent ceremonies, pregnancies and stolen babies, and ritualistic murders—ideas which Ofshe says were induced by the very therapists attempting to help. No evidence of these claims was ever produced, but the stories spread nonetheless. By the end of the decade, as more experts revealed the lack of foundation for Satanic ritual abuse, media coverage—and hysteria—died down. However, the public was left with a picture of Satanists as child-abusing monsters.

The "Satanic panic" of the 1980s may have been a revolt against the popular neopagan movement born in the 1960s, according to author Christopher Moreman. "A culture of conservative Christianity thus responded in an extreme way," Moreman wrote in his article "Devil Music and the Great Beast." "It has been suggested that a declining social system combined with a growing sense of helplessness and lack of faith in big government provoked the need for a scapegoat of some kind."

America found another bogeyman in Ozzy Osbourne. The heavy-metal singer and former Black Sabbath frontman's musical career took off in the late 1970s and early 1980s. Like Crowley, Osbourne courted a reputation for evil. He notoriously bit the head off a dove during one event, and bit the head off a live bat during another. In the 2000s, Osbourne starred in his own reality TV show with his wife and children, revealing himself to be an average, if eccentric, family man.

"Through a brief biographical sketch, it becomes obvious that Ozzy Osbourne is far from a worshipper of the Dark Lord, but simply a talented iconoclast with a flair for creating controversy, and thus publicity," Moreman wrote. While neither Osbourne nor Crowley worshipped the Devil, "their anti-authoritarianism, combined with such vices as drugs and women, made them both suitable straw men against whom conservative moralists might rail."

Anytime occult trappings appear at a crime scene, reporters play up that angle. Almost every day, news articles claim paganism, the occult, or specifically Satanism, is associated with some criminal act. In some cases, Satanism is no more than a headline—literally. In December 2007, the *Associated Press* ran an article on Robert Hawkins, the gunman who killed eight people at the Westroads Mall in Omaha, Nebraska. It sported the headline, "Mall Gunman Was Satanic, Suicidal," but failed to mention Satanism anywhere in the story. Putting Satan in a headline is a good way to get readers' attention, even if it isn't relevant.

If the press spun these claims about any other ethnic or religious group, it would constitute defamation or even profiling. Misinformation about occult groups is so widespread and so deeply entrenched in our culture that it is accepted as fact. Unfortunately, this can lead to long jail sentences for those who wind up on the wrong end of the mistake.

That's what happened to the West Memphis Three. In 1993, Jason Baldwin and Jessie Misskelley were sentenced to life in prison—and Damien Echols to death row—for the murders of three young children. There was very little evidence against them. The story of their trial has been told in several documentaries, including *Paradise Lost: The Child Murders at Robin Hood Hills,* which Emily Edwards covers in her book *Metaphysical Media: The Occult Experience in Popular Culture.*

"[The documentary] suggests there is a modern willingness to condemn witches, and that a jury in the 1990s might be as susceptible to a witch craze as one in the 1590s. ... One of the accused teens, Damien [Echols], wears his hair dyed black, admits that he practices the Wicca religion, and has an interest in heavy metal music. Damien's interest in the occult becomes a central element in his trial. Though the teen explains that Wicca is a religion that practices a close involvement with nature and teaches people to harm no one because 'evil you do will come back to you,' prosecutors question the benign nature of his beliefs. They exhibit books on Satanic witchcraft belonging to the teen and a piece of paper on which he had written the name 'Aleister Crowley' as evidence of Damien's Satanic orientation."

Later, DNA technology revealed that Echols, along with co-defendants Jason Baldwin and Jesse Miskelly, were not involved with the killings. After spending nearly half their lives in Arkansas prison, the men were released in August 2011; they entered Alford pleas, which allow them to assert their innocence while acknowledging that there is enough evidence to convict them. Echols has called West Memphis "A second Salem."

Along with the press, the police are a major source of misinformation about the occult. There are a number of so-called "occult experts" working around the country, many of them ex-police officers who have become fascinated with the topic, who provide police with seminars and other training. Unfortunately, at best these "experts" have an outsider's view of pagan, occult, Satanist or Diaspora beliefs and practices, and at worst their information is so wrong that it will wind up getting innocent people into trouble. They say they want to inform the police and assist them in telling the difference between peaceful spiritual practices and real wrongdoing, but when their information is confused and sensationalistic, it tends to have the opposite effect.

For example, the late Don Rimer, one of the best-known "occult experts" in the field, would teach officers the "signs" that teens are "dabbling" in the occult (attempted suicide, bizarre cruelty, running away) or symptoms of "occult ritual abuse" (harming family pets, preoccupation with death, or discussion of participation in religious ceremonies). Most of these are actually signs that a teen needs psychiatric evaluation, and the last example is too vague to be meaningful. Much of Rimer's presentation is a mishmash of different faiths and practices, with made-up "demon revel" holidays listed on the same calendar with the most significant Wiccan holidays. There's a mostly-factual but brief section in Wicca, followed by pages of supposedly demonic song lyrics. It's no wonder the police are confused about the relationship between crime and the occult.

In *In Pursuit of Satan: The Police and the Occult*, Hicks deconstructed the police world's "preoccupation with Satanism, Satanic crime, and occult and cult crime." Hicks described numerous cases in which officers' misreading of a crime scene leads them to believe there was an occult motive.

Police learn much of what they know about cults and the occult through seminars, Hicks confirms. But true occult experts are not the ones providing that information. "Some conservative fundamentalist Christian views drive the cult-crime model, insofar as cult officers frequently communicate fundamentalist concepts at seminars. Cult officers employ fundamentalist rhetoric, distribute literature that emanates from fundamentalist authorities, and sometimes offer bibliographies giving many fundamentalist publications," Hicks wrote. In other words, groups with a strong interest in maligning the occult are put in charge of teaching police how to understand it.

Meanwhile, officers are warned against studying the subject directly. "One law enforcement guide, an otherwise valuable exposé on con games and swindles, addresses Satanism as perhaps the biggest con of all and advises officers, 'Continue your education in this area by reading as widely as possible on the subject. But note: intense study of resource books and materials by occult sources is hazardous. Preferred is studying overviews and synopses by credible authors who have studied the occult traditions. The unknown realm of the occult beckons with many lures. Study and/or experimentation are to be avoided. There are safer ways to test for poisonous chemicals than by tasting them,'" Hicks quoted.

As a result, many officers who become "occult experts" don't actually know much about the subject, Hicks says. That's how you wind up with the Massachusetts police, for example, teaching that occultists and Satanists practice animal and human sacrifice, despite how rare this actually is.

Police sometimes meet violent criminals who do have a deep interest in paganism or the occult. These interactions may be officers' only contact with non-Christians, leading them to believe that the criminals are typical pagans, according to Hicks.

While some journalists get bad information from the police, police also "learn" about occult crime by reading newspapers, according to Hicks. After a rash of articles linking teen suicide to the occult, an article in *Law Enforcement News* blamed one teen's crime spree on some Satanic and occult books found beneath his bed. "A 14-year-old Jefferson Township, N.J., boy kills his mother with a Boy Scout knife, sets the family home on fire, and commits suicide in a neighbor's back yard ... investigators find books on the occult and Satan worship in the boy's room. But did the boy have a collection of spiders? A stack of pornographic literature under his bed? A girlfriend who just jilted him? Newspaper accounts never mention other possible explanations since only those touched by a nameless, faceless evil will explain why good boys go bad," Hicks wrote.

After being barraged by enough articles linking occultism to violence, it's no wonder parents come to the same conclusion when tragedy strikes. In another case, reported in *Denver* magazine, a mother described the suicide of her 16-year-old son: "From what we can tell, he evidently must have performed some kind of satanic death ritual. He was barefoot and we found symbols drawn on the ground. In his suicide note, he says, 'It is time for me to meet my lofty maker. I have now started the lonesome journey to the bowels of the earth; I travel that twisted road that winds its way down to the forsaken pit. My destination will be the foot of the throne where I kneel and greet my father.'" She said that her son listened to heavy-metal music, collected knives, played the *Dungeons & Dragons* roleplaying game, and owned several occult books, including the *Satanic Bible*—all of which she only discovered after his death. "At first we blamed ourselves," she told the magazine. "Then we started learning about similar deaths and seeing the pattern. Slowly, we realized we weren't responsible."

The boy's parents may not have been responsible for his suicide. But why did they know so little about their son's interests, hobbies, and apparently deteriorating mental state? By placing blame on the wrong things, we come no closer to understanding the real reasons why a few teenagers kill themselves or others. Many adults who long to understand these acts wind up looking in the wrong places. News outlets and law enforcement aren't helping. And there aren't enough sources of honest information for people who are looking for real, honest answers.

Magick in Theory and Practice

"Paganism" is sometimes used as a catch-all phrase for any non-Judeo/Christian/Islamic spirituality. Most often, it means any nature-based belief, particularly one with many gods and goddesses. It can include Wicca and other styles of witchcraft, as well as practices based on the Roman, Egyptian, or Norse pantheons. In a few systems, such as chaos magic, participants follow pop-culture "gods," from Bugs Bunny to Superman. In others, there are no gods at all.

"The occult" comes from the Latin word meaning "hidden." It can include paganism or activities such as Tarot, astrology, or runes. Basically, it refers to any practice designed to reveal hidden information, such as what's going to happen in the future or what someone else might be thinking. It also describes any kind of spell-casting. People cast spells for all kinds of reasons: to lose weight or find a girlfriend, to heal sick loved ones or rid the world of nuclear weapons.

If it sounds complicated, that's because it is; there are dozens, perhaps hundreds, of practices that can fall under the terms "pagan" and "occult." Even more confusingly, some of them may use the same terms or symbols, and occasionally the same practices. Partly that's because there has been a lot of cross-pollination, particularly among neo-pagan faiths such as Wicca, and other styles, like Thelema, which draws from Masonic practices as well as nature-based sources.

Possibly the most widely recognized pagan symbol is the pentagram, a five-pointed star within a circle. It has been used

—and mis-used—in so many places, including newspapers, book covers and horror movies, that people may think they know what it means. But its meaning and association depend on many factors: Does it have one point up, or two? Does it have other symbols or writing around it? In many ways, the pentagram is like the cross, whose meaning and association changes based on whether it's right-side up, upside-down, whether it depicts Jesus or not, or whether it has extra embellishments, as with the Celtic or the Russian Orthodox crosses. So many possibilities can seem confusing and overwhelming to outsiders, but the point is that not all pentagrams mean the same thing. If a teen in your life suddenly turns up with a pentagram on his or her clothing, books or other items, it's worth asking—gently—what it means.

There's no way to adequately describe every possible alternative spirituality in a single chapter like this one, but it's worth getting a taste of the breadth. The pagan, occult and minority-faith world includes a wide range of paths that appeal to teens looking for a change of spiritual scenery. On the neo-pagan tree alone there are dozens of branches and practices.

"Most Neo-Pagans sense an aliveness and 'presence' in nature. They share the goal of living in harmony with nature and they tend to view humanity's 'advancement' and separation from nature as the prime source of alienation. They see ritual as a tool to end that alienation," Adler wrote in *Drawing Down the Moon*.

Arguably the best-known neo-pagan branch is Wicca, a nature-based faith born during the 20th Century. Despite how new it is, followers celebrate eight holidays related to sun and harvest cycles, including the solstices and equinoxes, which have been honored for much longer. Wiccans generally believe in a God and a Goddess, and in the balance between masculine and feminine forces in nature. They may work with many gods and goddesses, and believe each one is a facet of the supreme God and Goddess.

Many are drawn to Wicca specifically because it honors women in a way that many dominant religions don't. Both teenage boys and girls practice Wicca, but it can be especially powerful for a teen girl to discover it. They often feel disempowered and confused about their roles as young women in society, as well their relationships to boys and men. Wicca can help them find strength and purpose. At the same time, Wicca appeals to young men because it encourages traits and talents generally forbidden to boys, including intuition, gentleness, and receptivity, Teresa Moorey wrote in *Spellbound: The Teenage Witch's Handbook.*

Wicca can be practiced in groups, sometimes called covens, or solo. Either way, the path has many qualities that appeal to adolescents. "Socially, witchcraft offers new perspectives, but it also has a specific personal relevance for teenagers. Because witchcraft encourages personal revelation, it offers a spiritual path free of dogma. No one tells you what to do. No one disempowers you, imposes sets of rules on you, or puts you at the bottom of a hierarchy that makes you feel defeated before you begin," Moorey wrote.

Wicca provides a backdrop for people to craft their own spells aimed at a specific goal, such as getting a job or passing an exam. Spells are a lot like prayers, but with different props. By performing spells to draw love, keep to a healthier diet, get rid of anger, stop gossip, find a lost pet, protect your bedroom, or just attract good luck, teens can feel like they can harness more control and success in their personal lives.

"Magick is the art and science of effecting positive change in your life," wrote Ellen Dugan in *Elements of Witchcraft: Natural Magick for Teens.* "You may attain this change by your will or desire to make those personal improvements and by working in harmony with nature. The only way you can really change your life is to change yourself."

Teens following Wicca may set up an "altar" in their bedroom with statues, candles, photos, or other symbols and mementos. Spells and rituals are based on the four directions (North, South, East and West) and five elements: earth, air, fire, water and spirit. Usually, altars will include items that symbolize each of the elements, as well as more personal items. They'll also likely include a pentagram, a small ceremonial knife called an athame (usually used for pointing and stirring, but not for harming anyone), and a cup.

Wicca is one of the most popular neo-pagan faiths, but it

is by no means only one. Most kinds of neo-paganism have a few things in common, such as respect for nature and its cycles and a belief in more than one god or goddess. They also have many differences. Some faiths are associated with a particular region's history and mythology; others use a more catch-all approach.

Neo-Druids follow a path inspired by the Iron-Age Celtic Druids, particularly those of Ireland and England. Like other neo-pagans, they hold nature as sacred and believe that the lives of plants and animals have deep value. Neo-Druidic ceremonies, particularly in Europe, are held in sacred groves and stone circles. Some groups have a particular uniform for ceremonies, such as cloaks and robes. Some of the gods and goddesses in Neo-Druidic and other Celtic pagan faiths include Cernunnos, Brighid, Lugh, the Dagda, Rhiannon, Macha, and Epona.

Asatru is a neo-pagan religion based on Norse and Germanic mythology. The word comes from the Norse word Æsir, a family of Norse gods, and "tru," the word for "faith." Asatru followers often believe in the presence of elves and spirits in stones, trees, and similar natural objects. They also find meaning in something called Wyrd, a word for fate or luck. Their gods and goddesses include Baldr, Thor, Odin, Loki, Freya, and Tyr. Asatruars often wear a small silver hammer on a chain around their necks. This is called the Mjolnir, or Thor's hammer.

Asatru features a variety of ceremonies. In a blot, people gather to feast and offer a "sacrifice" of something—a bit of food or drink, a story or poem—to the ancestors. Another Asatru event is called the sumbel, which is more serious. Guests pass a horn of mead and drink in honor of the ancestors; teens don't usually participate in sumbels. Asatru groups also sometimes hold seiðrs, which feature divine ecstasy and speaking in tongues, similar to some Christian and voodoo ceremonies.

In Feri, practitioners are initiated into a coven, where they learn the basic beliefs of the tradition. These include the concept of the Three Souls, including the "talker" (the conscious self), the "fetch" (a pre-verbal, childlike self), and the "Godself." Since the "talker" and the "Godself" cannot communicate directly, practitioners appeal to the "fetch" through the use of symbols and ritual, to make the connection. Deities of Feri include the Star Goddess, the Divine Twins, and the Blue God.

Wicca, and to some, extent, other neo-pagan practices, arose out of Thelema, a spiritual path crafted and inspired by British occultist Aleister Crowley. Crowley's name inspires plenty of preconceived notions, many of which he encouraged: By calling himself "The Great Beast" and publicizing his spiritual and romantic exploits, he invited others to think of him as dangerous, even frightening. More than 60 years after his death, many people still believe—mistakenly—that he worshipped the Devil. Instead, he wanted people to find their true purpose in life and to pursue it with passion.

In 1904, Crowley published the *Book of the Law*, also known as the *Liber AL vel Legis*. He claimed that the text was dictated to him by a spirit called Aiwass. The book describes a pagan religion focused on three Egyptian deities, Nuit, Hadit, and Horus. It also hailed the new age of Horus, in which "Do what thou wilt shall be the whole of the law."

"[This] is not interpreted as a license to indulge every passing whim, but rather as the divine mandate to discover one's True Will or true purpose in life, and to accomplish it, leaving others to do the same in their own unique ways," according to Frater Lux Ad Mundi, public information officer for the Ordo Templi Orientis USA. Many American Thelemites learn what they know by studying under the OTO.

The OTO takes members by initiation and bumps them up the ranks as they become more experienced Thelemites. However, the organization does not accept members under the age of 18, so most teens interested in Crowley's teachings must find another way to explore them.

"Do what thou wilt" has been interpreted by many as an encouragement to indulge in hedonistic behavior, "which is an understandable interpretation when Crowley's sexual proclivities and increasing drug use are taken into account," wrote Christopher Moreman in his article "Devil Music and the Great Beast." However, Crowley was much more interested in people's ability to use their Will to alter the course of their lives.

To find your purpose in life, you have to free the subconscious mind from the control of the conscious mind, Crowley said. He encouraged people to use magic and ritual to accomplish this. Some of the rituals Crowley wrote will help the practitioner find his or her guardian angel, an important step in discovering one's purpose. He also encouraged followers to keep a daily journal and to be skeptical about their magical work. That way, they could determine whether it was magic, or other factors, that led them to a specific result.

Thelema is very structured, and requires people to work hard to achieve their goals. But that hard work pays off. "The discovery of one's own, unique True Will usually involves a regime of self-analysis, discipline, study and practice that is empowering in its own right," Mundi said. "Some of these practices are the same, or similar to, the practices advocated by many of the great religions of the past and present, such as prayer, meditation, yoga, study of religious texts, chanting, symbolic and initiatory ritual, [and] devotional exercises."

Thelema encourages individualism, according to Mundi. In fact, it's so individual that not everyone who participates considers it a religion. For some, it's more of a personal philosophy. Either way, its encouragement to connect with one's purpose in life is powerful, especially for teens who are searching desperately for meaning and focus as they transform into adults. Thelema also teaches people that they have a duty to themselves, to others, to mankind, and to all other beings.

"Most young people go through a confusing, awkward, and sometimes painful process to establish their sense of identity," Mundi said. "That process can often be rebellion against the received wisdom and standards held by their families and imposed by society. Aleister Crowley was, first and foremost, a seeker after elusive and ineffable truths who defied societal conventions as necessary in that pursuit."

For rebellious teens, Crowley offers a potent example of someone striking out on his own. He gravitated to communities in exile, from Paris' Lost Generation to the decadence of 1930s Berlin. His life and philosophies have inspired a number of counterculture revolutions, including the Beats, hippies, and punks, according to Mundi.

Teens who discover Thelema may also explore related practices, such as Qabalah, a mystical offshoot of the Jewish Kabbalah; Enochian, a kind of angel magic developed by Queen Elizabeth I's astrologer John Dee and his associate Edward Kelley; or Goetia, a method of summoning demons. Finding out that a teen is studying Crowley's work may be upsetting, especially if you believe Crowley was evil. But adolescents who pursue his works are usually just searching for a way to make sense of life.

"Teens are looking for the same things spiritually as all sentient beings: an answer to the riddle of life—why are we here? What is the purpose of our existence?" Mundi said. "Being in the initial stage of their questing, it's a shocking, unsettling, and especially intense experience for them. Thelema's promise is: 'Certainty, not faith, while in life, upon death; peace unutterable, rest, ecstasy.' Also, Thelema helps provide both focus for someone seeking a direction for their life, as well as a sense of belonging and fellowship with like-minded individuals."

Of all the spiritual paths a teenager might choose, Satanism is has the potential to be the most alarming. After all, Satan is seen as the source of all evil, both in religion and in pop culture. The media links all sorts of violent crimes to Satanism; certain criminals claim "the Devil made me do it." Although most Satanists are not criminals and most criminals are not Satanists, that hasn't eased anyone's mind. Some Satanists actually encourage the public to see them as dangerous or evil. They may find that fostering a bad reputation allows them to live life without interference.

A teen who is exploring Satanism may be doing it just to get others to "butt out." However, there are plenty of valid reasons teens explore Satanism, similar to the reasons they check out any other spiritual path.

There are actually many varieties of Satanism. There's Luciferianism, inspired by the figure's history as a light-bringing angel. There's LaVeyan Satanism, based on the books by Anton LaVey. And there's modern or symbolic Satanism, in which Satan serves as a metaphor for the rejection of all spirituality and religion.

All three, but particularly LaVeyan and modern Satanism, encourage followers to put themselves first. This is a spirituality that celebrates materialism, individualism, and pleasure. Satanists often rebel against Christianity's suggestion that it's better to sacrifice the self in the service of others.

"[The Church of Satan] ... embraces diversity and sees Satan as a symbol of the rebel that has moved civilizations forward through invention and innovation, and not [as] an evil anthropomorphic deity," Steven Leyba, a former priest with the Church of Satan, told me. "It's a way of life, so you must learn from the lives of those who practice it, and when you do this, you will see it isn't about group-think. It's about living your life in the way you choose to live it."

Satanism has a strong anti-authoritarian streak. Satanists rebel against the status quo, and against messages that tell them to conform. In the *Satanic Bible*, LaVey teaches that all gods are created by humans, and that worshipping one of these gods means you're actually worshipping another human's ideas. He pushes readers to find godlike aspects within themselves and worship those instead.

He also strictly condemns killing or harming humans or animals for the sake of magical power. That's right: despite what police or newspapers often say when they find mutilated animals, this practice isn't OK with the Satanic Church. When murderers say they did it for Satan, their claims have nothing to do with this kind of Satanism. On the other hand, LaVey does encourage "an eye for an eye"-style treatment when someone has been wronged. He discourages Satanists from accepting mistreatment or disrespect, because they're supposed to be celebrating the divine within.

It's easy to see how these ideas would appeal to an adolescent, particularly one in the midst of a rebellious phase. "LaVey's *Satanic Bible* is required reading among alienated teenage rockers, but that's about as far as it goes," Gaines wrote in *Teenage Wasteland*. "Most kids like the hedonistic philosophy that condones doing what you want. This is something minors are rarely encouraged to do."

A faith that encourages individualism and hedonism can seem like a real relief to teenagers frustrated by a world of rules and expectations. Those who don't fit in with the mainstream crowd may feel especially at home, according to Gaines.

"Satan and sin made this scary social force simpler for adults to comprehend, and a lot more dangerous for kids to embrace. If partying was sinful, the flesh, the drink, the desire to be fully human could only be expressed by embracing the very evil you were condemned to. And if you were a kid, with no power and no voice in the social world that regulated you, Satan could help. For years, kids have beseeched favors, invoking his power, asking him to intervene on their behalf," she wrote.

Others may join up with Satanists to feel like they belong, or for protection. That happened to Jeff Harshbarger, who describes his experiences with Satanism in *From Darkness to Light*. Once he got involved, he discovered that the path bolstered his self-esteem and personality. "My view of life was different. My confidence had tripled. I felt more in control and more aware of my surroundings than before. A spirit of pride had entered me that I knew would never fail. Now I determined what was mine. I came first. I was my own god."

Although Satanism appears to offer power and freedom, the practice doesn't come easily, according to Leyba. "It is a great responsibility for anyone to be who they truly are, and it's much easier to have someone else tell you what to think and what to believe in," he said. "It's about becoming this figure of rebellion to grow, and to push civilization forward."

"Rather than providing a 'quick fix,' most magical orders emphasize discipline and hard work," Hicks wrote.

Among some Satanists, Satan or Lucifer is a symbol for the independent self. For others, the devil is the central god—a real, external power. There are some serious practitioners of this type of Satanism, often called Theistic Satanism. But among teens, it's frequently much more free-form, often cobbled together from old books, horror films, and word-of-mouth ideas.

When police or religious leaders discover graffiti involving pentagrams, or circles of candles, or mutilated animals, they point to "Devil worship." However, other explanations are more likely: kids love to paint or carve pentagrams because it freaks people out. Candles add a certain atmosphere to cemeteries and other places kids gather at night. But this isn't true spirituality.

Other kids may experiment with a hodgepodge of occult practices picked up from scary stories, schlocky books and horror films that might actually pass for "Devil worship." But for those who do, it's typically a phase. Teens who are serious tend to gravitate toward the kinds of Satanism described earlier. Those who are in it to experiment or for the shock value tend to move on quickly.

Many spiritual paths provide structure in the same way Christianity, Judaism, and Islam do. But for teens looking for something much more free-form, there's chaos magic. Chaos magicians will check out a number of different spiritualities, such as Wicca or Thelema, as well as spell-casting practices, and then use what they learn to create a mix-and-match system tailored for them. This can appeal to someone who has tried other pagan paths and found that none of them fit.

Sigilization, creating a sigil aimed at producing a specific outcome, is a core practice for many chaos magicians. Let's say a chaos magician wants to do well in a job interview. He or she would create a unique sigil or glyph that represents kicking butt at the interview. Chaos magic is different from other spell-casting traditions, in which magicians will focus lots of energy on a goal during the ritual, and then continue to focus on that outcome after the ritual is finished. In chaos magic, energy is poured into the sigil as it's created, but the sigil is meant to be so abstract that the goal and outcome are quickly forgotten. The theory is that one's conscious mind only gets in the way. By encouraging it to forget what the sigil means, this allows the subconscious mind to take over the job until the wish becomes reality.

Chaos magicians have been known to call upon gods from many world religions, but also characters from popular fiction—everything from *Lord of the Rings* to the Looney Tunes, depending on the purpose of the ritual. For example, if the *Star Wars* films meant a lot to your teen growing up, then he or she might work with the concept of Luke Skywalker when facing tasks in which bravery and heroism would be useful. Not all chaos magicians do this, but for those who do, the approach offers something more personalized and playful.

One popular symbol of chaos magic is the "chaostar," a sphere with eight arrows pointing outward in all directions. It was created by science-fiction author Michael Moorcock, who said it represents all possibilities. A common quotation used by chaos magicians is one allegedly taken from the historic Order of the Assassins: "Nothing is true. Everything is permitted." Both of these concepts encourage the chaos magician to be open-minded and to try things, even if they don't seem as though they would work.

Angelina Fabbro, who became a chaos magician in her early teens, described the practice this way: "Figure out the tools to change your way of thinking and the world around you, then you do it. I don't just mean waving a wand and hoping your wishes come true. I mean you invest every fiber of your being into the effort and belief of who you are or are becoming, and you never stop until you win. It's a toolbox of ideas. That's it. There isn't anything spooky about it. It's empowering. It's up to you."

"It's up to you" is definitely empowering for many teens, and chaos magic is an avenue that appeals to those looking for a less-mainstream spirituality. As Fabbro put it, chaos magic also has a "bad-ass" quality that can make teens feel powerful and self-confident. Teens spend their days going from one disempowering, demeaning experience to another. A spirituality that counteracts that can really feel good.

After working with chaos magic for a while, Fabbro discovered many things she liked about the practice. In particular, "It seemed to be free-form enough that I could be myself, take the toolset offered, literally build any kind of paradigm or worldview I wanted, and then set myself up to go for my goals," she said.

Recently, more teens are discovering faiths with their roots in Africa, South America, and the Caribbean, including Santeria, Palo Mayombe, and Candomblé. Although they're often mistakenly linked to criminal activity, these practices are generally peaceful. They're often shrouded in mystery because they're passed down within families through the generations and not frequently shared with outsiders.

Santeria was born in Nigeria, later moved to Cuba and is heavily practiced in some parts of the United States, particularly where Cuban-Americans abound. Santeria's followers believe in a group of gods called orishas. Believers must figure out which orisha they were born to serve: Ellegua, Oggun, Oshun, Chango, Oya, Obatala, Yemaya, or Orula. In Santeria, the spirits of the dead are honored in spiritual ceremonies—otherwise, they'll cause trouble for the living. In some rituals, people invite the spirits or orishas to possess them, a practice called "being ridden," as though they were the horse and the orisha is the jockey.

Voodoo (also called Vodou or Vodun) also originates in West Africa. Instead of orishas, Voodoo has the loa. The most well-known loa include Papa Legba, Erzulia Freda, Simbi, Kouzin Zaka, and the Marasa. Because Voodoo later merged with European cultures, each loa is now associated with a Roman Catholic saint. Ceremonies include processions with flags, drums, and ritual tools. Followers will then invoke the loa or ask to be "ridden." In some ceremonies, animals are offered food. If they eat the food, it means they accept their role as a sacrifice, according to Kail. There are many flavors of Voodoo from different parts of Africa, and from African-settled nations, each with its own practices and nuances.

Around the world, there are many faiths with roots in Africa. One is Abaqua, from Cuba, where practitioners serve the "power of the leopard" and sacrifice larger animals. There's Brujeria, from Mexico, centered on the Mother of Guadalupe and the Aztec goddess Tonantzin. Candomblé, from Brazil, is similar to Santeria. Hoodoo, based in the Southern United States, involves folk magic and rootwork. "Voodoo dolls" are part of Hoodoo folk practices (not Voodoo, as the name implies), but they actually come from European folk magic.

Palo Mayombe came from Congo, and later traveled to Cuba. A central concept of this religion is the nganga, a cauldron in which the spirits live. Herbs, dirt, water, shells, and animal blood are put into the cauldron in order to "feed" the spirits, according to Kail. Practitioners are initiated by having symbols scratched into their skin. "As the spirit is 'scratched in'" through this ritual, "possession may also occur," Kail wrote.

Palo, like Santeria and Voodoo, includes some animal sacrifice, including chickens, goats, and other small animals. In general, only priests or priests-in-training perform animal sacrifices. Young people will primarily offer water, food, and candles to the spirits. Most adults in the tradition may also make offerings of tobacco smoke and/or alcohol. It's worth noting that animal sacrifice is protected under the First Amendment of the United States Constitution. In 1993, the U.S. Supreme Court overturned a Florida law that had declared such sacrifices illegal, finding that the ban violated Santeria practitioners' right to religious freedom. As long as such sacrifices are humane and practiced as part of one of these faiths, they're legal.

Just as the priests of Santeria and Palo Mayombe are the medicine men and women of their communities, shamans—whose traditions stem from Native American practices—are healers who communicate with the spirit world and treat illnesses by healing people's souls. If you've heard of shamanism, especially through anthropology, it may surprise you to know that there are shamans practicing today. Some of them found their spiritual calling when they were teenagers or, in some cases, younger.

Modern shamans often adopt ideas from older traditions. For instance, many neoshamans believe that they are "called" to practice shamanism, typically through an illness or trauma. Dreams or visions tag along with the illness, telling the person that he or she is being called. Some are reluctant to answer this call, since it requires a lot of responsibility, and because in modern cultures these are not responsibilities that many people understand or accept.

Once called, the shaman-to-be then begins what is essentially "shaman school." The "classroom" is located in dreams, trance-work and vision quests. It also happens through interpreting signs and encounters with animals. Usually one or more spiritual guides teach the ins and outs of the practice, including how to heal parts of the shaman's own soul before healing others. This process can be very empowering and enriching, but also lonely, because not many people understand what it's like. For many pagan paths, there is a strong social aspect, but shamanism is much more of a solitary practice.

Shamanism is rooted in the idea of animism, which considers everything, from rocks to spiders, sacred. "Animism is the perspective that all things have a soul, that all souls are connected, and that all souls are equal," said S. Kelley Harrell, a practicing shaman. "Interacting in that connection is the role of the shaman. Traditionally, the shaman is described as an intermediary between the formed world and the unformed, willing a facet of the soul to journey into the spirit worlds to some intended deed. The outcome of this work is to bring the information back from the spirits to some betterment of community, individual, or self."

Shamans help people in a number of ways. One idea central to modern shamanism is "soul retrieval." When someone goes through a serious crisis or trauma, pieces of his or her soul are believed to go missing or be taken by force. It's the shaman's job to find those pieces and bring them back. This heals the trauma that caused the split. Shamans can also help others find their spirit animals or talk with spirit guides. They sometimes communicate with the spirits of the dead, and pass along messages to the living, who might not otherwise be able to hear or understand those messages. They help people understand the spiritual meaning behind illnesses, troubling dreams, or personal crises. They may also bring messages from the spirit world to the community in times of regional trouble.

Harrell was called to shamanism while healing from childhood sexual trauma, and found that the spiritual path was her unique road to healing. But doing so wasn't easy. "I knew that I was seeing a slice of reality that wasn't readily available to others," she said. "I had already clearly gotten the message that my abilities disturbed others and that I should hide them. The only resources available on paranormal or metaphysical experiences were fiction—in the form of horror books and films —or demonized perspectives on Earth religions and psychic ability."

Those resources scared her, and led to plenty of confusion. Ultimately she had to learn to trust herself. "The seeking soul must be soothed. My advice along that line is, any information or approach that doesn't feel right isn't. Hold out for what feels authentic," she said.

A teen who is exploring shamanism likely feels a strong connection to the spirit world, or to the world of nature. He or she may feel "called" to this path through dreams. The decision to answer that call can mirror the self-discovery of adolescence, according to Harrell.

"Perhaps the greatest rite of passage of adolescence is finding a sense of self through an intense feeling of isolation. Indigenous cultures recognize this transition to selfhood as the development of compassion, becoming a responsible adult in the connection with All Things, and specific tests have been honed over centuries to demonstrate to the community that the youth is ready to be an adult. In them, childhood has been spent preparing to pass the rites that make one a confident adult thriving for the benefit of the tribe," Harrell said.

Our culture lacks a lot of those elements. It doesn't provide structured spiritual development, nor survival skills in the way teens may need. "In the west ... children pass through this undefined, largely unmentored era of 'teen,' often without the tried and true spiritual and energetic support of their tribe," Harrell said. Finding that support elsewhere, including within themselves, can be a relief.

Wicca, neo-paganism, Thelema, Satanism, chaos magic, Santeria and shamanism are all spiritual and religious paths, of a kind. There are other occult practices that don't involve working with gods, spirits, or other higher powers. But they appeal to people—teens included—because they provide opportunities to ask questions about the future, talk to loved ones who have passed on, or learn about hidden aspects of current life. They can feel like a way to make sense of the world and its unknowns.

Many of these practices fall under the umbrella of divination, and one of the most popular flavors of divination is astrology. You're probably familiar with astrology through the horoscopes printed in newspapers. These horoscopes are based on your "sun" sign, determined by the month of your birth. While the sun sign is one element of astrology, it's a very general one. Astrology includes many other factors and offers a much more personalized description of a person's personality, tendencies, and potential destiny.

Astrologers draw up a complex "chart" based on an individual's birth date, time, and location. They can pinpoint where each planet was located in the sky at the time of birth. Those positions are thought to influence one's temperament and future. Each planet, including the sun and moon, is associated with a unique aspect of life. The Sun represents the self, the Moon relates to emotions, Mars describes physical energy and power, Venus relates to love and beauty, and so on. Meanwhile, each sign correlates to several attributes: Leo is outgoing and generous, while Pisces is shy and dreamy. If your Moon is in Leo, your emotions would follow Leo's magnanimous nature, but if your Moon is in Pisces, you may be more sensitive emotionally.

The planets closest to the sun move quickly through the sky, changing positions every day, so they are the planets that make each person unique. Planets with longer orbits, such as Uranus and Neptune, move slowly through the heavens. Their positions are thought to influence whole generations.

Astrologers also consider the positions of planets in relation to each other, and whether they are beneficial or challenging. It takes work to learn to interpret astrological charts. Teens who study astrology are likely looking for more insight into themselves, as well as the future. They may also want to overcome some of the personal tendencies astrology tells them they have. Or, they may want to help friends and loved ones by reading their charts for them.

Another popular divination tool is the Tarot. This collection of 78 cards, developed in Europe in the late 14th Century, has been used for games and fortune-telling; our modern playing cards are based on them. The Tarot has four suits: swords, wands, cups, and pentacles or coins, which have become the spades, clubs, hearts, and diamonds. Each number and royalty card in the four suits has a specific divinatory meaning. The Tarot deck has 22 additional cards. In order, these cards describe a man's journey from "Fool"—the very beginning—to "The World," which represents the achievement of worldly knowledge and experience. The Fool mas many adventures, learning about love, death, strength, justice, and fate along the way. When one of these cards turns up in a reading, it means the querent is in a similar place in life.

A Tarot reading begins with a question. Then, the cards are shuffled face-down and laid out in different patterns. As they're turned over, the cards are interpreted both individually and in concert with one another. This interpretation may answer the question and indicate a little bit about the outcome of the issue. Often, the Tarot does not predict the future so much as provide a different perspective about a problem. It can suggest motivations and solutions that are not already obvious to the person asking the question. You can read the Tarot cards for yourself, read for someone else, or ask someone to read them for you.

Some people use runes for divination, which come from an early Germanic alphabet. Each letter has its own meaning, making it possible to use them for divination. Some cultures who used the runic alphabet believed it had supernatural powers. The letters could be scratched onto objects and used as magical charms. Some even thought that the right combination of runes could bring the dead back to life.

There are 24 runes in what's called the Elder Futhark alphabet. These are written onto wood discs, ceramic tiles, or similar small objects and held in a small bag or pouch. As with the Tarot, someone can ask a question, then draw several runes and spread them out face-down in a variety of patterns. Each rune has a meaning, as does each position in the spread. Together, these can reveal information about the situation in question, the person asking the question, and the outcome of the situation. Runes may have special meaning for anyone involved with the Asatru faith, or for folks are descended from Scandinavians. They were also used in J.R.R. Tolkien's *Lord of the Rings* books, so fans of his work may become fond of them.

Another form of divination is dowsing. Most people, when they hear of dowsing, think of someone meandering through a backyard with a forked stick, looking for water. But there are many tools for dowsing, such as the pendulum. A pendulum can be any kind of weighted object on a string or chain: a crystal, a metal weight, a ring. Just about anything can work.

The idea is, you hold the pendulum by its chain or string in one of your hands, and let the weight dangle. It will seem to swing side-to-side or in circles by itself, although it's actually controlled by subtle muscles in the hands. It may swing one way for "yes," and another way for "no," providing answers to simple questions. They can provide particular movements for any pair of opposites, such as "boy" and "girl." This is sometimes used to predict the gender of an unborn baby. Pendulums can also be used over maps in order to find lost objects and people. Writer and archaeologist T.C. Lethbridge used different lengths of string for different kinds of objects—metals, ceramics, etc.—and counted the number of swings. This would tell him how old an artifact was.

Many teens explore psychic phenomena, including lucid dreaming, astral travel, ESP or mind-reading, telekinesis, and communication with ghosts. Like divination, most of the time these practices are not part of any specific pagan religion, but they're part of the larger occult world.

No one knows for sure what happens when someone attempts to communicate with the spirits of the dead. There have been a number of famous mediums throughout history, each one with his or her own techniques for receiving messages from ghosts and passing them along to the living. Whether or not these mediums are the real deal, belief in ghosts is incredibly common, even among people who say they don't believe in the occult.

There are two main methods that nonprofessional mediums use to communicate with spirits: séances and Ouija boards. In a séance, a group sits with the medium and they work together, often in silence, to invite a specific spirit or spirits to come forward. Sometimes, the spirits communicate verbally with the medium in a way that only he or she can hear. Other times, ghosts will flutter candles and curtains, knock on or overturn tables, turn warm rooms freezing, or create breezes and winds. Many have claimed that these events are actually hoaxes organized by the medium or by others in the room. But that doesn't prevent many teenagers from attempting séances on their own. Some do it simply to see what happens, or to find out information that they wouldn't be able to know otherwise.

Others attempt to contact the dead because they have lost a loved one and wish to talk to him or her. In the latter case, teens may reach out alone, rather than with a group, for more privacy and intimacy.

Ouija (pronounced WEE-jee) boards are marketed and sold as games. They include a board decorated with letters, numbers, and the words "yes" and "no." Boards can be used by one or two people. They lightly touch their fingers onto a small pointing tool placed on the board, called a planchette. One or both of them will call out questions. In theory, the spirits guide the planchette—and the querents' hands—to different spots on the board, answering questions. Many teens use Ouija boards to quest for information, and they take it seriously. Others use them to frighten themselves at slumber parties. These tools are often frowned upon in the occult community. Some say they're like dialing a random telephone number and taking the advice of whoever picks up the phone.

Astral travel, also called astral projection, is often part of shamanism, but is used by others as well. It's based on the idea that your spirit can wander around—or traverse long distances—while your body rests in place. The person attempting to travel on the "astral plane" will sit or lie comfortably and enter a relaxed trance state. Meanwhile, the astral traveler pictures his or her spirit floating away. The traveler can stick close to home, visit a nearby friend, explore the house of someone who would not otherwise let them inside, attempt to write messages, or even cross the globe to see far-away friends. Some people believe they travel to other worlds.

Teens often feel as though they don't have enough mobility and freedom, especially if they live in rural areas. For them, an astral journey can seem very appealing. It can also be tempting to try astral projection "just to see what happens." Some might try meeting with friends "in the astral," and then swap stories the next day at school to see if they match up.

Many people have recurring bad dreams and wish they could steer those dreams to a happier ending. Or, they have boring dreams they wish were more thrilling. In lucid dreaming, the dreamer becomes aware he or she is dreaming, then controls the rest of the dream. Friends may agree to meet up in lucid dreams and share information. When they wake up, they can find out if they really shared that information. Lucid dreaming can make a lot of sense for teens who already have vivid dreams and want to explore them more consciously.

Extra-sensory perception, also called ESP, telepathy, or sometimes simply mind-reading, is the ability to know what others are thinking. In ESP experiments, one person holds an idea in his or her mind, and then the other person attempts to identify that thought. This is how someone can train to become a better mind-reader. Even without training, some seem to have an uncanny ability to know what others are thinking. They may know who is calling before they answer the telephone, or who is at the door before the doorbell rings, when they are not expecting someone. Others will get "hunches" about something that is about to happen, or about something that has recently happened without their knowledge.

Some teens feel they have this kind of intuition. For them, it can be comforting to know that there is a name for it, and a tradition of psychics that goes back for generations. It can be frightening to see flashes of events, only to find out they really happened. It's a relief to know others experience it, too.

Telekinesis, or psychokinesis, is the ability to move objects with one's mind. Although it is mostly the stuff of scary movies and books, plenty of people believe they have this power. They work hard to train themselves to shift or lift objects simply by thinking about it. Someone might use telekinesis to control the way dice land, to create wind or stop the rain, to light candles—the possibilities are endless. Some believe that telekinesis causes incandescent lightbulbs to blow out when a telekinetic person flips a light switch. For some teens, being able to do these things—or claim to be able to do them—may make them seem more interesting and more powerful to their friends.

The Spiral Dance

Abel Gomez was 13 when he discovered paganism. He looked into a number of disciplines, including Witchcraft, Hinduism, Buddhism, Qabalah, shamanism and ceremonial magic before he joined the Reclaiming Collective, a Wiccan group.

"I wanted something fresh, something that spoke to my deep yearning for connection to mystery and the unseen world," Gomez said. "All of these traditions spoke to the same fundamental yearning [for] a deeper sense of connection."

He chose Wicca because it's based in nature, and for its connections with ancient, mythic gods. He chose Reclaiming because it provides a community framework for his spirituality, Gomez said. He was looking for a path that helped him better understand the world around him.

"At a time of questioning and stripping away of idealizations in search of deeper truths, teens seek spirituality that is both moving and relevant," Gomez said. "Amid war, environmental destruction, and poverty, teens ask how spirituality can help to create a better world and more complete, integrated people. In pursuit of deeper truths, greater autonomy, and connection to the natural world, many modern teens are exploring esoteric and Earth-based spiritual paths."

When Gomez joined Reclaiming as a teen, he realized its combination of witchcraft, community and political activism was "powerful," he said. As he began attending regular rituals and other events, "something struck a chord with me. I loved the simplicity and profundity of a group of people gathered together to sing, honor the old gods, make magic, and celebrate the turning of the Earth."

Though Reclaiming, Gomez felt transformed. "It has given me a greater sense of connection to the gods, to the world around me, and to my own heart's yearning. This sense of connection has been the motivation to become a vegan, volunteer in my community, work toward environmental sustainability, and get involved with social-justice movements," he said.

There are a mind-boggling number of alternative spiritualities out there, and teens, like adults, check out any or all of them in the hope of finding something that's right for them. Nationally, it's tough to find good statistics on just how many teens are exploring or following pagan beliefs.

For one thing, data can be useful (or not) depending on

how people describe themselves in surveys. Many Americans believe that the occult is sinister, amusing, or neurotic. And they think occultists are weird, disturbed, or even dangerous, Emily Edwards wrote in *Metaphysical Media*. But these same people might believe in something considered "occult," such as ghosts. If you ask them whether they're pagans or occultists, they would say no, but their beliefs tell another story.

David Kinnaman and Gabe Lyons went in search of hard data on young people and spirituality when they co-authored *unChristian: What a New Generation Really Thinks About Christianity and why it Matters* in 2007. Before writing the book, they polled Americans age 16 to 29, a group of 29 million people. Forty percent of them identified themselves as "outsiders to Christianity," meaning they practiced anything from paganism to Islam and Judaism.

In 2008, 24 percent of Americans age 18 to 29 were following a "new religious movement or other religion," according to the massive American Religious Identification Survey conducted by the Trinity College of Hartford, Connecticut. This gives us a peek into the lives of older teens, but doesn't describe what younger ones believe. In my own research, I found that some youth discovered paganism or the occult at young ages; most were introduced to it between 10 and 14. The youngest was 5.

My sense, based on research and discussions with adult and teen pagans, is that the number of adolescents who check out paganism is relatively small—less than 10 percent of the overall teen population. At the same time, it's not uncommon for youths to try it. Some read a few books, attempt some spells and then move on. Others develop a deep connection to a spiritual practice that stays with them for years.

Many adolescents, like many adults, long to make sense of their existence. They want to know why they're here, why the world is often such a confusing place, and whether they have some spiritual purpose. At the same time, adolescents are all about breaking away from the patterns of childhood and striking out on their own. Many teens are exploring their identity in a way they haven't before, and beginning to discover who they'll become as adults. It's also a time of intense emotional and hormonal upheaval. That can make teens feel as though the need for a spiritual path is urgent. As they cast aside the traditions of their parents, they may abandon the church they grew up with.

In *unChristian*, Kinnaman and Lyons discovered a number of reasons why teens break away from the church. Many have lost respect for Christianity because they find it anti-homosexual, judgmental, or hypocritical. Other teens felt that many Christians were out of touch with reality and too focused on converting people.

While Kinnaman and Lyons' research showed that many teens "tried Christianity on for size," a good chunk of them didn't stick with it because of their disillusionment. "[Christians] have become famous for what we oppose, rather than what we are for. We are known for having an us-versus-them mentality. Outsiders feel minimized, or worse, demonized, by those who love Jesus," Kinnaman and Lyons wrote. "A huge chunk of the new generation has concluded that they want nothing to do with us." At the same time, they found that youths are hungry for new experiences and new sources of motivation—particularly ones that allow them to try things for themselves, without "experts" or "talking heads" getting in the way.

They weren't the only ones who learned that teenagers mistrusted the Christian church. Jeffrey Jensen Arnett interviewed hundreds of heavy-metal fans in the 1990s, and shared his findings in *Metalheads: Heavy Metal Music and Adolescent Alienation*.

"There are some [teens] who are contemptuous of [religion], who cite the hypocrisy of televangelists and the acquisitiveness of organized religion as evidence that all religion is a sham, but most are simply indifferent to it. It does not move them. It adds to their alienation for what it *fails* to provide for them: it does *not* give them comfort, reassurance, a stable social network outside the family, a ready source of meaning—the way it has in virtually every other society historically and cross-culturally," Arnett wrote.

Many of the teens and former teens interviewed for this book gave up on the church and struck out in search of something more comfortable for a variety of reasons. "I had some significant issues with mainstream religion," said an Atlanta, Georgia, resident who began exploring the occult at age 16. "I couldn't deal with the falseness and the hypocrisy between what was preached and what the priests actually did in their day to day lives."

"I became disillusioned with Catholicism because it tended to be very hypocritical. I became an atheist due to my small-town upbringing. I didn't know there were any other choices," said a pagan who grew up in the Midwest and discovered the occult at 14.

Until Kinnaman and Lyons wrote *unChristian*, little was known about teens and their relationship to spirituality. Few people have thought to study teens' religious leanings, according to Charles Shelton, who wrote *Adolescent Spirituality: Pastoral Ministry for High School and College Youth* in 1989. Shelton, too, found that teens needed religion and religious commitment, but had serious issues with the church. Those who remained Christian developed their own unique bond with Jesus Christ.

Teens are driven by "personal relationships and the meaning that those relationships give to their own lives," Shelton wrote. As part of those relationships, adolescents engaged in sexual activity to meet a number of needs, including intimacy, belonging, identification, and imitation, and the desire for dominance, submissiveness, passion, and intensity. They were also curious, looking for competence, and hoping to rebel, according to Shelton. All of these needs, desires and motivations also explain why teens explore and choose the spiritual paths they do.

The search for identity during the teen years provides the perfect backdrop for spiritual experimentation, according to Sharon Parks, who wrote *The Critical Years: The Young Adult Search for a Faith to Live By*. Teens are just beginning to reflect on the meaning of life, and with that comes a whole avalanche of spiritual questions.

"To attend to faith is to be concerned with the questions so familiar to those who grieve and to others who suffer meaninglessness: 'Why should I get out of bed in the morning?'

'What is the purpose of my existence and the existence of others?' 'Does anything really matter?' 'What can I depend upon?' 'Are we ultimately alone?' 'What can be trusted as real, and what is my relationship to that?' 'What is the ultimate character of the cosmos in which I dwell?'" Parks wrote.

Younger children in faith often start out by believing there is a supreme authority. As they become teenagers, they learn that all information, including spiritual information, is relative. This discovery kicks off a search for personal truth, according to Parks. At the same time, teens are struggling with a relatively fragile sense of what she calls "inner-dependence," one that is vulnerable to disappointment, failure, exclusion, abandonment, emptiness, and hopelessness. Many times, they will choose a spiritual path that gives them a hands-on feeling of success, belonging, satisfaction, and optimism. Most pagan and occult paths offer just those kinds of feelings.

Teens' delicate, emerging personalities—and their need for meaning and a sense of belonging—can also make them prone to idealism, even zealotry and fanaticism. Anyone who has seen a teenager plaster her walls with music posters knows about fanaticism. Young people also lend this kind of zeal to their spiritual pursuits. They may fall hard for a particular path, including a pagan path, because it may be the first thing to answer all of their longings, needs, and vulnerabilities.

In *Real Boys' Voices*, William Pollack found that spirituality was a major source of stability for teens. In fact, their faith—whether in organized religion or an alternative—surprised him. "For many boys, such a spiritual core is not only profoundly meaningful but also emotionally sustaining, leading to hopefulness and renewal when perhaps all other avenues and possibilities seemed compromised or even lost."

Fabbro, a co-founder of the now-defunct chaos magic-based site Irreality, was 9 or 10 when she discovered books on lucid dreaming and the occult at her local library. Fabbro had experienced vivid dreams and wanted to understand them better. Books on "lucid" dreaming teach the ability to move through one's dreams more consciously, as well as control them.

Always a bit of a nerd, Fabbro spent her school

lunchtimes chatting with friends and searching the Internet. After she and a friend discussed so-called "psychic vampires"— people who claim to "drink" the energy from people nearby— she went online to explore the topic. There, she stumbled across a site that offered texts on psychic vampires and chaos magic. It defined chaos magic as an eclectic form of paganism that encourages people to experiment with spell-casting from a variety of traditions. It also suggests adopting playful ideas from the imagination. From there, chaos magicians craft a personalized path that works best for them.

Fabbro loved it. "The act of taking ownership of your own fate—your actions, reactions and consequences, no matter what they might be," was important for her. "Chaos magic, in particular, seemed to be free-form enough that I could be myself, take the toolset offered, and literally build any kind of worldview I wanted, and then set myself up to go for my goals."

Teens, in general, need to be encouraged to become the person they want to be, take ownership of their lives, and understand that they have the power to shape their future, according to Fabbro. The spiritual path they take doesn't matter. What matters is the process of challenging tradition so teens can understand themselves better, she said.

"[Teens] want to figure out who they are, and how to connect with something, anything—to know more and be more," Fabbro said. "To assert and establish themselves even if they pretend it's to 'look cool' ... or to annoy parents or get a reaction."

Like Fabbro, Steven Leyba was something of a nerd growing up in Camden, Arkansas. And, like Fabbro, his introduction to the occult was his town's public library. At the time, he was curious about the meaning of life and the beliefs of people across the globe—and he was disillusioned by what he saw as the dishonesty of the Christian church.

"I was appalled at what the Baptists and other Christians were calling Christianity, and by how controlling religion was and wondered why people called that 'spirituality,'" he said. In contrast to what he experienced in the Baptist South, Leyba was looking for a path that held personal meaning.

Ironically, it was the messages of the Baptist church—particularly those describing the supposed "Satanic" messages in popular music—that drew Leyba's interest. He discovered a copy of Anton LaVey's book *The Satanic Bible* at his aunt's house. He was intimidated at first by the idea of the Church of Satan. But he read the book anyway, and sympathized with its critique of Christianity.

"It was a great inspiration for my art, and my own personal philosophy of self-reliance," Leyba said. "It helped give me the confidence to pursue the kind of art I wanted to do."

At the same time, Leyba was unearthing his Apache heritage and the mistreatment of Native Americans by Christian missionaries. He was incredibly angry at the church for what it had done to his ancestors. He felt they had been treated as though they were "devils." To him, embracing Satanism felt like reclaiming that demonization from the people who had driven the Native Americans down.

Leyba also had more traditional teenage reasons for exploring Satanism. "For me, the occult was about taking emotion and desire and the energy around that, and concentrating it on the things I wanted on my life and the world," he said. "It was also dangerous, chaotic, and taboo. Occult means the unknown, and I wanted to know the unknown. Satanism was the darkest and most taboo and misunderstood." To Leyba, the *Satanic Bible* is a book about self-reliance.

As an adult, Leyba got to know LaVey personally. LaVey named him a Reverend in the church. Now a successful mixed-media and performance artist, Leyba founded the Coyotel Church, a Native American-based Satanist group that works with plenty of teens and young adults, helping them to find their spiritual paths.

"There isn't much in a young person's life that truly empowers them," Leyba said. "They are looking for examples and not experts, priests, dogma or doctrine. They are looking for deeper meaning—and in our consumerist, global 21st Century, there isn't much of that. Spirituality is the most important thing for a young person because it helps to create who they are and establish their identity. That is why you can't force religion and spirituality on children. They have to find it on their own."

The need for empowerment and meaning: I heard these kinds of messages repeatedly as I interviewed people for this book.

"My exploration of the occult made me feel better about myself, since it gave me the power to change myself," said a 19-year-old from Northern California who started exploring the occult at 10. "I also felt like I had an important role as a go-between with spirits and humans. It gave me a purpose and a reason to keep living when things got tough."

Discovering paganism was "definitely more empowering and confidence building," said a Londoner who started exploring the occult at 11. "It makes you feel more self-worth and helps you affirm your own divinity and personal agency in the world. It also helped me realize my personal responsibility for my own faults and gave me tools and ideas on ways to work through those, both mundane and occult."

"Most of the occultists I know have a deep and profound love for the divine mystery, without getting hung up on the specifics," the London pagan said. "Most likely kids will be lead away from their traditional faiths if they explore deeply ... but simply because those faiths tend to fall apart on close inspection and it's the fault of the belief system, not the child, when he or she starts to see the inconsistencies adding up."

"[I liked] the idea that religion could be more personal, more about your connection to nature instead of just going to church and saying the right words," said Elise, whose story opened this chapter. "I was sort of forced into Catholicism growing up, and was bitter about it. [With Wicca], I was attracted, at first, to the idea of a spiritual connection not associated with a particular god. As I matured and began to recognize what Wicca was about, the peace appealed to me in a world of chaos. There wasn't anything that I really disliked about Wicca, because it was meant to be personalized."

After trying a number of spells, "I felt very successful. I knew the more confident I got, the more successful they would be," said a pagan from Toronto who started exploring the occult at the age of 12. "I also found very early on that I could change myself just as well as I could alter the world around me. This was one of the most powerful self-help concepts I've ever learned."

Although many adolescents take their spirituality seriously, there's also the possibility that a teen is just using the occult to keep adults—or other kids—at bay. The books, symbols, clothing and other paraphernalia can seem frightening on the surface, so teens sometimes use them when they want a bully or parent to leave them alone.

"I remember in the Rockaways, when I was about fifteen, there was a dorky guy who used to tell people he was Satan. It was basically his way of scaring girls into respecting him," Gaines wrote.

Kail recalls a boy who was stopped by police—and happened to be carrying a copy of *The Satanic Bible*. "When the boy was questioned about his involvement with Satanism, he smiled and shook his head, saying, 'If you're talking about that book I carry around, I don't even know what it is about. I just know that it scares people. I used to get beat up by these guys in my class, but ever since I started carrying that book around, nobody messes with me!' Using the occult as a security blanket is very popular. I have had teachers, parents and even police officers tell me that they were scared to deal with juvenile occultists," Kail wrote.

Parents who are confused by their teen's activities may be unsure what to do: intervene? Ask questions? Many times, parents found if they took a more hands-off approach to their kids' occult interest, it would fizzle out on its own. Edwards tells the story of four teenage girls who watched the Wicca-based film *The Craft* often during sleepovers, and watched certain scenes repeatedly. The mother of one girl said all four sets of parents were aware of their daughters' interest in the movie. Although they weren't happy about it, they decided not to make a big deal about it. One of the girls' fathers, a teacher, was sure that his daughter's interest in witchcraft was only a phase. He was right. As the girls graduated from high school and moved on to college, they lost interest. "The lure of both film and ritual seems to have been temporary," Edwards wrote.

Furthermore, one of the moms told Edwards she realized the girls' fascination with the film had less to do with Wicca, and more to do with adolescence itself. "[She] felt that teenage girls and young women may become attracted to witchcraft as a way of rebelling against authority and social conditions that seem stacked against them. She believed her daughter and the other girls used rituals learned through books and movies to create tight friendship bonds and a sense of community that was important to them during a stressful period of change," Edwards wrote.

While some teens only dip their toes into the occult pool, others find path to call their own. "During high school, some teens will 'try on' the occult. They might even dabble in different practices, which may or may not lead to more serious involvement. ... The occult appears to offer answers to the teen who questions, acceptance to the misfit, and power to the powerless," Harshbarger wrote.

When teens are serious about an alternative spiritual practice, parents may find themselves put off—in large part because of what they've heard, either through popular culture and the news, or through their religious background. That can make it difficult for them to respect their children's practices, or be compassionate about them.

"At first, [my parents] were very much against it," said Fabbro, whose parents discovered her interest in Wicca before she moved on to chaos magic. "My mother was raised Catholic. They thought the worst at the beginning. They found one of the more tame books on Wicca and had some freak-outs."

However, her parents soon understood a couple of things. One, Fabbro's exploration wasn't hurting her. Two, she was stubborn enough that they wouldn't be able to make her quit. "They realized it wasn't a big deal. I wasn't a bad kid by any means, I didn't fall in with a cult, or drugs, or anything that might mean for proper concern," she recalls. "One birthday my mom gave me a card with a witch on it and some witty quip, along with a small book on fortune-telling. I knew that in that indirect way, my mother was telling me that she loved me the way I was."

However, things didn't go smoothly with other parts of

her family. During a holiday meal, Fabbro's mom mentioned, almost proudly, that her daughter was exploring alternative religions. Fabbro's aunt said that she was never to see her cousin again—one of her closest friends at the time. The two have not spoken since.

Gomez had similar experiences with his Catholic family, at first. "My parents were not happy to learn of my interest," he said. "My mom discouraged it and my dad tried to ignore it." His family was not entirely immune to the fear and misunderstanding our culture has about paganism, but they tried to understand. "They feared that the Craft was inherently linked to Satanism, and that ongoing practice would essentially lead to self-destructive behavior. Luckily, as I continued to read and become more knowledgeable about witchcraft, I was able to have conversations and explain to them what it is really all about."

Over the years, Gomez was able to bring his family to some public rituals and other Reclaiming events so they could see his new community for themselves. Eventually, they came to understand how much this faith meant to their son, whom they had raised to embrace religion and ceremony.

A teen's serious interest in an alternative spiritual path —especially one that comes so loaded with misinformation as Satanism—is bound to give parents pause. "My mom was very worried," Leyba said. "I tried to explain it to her. I told her about *The Satanic Bible* but she wasn't interested in reading it. My father read it and he could see why I was interested in Satanism and how it was helping me have confidence with my art and myself."

However, Leyba was able to show his mom that his beliefs were having a positive effect. "I had a lot of self-esteem issues and I didn't like doing many of the things most kids did *The Satanic Bible* helped me be myself. Later my mother could see how I applied the philosophy and how it helped me have great successes in life," he said. "I wish she had read *The Satanic Bible* so she could have at least known what the book was about and why I was drawn to it rather than assume I was being manipulated. Ultimately it deepened my relationship with my parents because they learned to trust my judgment and see the outcome of my actions and not alienate me."

There's good reason to trust teens' judgment: they know their limits. There are paths for all personalities, and many teens I interviewed had the same reservations about some of those paths that adults do. When asked whether there were any parts of the occult world that were too scary for them, several named Satanism, Goetia, demon-summoning, chaos magic, voodoo, or blood magic. A few also said Ouija boards were too much.

Teens had a variety of reasons for these reservations. "I've never been keen on the idea of harming others, especially for self-gain," said a Northern California resident who started exploring the occult at age 12, and who objected to the use of black magic.

"I've had some Satanic friends, and I respect them and their beliefs but it's not for me. I agree with some of their teachings, but I also find it's based too much on personal selfishness. I don't believe in using magic for vengeance against another person like they do," said a Colorado resident who got into the occult at the age of 8.

On the other hand, a few of those who were initially uncomfortable with Satanism, black magic, and what's known as the "Left-Hand Path" eventually found a home among those faiths. "As I became more comfortable with my own practices and allowed myself to explore it academically, I realized most all of the things I was told as a child about Satanism were either lies or simply untrue," said a Tennessee resident who began studying the occult at 12.

Whatever a teen is studying, chances are good he or she knows why it appeals, and when a practice or path is too much. Many pagan practices not only encourage but require self-reflection. None of the teens I interviewed became blindly enthralled with any practice; that scenario takes place in the minds of tabloid journalists like Geraldo Rivera, not in the real world.

"In many ways, [my exploration of the occult] lead to my self-acceptance," said a Memphis, Tennessee, resident who began exploring the occult at the age of 12, told me. "It allowed me to be realize that it was OK to be who I am, whereas in Christianity, I felt pressured to conform and deny my identity, which lead to three failed suicide attempts. I think, in many ways, paganism saved my life."

Adventures in Imagination

Chris' first time playing *Dungeons & Dragons* was a bit unusual. He was 12 years old when a friend brought one of the *D&D* books along on a school field trip. Chris had never seen anything like it before, but after looking through the book, he immediately wanted to play it. There was just one problem: his friend wasn't interested in leading the game. So Chris volunteered to lead—also known as acting as the Dungeon Master, or DM.

Typically, players don't DM until they've played a game for a while. That gives them time to learn how the rules, characters, and potential storylines can interact. But Chris dove right in, crafting the first of many "dungeon crawls" he designed in those early years—a trek through a fictional world filled with monsters, treasure, and other surprises for the players.

D&D entered Chris' life at a crucial time. As a junior-high student, he watched his classmates join different cliques: jocks, hippies, the "smart kids." He was recruited for the basketball team on account of his impressive height. But joining the jocks didn't feel quite right. Gaming introduced him to a group of people who shared his love of storytelling, as well as his slightly misfit nature. Over time, he branched out into other gaming systems, including *Battletech*, *Cyberpunk*, *Rifts*, and *Heroes Unlimited*.

"[Gaming] gave me a group of friends to hang out with and do stuff with, and a constant social interaction that I didn't have," he said.

It also provided a respite from the real-life depression

Chris developed in high school. He began to feel suicidal. His mom, afraid that role-playing games might be contributing to her son's self-destructive thoughts, asked him if the two were connected. Although he couldn't articulate it at the time, Chris realized years later that the opposite was true.

"[They asked me], 'Is the roleplaying too much, is that why you are the way you are, is it causing you to be depressed, are you having a hard time keeping a grip on reality?' and to be honest, roleplaying is actually one of the things that keeps me grounded," he said. "It's the one constant thing in my life. It's the one thing that doesn't need to have any other meaning to it. I don't have to read into it. It's a time to do something fun and let loose. ... I never lose reality in the gaming."

RPGs have allowed Chris to develop his creative side. In academics and work, he has focused on math and science. But inventing new role-playing adventures gives him the chance to flex his imagination. Gaming has also bolstered his tendency to take on leadership roles, which has come in handy in work and social situations.

After high school, Chris discovered *Vampire: The Masquerade*, a horror-based game from White Wolf. The story sparked his interest, helping him create more sophisticated adventures for his friends and their RPG characters. As an adult, Chris continues to lead role-playing games on nearly a weekly basis. Occasionally, he GMs a game for his teen son.

"Whenever I run a game, I always try to cater to the people's characters as much as possible, try to give them something cool that they like about their character that makes them remember [it], so they walk away from the game remembering how much fun we had doing it," he said.

Mazes and Monsters

One June afternoon in 1982, Irving "Bink" Pulling, a 16-year-old resident of Montpelier, Virginia, took his family's loaded handgun and shot himself in the chest. His mother, Patricia Pulling, found him dead in the front yard when she returned home that evening.

Pulling claimed that Bink's suicide was a complete

surprise to her. While going through her son's belongings, she found a handful of *Dungeons & Dragons* books and asked around to find out what they were. At a local shop that sold role-playing supplies, she asked a clerk how she could learn more about the game. Eventually, she wound up connecting with a handful of gamers at a local college. They played *D&D* with her for more than a month, according to her book, *The Devil's Web*.

According to newspaper reports, Bink's friends and teachers said he was suffering from depression, isolation, and instability. Despite this, Pulling became convinced that *Dungeons & Dragons* had made her son want to kill himself. She sued Bink's school, where he had occasionally played *D&D* in the gifted-and-talented program. She claimed that a teacher had placed a curse on him that caused him to commit suicide. When the case was thrown out of court, Pulling didn't give up. In 1984 she founded Bothered About Dungeons & Dragons, or B.A.D.D., an organization she hoped would raise awareness about the supposed evils of role-playing games.

Bink wasn't the first boy whose suicide was blamed on gaming. In 1979, James Dallas Egbert III, a student at Michigan State University, ran away from school with the intention of ending his life. He left behind a note mentioning the steam tunnels beneath the school, as well as *Dungeons & Dragons*. Local reporters claimed the game inspired him to run away. He returned, but the 16-year-old college prodigy was facing more than his fair share of stress. Egbert had become unstable and was allegedly battling a drug addiction. He succeeded in ending his life a year later. Many believed D&D was at least partly responsible.

Egbert's story inspired a novel by Rona Jaffe, *Mazes and Monsters*, as well as a film starring Tom Hanks. In the movie, Hanks plays Robbie, a college student who joins his peers in a game of the fictional *Mazes and Monsters* RPG. He suffers a psychotic break while playing a live-action version in the caverns near their university. Robbie begins behaving like his *M&M* character in real life, and will only respond to the character's name. Disoriented, he treks to New York City in search of his estranged brother, and nearly commits suicide.

Released in 1982, the film convinced many parents that role-playing games would cause their children to lose touch with reality.

Media reports linking Egbert's death with gaming died down, but the idea of a connection lingered. Even though there was no solid evidence that Egbert's love of *D&D* had anything to do with his suicidal feelings, journalists made it sound like the hobby was to blame. Reporters glossed over the obvious signs that he was psychologically troubled and needed help.

In later articles, journalists continued to connect RPGs with violence or suicide, launching a moral panic, according to J. Patrick Williams and others in *Gaming as Culture*. "*D&D* was defined as a threat to societal values and interests soon after it emerged on the American mainstream cultural radar in the late 1970s. The threat was manifested primarily in fears of occult worship ... and negative psychological conditions including suicide, all of which the mass media presented in a stylized and stereotypical fashion." As a result, many parents believed that these games were dangerous, even deadly.

Pulling was one of those parents. In *The Devil's Web*, her book on the dangers of RPGs, she argued that many gamers were susceptible to the games' dark influences. "Sadly, there are those who, for a variety of reasons, do not have a solid grasp on reality. Some of these individuals find the fantasies of childhood far more rewarding than the day-to-day details of their lives. There are those who are functioning happily and have a world of endless possibilities ahead of them, but who occasionally look for a little extra 'kick,' a temporary yet powerful rush of excitement. For all of these people, fantasy role-playing games present a very dangerous and very real threat," she wrote.

To bolster her argument, Pulling quoted from Dr. Thomas Radecki, MD, chairman of the National Coalition on Television Violence—another one-man "coalition" similar to B.A.D.D.: "There is no doubt in my mind that the game *Dungeons & Dragons* is causing young men to kill themselves and others. This game is one of nonstop combat and violence. Although I am sure that the people at TSR mean no harm, that is exactly what their games are causing. Based on player interviews and game materials, it is clear to me that this game is desensitizing players to violence and also causing an increased tendency to violent behavior."

B.A.D.D.'s anti-gaming pamphlets and media appearances gave weight to the idea that RPGs could lead vulnerable adolescents into trouble. Eventually, parents were not the only ones to mistrust these games; police began to question whether RPGs could inspire criminal activity. That was partly Pulling's doing, too.

Pulling became an "expert" in this supposed link between gaming and violence, and testified in numerous trials. In 1984, she participated in the trial of Darren Molitor, accused of murdering a young girl during a Halloween joke. In the course of the trial, Pulling convinced Molitor that his deep interest in *D&D* was a factor in the crime. He wrote an essay in which he claimed, "the game is played or imagined entirely in the mind. If it is played, let's say three to five times a week, four to eight hours each time, the conscious mind becomes accustomed to the violence. Suddenly you are no longer in total control of your mind. The 'fantasy game' becomes a 'reality game.' You begin to live it for real. Everything you do or say involves ... the game itself. You no longer play the game for enjoyment; you play it because you feel you have to. [Your mind] is possessed by the game. It is more dangerous than I can fully explain."

Molitor later retracted those claims and said, "I no longer feel the game is dangerous for everyone." But the incident suggests that Pulling was able to brainwash Molitor and others into believing her agenda. It's also misleading that, instead of quoting gamers who *hadn't* gone to prison, Pulling used quotes from Molitor in her book on the dangers of gaming. The convicted killer doesn't resemble the large majority of role-playing game fans in any way.

After founding B.A.D.D., Pulling went on to gather information on more than 100 cases, like Molitor's, in which role-playing games were supposedly linked to teen victimization, violence or suicide. However, even in her own descriptions of these cases, it's clear that other factors were also at work.

For example, she cited an instance in which two adults used *Dungeons & Dragons* to entice a 15-year-old into a sex act. It's more likely that the game was bait, not the inspiration for the crime. In another instance, a 16-year-old Pulling described as "legally insane" killed a store clerk in Orlando. Despite that description, she connected the murder to his "obsession" with *D&D*. She mentioned a 14-year-old's suicide note, in which he said he wanted to go to a fantasy world where the elves are. In that case, it sounds like the game was providing relief and respite from the real world.

"As the result of a number of cases that have been made public in the last few years, many parents, educators, and mental health professionals have come to agree that this is a violent game and that youngsters who play it can over-identify with their characters to the extent that their safety is in jeopardy," Pulling wrote.

B.A.D.D. petitioned the Consumer Product Safety Commission, claiming that the games were dangerous. The Games Manufacturing Association responded with its own research. Numerous studies of gamers followed. None found a serious link between RPGs and violent activity among teens— let alone proof that gaming caused problems. GAMA commissioned Michael Stackpole to examine Pulling and her organization. In 1990 his "Pulling Report" was released, detailing the manipulative methods she used to further her belief that gaming is dangerous.

In it, Stackpole described how Pulling wrote up interrogation methods for police, to be used when interviewing criminal teens who play RPGs. She provided police with ridiculously broad descriptions of teens who were vulnerable to Satanic brainwashing. Stackpole also showed how she revised newspaper articles about supposed game-related crimes (including her own son's death) in order to support B.A.D.D.'s agenda. "She has engaged in unethical and illegal practices. Her methods and tactics, at their very best, taint any evidence she might offer and, at their worst, construct a monster where none exists," Stackpole wrote. B.A.D.D. disbanded after the report was publicized. Pulling died in 1997 of cancer.

Following on Stackpole's work, studies in the 1990s

continued to find no link between RPGs and troubling behavior among teens. In fact, in one study, researchers Suzanne Abyeta and James Forest found that non-gamers were more prone to criminal activity than gamers.

However, the link between RPGs and violence has not disappeared. Even now, the famous Chick.com website—home of the "Chick tracts," small booklets that detail the perceived evils of everything from Wicca to Halloween—hosts essays by William Schnoebelen describing the dangers of role-playing games.

In "Straight Talk on *Dungeons & Dragons*," Schnoebelen described the game as a "tragic and tangled subject," and "a feeding program for occultism and witchcraft." He also wrote that the game violates Biblical commandments that warn Christians against all appearance of evil. Schnoebelen, a former Wiccan and Satanic priest, more recently published a second essay, "Should a Christian Play Dungeons & Dragons?" In it, he argues that *Dungeons & Dragons* helps new-age and Satanist groups introduce anti-Christian ideas to gamers.

"Just because the people playing *D&D* think they are playing a game doesn't mean that the evil spirits (who ARE very real) will regard it as a game. If you are doing rituals or saying spells that invite them into your life, then they will come— believe me! We have prayed with enough people our age and younger who were former *D&D* fans, and they were totally in bondage to it," Schnoebelen wrote. He goes on to argue that fantasy role-playing games use brainwashing techniques, including fear, isolation, physical torture, erosion of family values, degradation, and loss of self-control to gain followers.

Pulling's material is not totally devoid of value. She encourages parents to learn more about their kids' gaming habits, and to talk with them openly about their interest in RPGs. She also says the problem is not games themselves, but obsession, definitely a worthy distinction. "I don't want to imply that the youngster who watches one or two occult movies, reads an occult book, attends a few heavy metal or black metal concerts and buys these groups' albums, or plays one fantasy role-playing game, is in serious danger of becoming a teen Satanist," she wrote. "I emphasize the word obsession. Many parents do not notice the gradual transition from a child's curiosity about occult entertainment to true obsession."

Pulling—and others like her—had a tremendous effect on *D&D* and gaming as a whole. Many smaller game companies went out of business, and some game shops went bankrupt after gaming received so much negative attention. *Dungeons & Dragons* publisher TSR removed all references to "devils" and "demons" in its second edition—though those references returned in its third edition, released in 2000.

While Pulling did plenty to stir up parents' fears about role-playing games, she isn't the only source of misunderstanding. The behavior parents see in their own teens may be enough to make them think something is wrong with RPGs. For instance, when players spend enough time in-game together—and not much time socializing as their real selves—then the RPG becomes the primary foundation for conversation. This can be confusing to parents who might witness such exchanges.

"There was a period during the live-action [*Vampire: The Masquerade*] years where I would run into people in the mall, who would call me by my character name and start in on some huge spiel about how I had done something that they didn't like and we should plan to overthrow the prince," said Cisco, an adult gamer who began playing in her teens. "It's like, this is the *mall*. This is not game." Even though some players will behave this way when they talk with fellow RPG fans, it doesn't mean they have thrown reality out the window. In some cases, players may not even know one another's real names, only their character names. In other cases, players love the in-game story so much, they look for any opportunity to dive into it.

The stigma surrounding these games often causes deeper frictions between players and their parents, which Cisco experienced with her father. "I would take my *Vampire* books to his house for the weekend, and he thought I was going to join a Satanic cult and become a blood-drinking freak goth person," she said. She admits that she had a fondness for going out at night with friends, dressing in black, and wearing custom-made fangs over her teeth, which likely worried him. But she felt like the "cult" invention was going too far, she says.

Parents may see changes in their teen's behavior when fellow gamers are around, particularly during gaming sessions. Mark Barrowcliffe, author of *The Elfish Gene,* lamented that he and his friends behaved a bit like pigs while deep into the RPGs they shared. However, he doesn't blame those effects on games —but rather on too much percolating testosterone. "The fact that most people turned out to be decent human beings away from the [D&D] group and under the influence of women leads me to conclude that it wasn't really *D&D* that had caused us to behave so vileley to each other but masculinity itself. Shutting ourselves away in male-only company for our entire youth was like distilling that maleness, taking all other influences away and just leaving us with our dark selves. The only way that *D&D* was to blame is that it gave us a reason to be in those rooms, face to face for all those years, like an extended reality TV show that you couldn't be voted off."

Corey, another adult gamer who started playing in his teens, said that parents may feel like RPGs are the cause of many adolescent problems because teens become interested in gaming at the same time they're beginning to experience puberty, which can make both them and their parents feel off-kilter. As kids encounter hormonal and mood shifts, make new friends in middle school and high school, and begin trying on new personalities, tastes, and hobbies, they can seem like strangers to their parents. Taking up role-playing games at the same time can certainly make it seem as though RPGs can be influencing teens in unsettling ways.

Charisma Points

These days, it seems like plenty of people are "coming out of the basement" about their former lives as teen role-playing gamers. In the early years, playing RPGs earned you a reputation as an incurable nerd at best, or—thanks to years of moral panic and media hysteria—someone on the verge of coming unhinged. This "coming out" phenomenon has produced books like Barrowcliffe's, and articles like "Dungeons and Dragons: My dorky literary muse," Samuel Sattin's piece for Salon.com about how reconnecting with his inner RPG player helped him write his first novel, *League of Somebodies*.

Sattin was struggling with the book when he recalled a creative writing teacher's advice: "writing is all about character." Sattin knew about creating characters; it was the core of *Dungeons & Dragons*, which he'd played for many years as a teen. Before he made that realization, his books and stories were just copies of other people's books and stories, he wrote. Once he "met" his main character, inspired by one he developed in those long-ago *D&D* sessions, he scrapped 600 pages of a work-in-progress and started over.

"I'm not arguing that D&D, while requiring finesse to play, is society's greatest form of expression," he wrote. "It is a story-telling game, impermanent as Buddhist sand-art, or coyote tales grumbled around a campfire. But it is from these platforms of interactivity, these sophisticated games we create for an allotment of dopamine, that we teach ourselves ways to deal with the real world."

Fellow writer Ethan Gilsdorf wrote a similar article, also for Salon.com, called "How *Dungeons & Dragons* Changed My Life." In it, he describes how he spent every waking moment of his teen years—when he wasn't in school, anyway—thinking about, planning, or playing the game. He drew maps, created characters, and just about lived in *D&D*. And, when he was 40, he returned to the game. That return inspired him to write, but it also allowed him to "reconnect with his inner geek" in a world that's much more forgiving of such quirks today than it was in 1979.

"Pure and simple, for many, *D&D* represents a lost age: It was an individualized, user-driven, DIY, human-scaled creative space separate from the world of adults and the intrusion of corporate forces," Gilsdorf writes. Even today, in a much more intrusive world, the immersive nature of RPGs can still offer that kind of escape.

This "coming-out" has sparked a kind of revival, inspiring many reporters to go "undercover" with various role-playing groups to discover and write about how they work—and why they appeal. One of the most fascinating is an article by Nathan Thornburgh for *Time* about the prevalence of live-action role-playing games in, of all places, Denmark. This kind of gaming is rumored to be the third-most popular pastime among the Danes, who not only indulge in fantasy gaming but also re-create scenes closer to world history.

For example, in one game, children assumed the roles of Communist and Nazi soldiers, while in another, adults played out an alternative history in which Germany had won World War II. When games hew so close to reality, it can bring out opportunities for intense psychology, Thornburgh writes. However, when he and a fellow writer joined the Danes for an afternoon of live-action role-playing, they joined fantasy battlegrounds where adults and children played together.

"By the end of the morning, the weaponry and the exercise had transformed these children from undifferentiated mumbling adolescents into their truer selves: hellions, heroes, cowards, and even some psychopaths," he writes. But all that is in the context of a fantasy—and kids know it. When the game is over, they return to themselves, informed by the roles they've played.

Fantasy role-playing games emerged with the 1974 release of *Dungeons & Dragons*, created by Gary Gygax and Dave Arneson. Inspired in part by J.R.R. Tolkien's *Lord of the Rings* trilogy, it also cribbed from Jack Vance's *Dying Earth* novels and the books of Edgar Rice Burroughs, H.P. Lovecraft, Roger Zelazny, and Michael Moorcock, among others.

In *D&D*, players create characters that are human, dwarf, elf, or halfling, and either a fighter, rogue, sorcerer, or cleric. They can decide whether their character is good, neutral, or evil, and lawful or chaotic. Finally, they roll dice to determine how much—or little—of six qualities their character will have, including strength, constitution, dexterity, intelligence, wisdom, and charisma. Characters start out the game with a certain amount of health called "hit points." Battling villains and monsters—and getting hurt—can reduce these hit points, while surviving fights and progressing through the game will earn more hit points, as well as "experience points," which strengthen the character overall.

The Dungeon Master leads the characters on an imaginary quest, one that's either predetermined by the game authors or one invented by the DM, following the rules of *D&D*. Players take turns, deciding what their characters will do next and rolling dice to determine how successful that course of action will be. Games can take weeks or months to finish, depending on how often and how intensely they're played. Players usually become heavily invested in the games, in their characters, and in the relationships between both the characters and the players controlling them.

The *D&D* model has become a kind of template for many role-playing games. In the past three decades, hundreds of such games have hit the market, borrowing themes from science-fiction and cyberpunk to gothic and horror themes. RPGs have branched out from their birth as "tabletop" games (though many are still played this way) into live-action role-playing games, or LARPs, as well as virtual RPGs, or video games, such as *World of Warcraft*.

With hundreds of games on game-store shelves, it's tough to tell just how many RPGs are sold—or how many people are playing them. However, *Dungeons & Dragons* remains the most best-selling game in the field. By 2006, it had sold more than $1 billion in books and accessories, and some 20 million people had played the game.

In 1991, White Wolf released *Vampire: The Masquerade*, a tabletop and live-action RPG in which players portray a variety of vampire characters in a modern world rich with gothic and punk elements. It became one of the most popular role-playing games of all time, spawning second and third editions and winning a "best role-playing rules" award in 1992. Although essentially all the characters are undead, and must "drink blood" to survive, they are still in touch with their human sides—and have a "humanity score" that describes just how human they still are. Through the game, players explore concepts of morality, personal darkness, sense of self, and sanity. As with many other RPGs, collaboration with and opposition to other characters is key. In live-action versions of the game, players dress and act in the roles of their characters in a kind of improvisational theater, gathering frequently to enact the game and move it forward.

Cisco began playing a tabletop version of *Vampire* when

she was 15, though the game didn't go very far "because nobody knew how to run it," she said. She and her friends spent time crafting characters and holding "long story sessions," then abandoned it, but adopted the characters and ideas. In a kind of ad-hoc RPG, they would run around town pretending to be vampires.

"We kind of played our own version of live-action *Vampire*, in the sense that we all dressed up and had the fangs," said Cisco, who was already immersed in goth culture before encountering the game. "I didn't really change that much to play the *Vampire* game. It was like, 'Ooh, I add another lace petticoat over the one I'm already wearing. And I put my fangs on again because I took them off to eat dinner. So in that sense, my early gaming experience was very different from [other people's], because I wasn't trying to escape from what I was living. I was extending what I was living."

White Wolf released a number of other popular games inspired by horror fiction, including *Werewolf: The Apocalypse* and *Mage: The Ascension*, providing a darker and more modern setting than the medievalesque fantasy world of *Dungeons & Dragons*. But game producers offered plenty of variety for gamers of all mindsets. For example, Steve Jackson Games wrote and released *GURPS*, or *Generic Universal RolePlaying System*, in 1988. It offers a system so open-ended that players can adapt stories and concepts from the real world, other RPGs, or their imaginations.

Cyberpunk, released in 1988, takes players into a world based on the novels of William Gibson, Bruce Sterling and other writers of high-tech science fiction. Players can portray a cop, a corporate leader, a journalist, a street criminal, a hacker, or a handful of other characters in a dark, fictional West-Coast city where mega-corporations are in control. *Rifts*, released in 1990, combines sci-fi, horror, mythology, and other elements in a futuristic setting where characters move between different universes via portals called "rifts." Other role-playing games, such as *Call of Cthulhu* and *Star Wars*, allow players to enter and reinvent worlds they had otherwise only experienced passively through movies or books.

While RPGs saw their heyday in the 1980s, they have

maintained a steady following into the modern day. Gamers are still having fun creating characters and storylines with their fellow players. In fact, with the popularity of fantasy-based fiction such as *Harry Potter* books and films and the *Lord of the Rings* movies, fantasy RPGs are moving out of the subculture and into mainstream, according to Williams.

Being able to create characters and design adventures in a variety of settings give RPGs plenty of appeal, but there's still more to like. Many other types of games are competitive, but RPGs require collaboration. They do not ask gamers to keep score, and there is no such thing as "winning" or "losing," except when a character dies, Denis Waskul wrote in "The Role-Playing Game and the Game of Role-Playing." The "rules" gamers follow are not for regulation—they simply help establish the conventions and guidelines of the in-game world. "Teamwork, cooperation, and survival are the organizing themes," Waskul wrote.

The fact that RPG stories are so unpredictable makes them exceptionally life-like. A player can announce the action his character is going to take, but it takes a roll of the dice to determine whether the action will be successful. If it works, another dice roll can bring unexpected consequences. Two players could portray the same character, but due to personality, differences in imagination, and the whims of the dice, those characters would have very different adventures, according to Waskul.

Spending hours pretending to be a character on a quest, either by rolling the dice or dressing up and acting out the part, might seem like an odd activity. What is it about RPGs that inspires some teens to spend countless hours gaming? For some, as for Chris, it's about finding a social setting that feels comfortable and rewarding after years of loneliness and isolation. For others, such as Cisco, RPGs provide an opportunity to explore characters that resemble fictionalized, enhanced versions of themselves.

For Corey, role-playing games offered the chance to develop his writing and storytelling abilities. He got his start at 14, playing *Teenage Mutant Ninja Turtles & Other Strangeness*. Corey had already fallen in love with the *Teenage*

Mutant Ninja Turtle comics, so playing an interactive version of those stories appealed to him. He moved on to *Heroes Unlimited* and *D&D*, and each time, he was more interested in creating characters and designing stories for them than in playing games with others. In fact, the times he acted as the Game Master, he grew frustrated that he couldn't control the direction of the story—too much was up to the decisions of other players, as well as the dice.

"[I wanted] to live a different life, to tell stories, to have characters," he said. "I was an only child. I spent most of my free time living in my own head. I didn't have a lot of friends. I didn't go out. So even when I started to have friends and they yanked me out into other things, it was—as much time as I could spend living in my own head, I did. I like making up characters. I like having this more superheroic world, and then fantasies that went on in *D&D* and stuff, but I always had a story that was behind these guys, and to me it was like trying to get to the point where I could tell that story somehow."

Scott was 10 when his aunt gave him a copy of *Dungeons & Dragons* for Christmas. The game excited him, not only for its fantasy elements but for the fact that it was for ages 12 and up. The gift made him feel mature. He began to follow the instructions, make characters and develop stories, but his friends at the time didn't want to play. "They just didn't get it," he said. "So I would play *D&D* by myself."

For years, Scott spent hours alone, rolling dice and following the modules designed for solo gamers. He designed numerous characters and led them on quests. Sometimes he merged multiple characters into one, creating mega-avatars with odd combinations of traits. After many years playing on his own, he managed to make friends with a handful of folks who also happened to play RPGs. Suddenly, gaming was his way into a new social circle—one that continues to be his core group of friends 20 years later.

"People that roleplay almost always have something to talk about. They have a common form of expression that they can understand," he said, adding that it was liberating to finally play with other gamers after years of isolation. "It didn't really matter what I was playing, as long as I was playing."

Corey's parents were thankful that their son had found a hobby that allowed him to make friends. He had been isolated for so long that role-playing games provided him with the first kids who invited him out. "My friends rescued me, and rescued my mother probably, from having the worst time with me," he said. "If it hadn't been for them I would still be locked in my room, reading my comics, [playing] on my Commodore 64."

For all of these gamers, RPGs provided an activity that they could share with other people. Sometimes those people were already their friends, but other times the games introduced them to new people and gave them something in common with those people. Since teens who are drawn to RPGs are often more socially awkward, and may be shy or have other problems making friends, these games can be a gateway to friendships and a social life.

There are as many reasons to play RPGs as there are gamers. But is there a type of person who plays role-playing games? Some researchers seem to think so, according to Williams. Psychologists Neil Douse and Ian McManus found that gamers tended to be more introverted than their non-gamer counterparts, while Lisa DeRenard and Manik Kline "found that more players of *D&D* expressed feelings of cultural estrangement than controls, but fewer players expressed feelings of meaninglessness in their lives," Williams wrote.

Or, put more simply, "Everyone who ever played [*D&D*] more than once was a nerd," Barrowcliffe wrote. And, no, being a nerd isn't a bad thing.

Role-playing has been around a very long time. It was developed in psychological contexts to allow clients to act out aspects of their own lives—often through the roles of other people in their lives—in order to better comprehend conflicts and struggles. Since then, it has been adopted by the educational world. In the classroom, asking students to act out various lessons—from historical re-enactments to mathematics —provides them with a boost of motivation, a safe fictional context in which to learn, and plenty of fun, according to Williams.

As with books, much of the experience of the role-playing game takes place in the imagination. Barrowcliffe recalled how his favorite games engaged his imagination—often without his realizing it: "I spent a lot of time wondering what the clean on +3 armour looked like to the edge on a flaming sword. When I was having these thoughts, though, I wasn't aware I was purely exercising my imagination. To me, I was involved in a deductive process ... I was referring to a world that, in my mind, actually existed."

Barrowcliffe also found himself taken with the fictional language used in *Empire of the Petal Throne*. He began learning the language during periods when he couldn't actually play the game with his friends. "I think this is the soul of why role playing games like *D&D* and *EPT* were so popular with young boys. They provided a trellis work for the imagination to climb upon and thrive. Unsupported, your day dreams can wither; backed up by rules, pictures, model figures and the input of others, there's no end to the amount of brain space they can consume."

Unlike books, in role-playing games, players are helping *write* the story as they go. This process helps players access different parts of their minds, Sarah Lynne Bowman wrote in *The Functions of Role-Playing Games*. "The content of these narratives often emerges from deep, archetypal symbols cultivated from the wells of collective human experience. Myths, epics, and fairy tales tell recurring types of stories that appeal to universal aspects of the human condition." In other words, our culture is full of parallel stories—for example, about dragons, such as Smaug guarding his treasure in *The Hobbit* or Godzilla destroying Tokyo. These stories sell well because they're fun, and because at the same time, they appeal to humans on a subconscious level. *Dungeons & Dragons* offers the opportunity to go head-to-head with an actual (if fictional) dragon—and win.

Because of this, RPGs can provide players with the opportunities to experience what Bowman calls "ritual storytelling"—stories in which the players face their dark sides, overcome fears, and emerge as heroic, victorious figures, just as in old myths, according to Bowman.

Much of this happens through character work. In "Playing with Identity," Michelle Nephew found that characters often represent a player's unconscious desires, in part because the player can hide within his or her character. Players will frequently write their own strengths into their characters—as well as strengths they wish they had. However, they are unlikely to give their character their own weaknesses. More often, they will choose the weaknesses of others. Some gamers particularly enjoy adopting the role of a villain.

"Role-playing allows the players to escape a sometimes harsh reality into a dreamworld in which they can re-assert their personal power and individual sense of worth," Nephew wrote. "Being able to take on the role of someone with superior abilities to your own is an escapist draw for many players."

Characters may allow players the chance to escape or transform their personalities. At the same time, players identify strongly with the characters they create and play. It can be a serious blow when something irreversible happens to that character. "In *D&D* if your character dies, he's dead, which usually, but not always, is a serious threat to his future. Losing a character that you've had for some time, maybe years, can be a major emotional experience. At 14 years old it can be the first real grief you've known in your life," Barrowcliffe wrote.

At the same time, RPGs provide a safe and relatively consequence-free place where gamers can explore and enhance aspects of themselves, according to Bowman. By playing a variety of characters, they also get to peek into the headspace of someone else, which can develop players' empathy.

Scott found that playing different roles helped him develop his personality and sense of self. "It gives you the freedom to express yourself where you're not really you. You can just mess around and be someone else. Since I was the typical depressed teenager and loner, it was liberating to be able to be someone else," he said. "You could pretend that you're not only cooler than you are, but smarter than you are, [and] wittier than you are."

Role-playing also requires teamwork, which builds bonds between players. "The shared, performative experience of RPGs provides a ritual atmosphere for players to enact compelling stories or perform unusual, extraordinary deeds. In this way, RPGs help encourage a sense of community, by teaching individuals how to function as a group," Bowman wrote.

These lessons—along with creativity, self-awareness, and "out-of-the-box" thinking—all encouraged in role-playing games—are incredibly useful in real-world situations, according to Bowman.

Researcher Heather Mello polled gamers to find out more about what skills they admired most in their fellow players. Among them, 65 percent said they appreciated their peers' ability to role-play; that is, to get into character and play the game. Another 38 percent said creativity was the skill they admired most, while 25 percent named teamwork, 16 percent said analytical thinking, and 16 percent said humor.

She also asked players to name the skills they acquired in game that came in handy outside of gaming. Almost half said that vocabulary and trivia were useful, followed by 41 percent who named social skills, 29 percent who named knowledge of mythology, and 24 percent who said knowledge of history was most useful. Other skills the players said were helpful included research ability, critical thinking, empathy, reading and writing, probability and statistics, leadership, acting and public speaking, and martial arts.

Social aspects can be especially beneficial. "Introverted persons may learn to cooperate or come out of their shells in pursuit of amiable, fun gaming. Extroverted gamers may tone things down in order to create a cohesive, satisfying gaming experience," Mello wrote in "Invoking the Avatar."

Parents may worry when they see their teens spending hours in an apparent "fantasy world," rolling dice or dressing up as a warrior or vampire. But RPGs offer countless psychological riches—from the chance to explore different personalities and emotions to the possibility of making friends and overcoming shyness. Players often come to a better understanding of themselves, and develop skills that will aid them for the rest of their lives. And they usually have a lot of fun doing it.

Now that role-playing games are less stigmatized, old and young gamers are finding new ways to apply them to all sorts of problems, big and small. When Heikki Holmås became

Norway's minister of international development in 2012, he revealed his longstanding interest in *D&D*—and told a writer at Imagonem.org how role-playing could help resolve one of the world's most deadlocked situations: the Israel-Palestine conflict. In fact, he had high hopes for a Norwegian LARP project taking place in Palestine that year: "There's no doubt that you can put Israelis into the situation of the Palestinians and vice versa in a way that fosters understanding and builds bridges. Those things are an important aspect of role playing games which makes it possible to use them politically to create change," he said.

Role-playing games have a special kind of power because they create "real emotions that stick" with the players, which simultaneously makes the games more intense and makes it possible for them to change the world, Holmås said. That's because they help people understand how humans under pressure act differently than they do in everyday life, he explained.

RPGs aren't just a nostalgia trip; plenty of young people still play them, and sometimes that gameplay spills out into other contexts. In Canada, 12-year-old Julian Levy was showing his dad, psychologist Alan Kingstone, pictures from one of his *D&D* monster books when Kingstone had a kind of epiphany. Kingstone's research at the University of British Columbia centered on whether humans will naturally look at another person's eyes to see where they're looking, a phenomenon called "gaze-copying." But he wasn't sure whether humans are drawn specifically to people's eyes, or to their faces overall. Monsters provided the answer.

Levy suggested that Kingstone have people look at the pictures—many of which depict monsters with eyes on their hands, on the ends of tentacles, and elsewhere—to see where they would look. Sure enough, the subjects looked at the middle of the picture, as with humans, and then hunted around for the creatures' eyes, whether or not they were on their faces.

"If people are just targeting the centre of the head, like they target the centre of most objects, and getting the eyes for free, that's one thing. But if they are actually seeking out eyes that's another thing altogether," Kingstone told *Discover* magazine.

Even for non-scientists, RPGs can help connect the generations. Thanks to Chris' passion for the games, his son has started playing. Although he won't let the teen play with adult gamers that gather regularly at their house, Chris occasionally organizes adventures specifically for the boy. In that way, Chris can help craft the kind of story and experience his son encounters in the role-playing world, and watch first-hand as he explores his character and brings new aspects of his personality to life.

The Fiercest Calm

The day started out beautifully enough. It was a warm, sunny Saturday morning, and Vincent was helping his mom and grandfather around the house. One of his chores for the day was to burn some old trash that had been piling up. He stuffed the trash into a metal can, and then sprinkled it with a mixture of oil and gasoline to help it ignite—a decision he admits was unwise.

"At the time, I figured it'd just catch quick and I'd be done," he recalls. "I lit it. There was a very loud sound and I found myself surrounded in flames." His arm burned and his t-shirt caught fire, only extinguishing when Vincent ripped it from his body. It seemed to take forever for the ambulance to arrive, and for paramedics to transport him to the emergency room. That's where he learned that he had second- and third-degree burns over 18 percent of his body, requiring skin grafts to his arm and chest.

Although the burns themselves were painful, healing was worse. "If being on fire is a 10 on a scale of 1 to 10, then recovering from skin grafts was a 12." Also, since the skin grafts were taken from his legs, it would be a while before he could walk again.

Doctors and nurses gave him morphine, but Vincent discovered that the drug didn't kill the pain —it just distracted him from it. He asked his mom to gather all the music she could find in his bedroom and his car and bring it to the hospital, where the nurses let him listen in his room. Heavy metal was Vincent's music of choice.

"I found that softer songs didn't do much for me," he says. "But the harder ones, especially the ones about pain and suffering, helped tremendously. Singing along with Glenn Danzig, feeling the power in my voice, I could overcome the pain. I could ride it like a wave, using it to propel me higher, away from the limitations of my body."

Those songs were Vincent's constant companions for the two weeks he was hospitalized. Pain prevented him from concentrating well on television or books—even comic books. Only in his favorite music was he able to find comfort and distraction from the intense sensations in his body, and the slow healing in his chest, arm and legs.

Some songs, such as Manowar's "The Power," soothed Vincent with their messages of allegiance and triumph: "Our hearts are filled with metal! And masters, we have none. And we will die for metal! Metal heals, my son."

A Twist in the Myth

Elyse Pahler was 15 years old when three Slayer fans ended her life. She was drugged, stabbed, and raped, allegedly as a sacrifice to the Devil; the killers claimed that the act would give their band, called Hatred, the boost it needed to hit the bigtime. Her body was found eight months later near her California home.

Pahler's parents sued Slayer in 1996, claiming that the band and its record company were responsible for "unlawfully marketing and distributing 'harmful' and 'obscene' products to minors," Karen Sternheimer wrote in It's Not The Media: The Truth About Pop Culture's Influence on Children. Specifically, they claimed Slayer's songs "Dead Skin Mask" and "Postmortem" gave the killers specific instructions on what to do.

After the killers' trial was concluded, a judge dismissed the case against Slayer in 2001, saying, "There's not a legal position that could be taken that would make Slayer responsible for the girl's death. Where do you draw the line? You might as well start looking through the library at every book on the shelf." The Pahlers sued again; this time, when the judge dismissed the case, he said he didn't consider Slayer's music obscene, indecent, or harmful to minors.

The killers themselves said Slayer's music had nothing to do with the murder. "One of the boys said, 'We never listened to the lyrics before the murder. The fact is Slayer music didn't have anything to do with the murder. The police went into my house and saw some Slayer posters and records and they made up a motive.' [Another said] 'The music had zero influence on me going out to kill somebody ... Those allegations were put together by lawyers to make money,'" Sternheimer wrote.

Heavy-metal music has had a bad reputation—and has often celebrated that bad reputation—since its raucous early days. Parents and political leaders scorn it for its notorious noise levels, confrontational lyrics, and ability to turn listeners into a veritable army of die-hard fans. Detractors argue that the genre inspires violent, suicidal, or immoral behavior—even though those arguments have been disproven.

There's no denying that heavy metal has been at the scene of many teen suicides, and that some violent or law-breaking teens have called this music the soundtrack to their lives. A handful of those cases grabbed headlines around the world. There's also no denying that heavy metal has practically made its name by scaring adults with its dark costumes, shocking makeup, ear-splitting sonics, and lyrics that explore subjects darker than you'll find in the average pop song. However, millions of teens have loved this music without going to such dark places. And for teens whose lives have been especially rough, music that matches their lives' intensity is often a balm.

Most metalheads (as fans are often called) say the music comforts and energizes them, bolsters friendships, and provides its own kind of friendship and healing when nothing else is available. Instead of sparking violent or suicidal thoughts, many say the music is the one thing that prevented them from becoming violent or suicidal in dark times. Many adults have tried to take this music away from teens, arguing that it is dangerous. But teen metalheads say that separating them from their favorite tunes is much more dangerous.

Almost as soon as rock and roll was invented, it was scorned, criticized, and feared. Often, that fear came from those in power. In 1955, the Houston Juvenile Delinquency and Crime Commission named 30 songs that were "lewd" and "unfit for young listeners," according to Eric Nuzum's book *Parental Advisory: Music Censorship in America*. Every musician on the list was black, including the Drifters, Ray Charles, and the 5 Royales. Radio stations banned these and other artists—all of whom were black.

In the 1970s, a Christian anti-rock movement emerged, bolstered by religious leaders such as Arizona minister Bob Larson, now a radio personality and self-styled exorcist who has also trained his teen daughter and two of her friends to perform exorcisms. Larson's books on rock music detailed the evils he perceived in the genre. Scores of preachers echoed Larson, calling rock and roll dangerous, corrupt, and anti-Christian, according to Nuzum. These preachers traveled around the country, speaking to church groups, presenting films and slide shows, and writing books. "Most proclaimed that rock was the devil's music ... while others professed that sin was so deeply engrained in rock music that it was nearly impossible to separate the two. Initially considered fringe kooks, as rock music (especially heavy metal) became more defiant and rebellious, these crusaders were taken more and more seriously," Nuzum wrote.

Larson was the most prominent of these crusaders. He penned several books describing—in great detail—specific songs, bands, and the unsavory themes and lyrics he found within them. He painted himself as a former rock-and-roll fan who no longer listened to the music, except to learn exactly what he's arguing against. While some parts of his books are informative, others are over-the-top in their criticism of rock. He claimed the genre can be "pornographic, can incite listeners to homosexuality or drug use, extolls the dangers of Eastern mysticism and the occult," and, in some cases, opens listeners to demonic possession. That's right: he actually said rock music makes people possessed.

With each new generation of rock-and-roll listeners, there is also a new generation of parents who are driven crazy by their teens' music. It's almost as if it's part of rock's mission to evolve so that it can offend the next wave of parents. "Rock music continues to play a central role in youth culture in part due to its confrontational and antagonistic stance toward adult values. As generations of rock fans grow up, and have families of their own, they bring their music with them into adulthood.

That makes it necessary for rock music to change, to mutate, in order for it to remain a viable center of youth culture," wrote Jonathan Epstein in *Adolescents and their Music: If It's Too Loud, You're Too Old.*

By the time rock and roll had spawned heavy metal, the bar for shocking parents was already pretty high. But heavy metal added makeup and theatrics to the mix, drawing plenty of misguided press coverage that focused more on the spectacle than the truth of the music.

That media storm really got underway in the mid-1980s, when the Parents Music Resource Center, or PMRC, set its sights on the genre. The group of Washington wives claimed that there were five persistent, objectionable themes present in rock music: rebellion, substance abuse, sexual promiscuity and perversion, violence, and the occult. Heavy metal was a major player among the music they objected to, even after metal musicians pointed out that their videos, album covers, and lyrics were being blatantly misinterpreted. Nine of the PMRC's "filthy fifteen" songs, a list of tracks they found unfit for young listeners, were from heavy-metal bands. While it's true that metal does frequently address the themes listed by the PMRC, it's often in a more philosophical manner than adults might think.

The PMRC's claims kicked off a moral panic, drawing a line between what could be considered "respectable" or "deviant," according to author Stephen Markson. "Those who argue that AC/DC stands for 'Anti-Christ/Devil's Children,' that KISS stands for 'Knights in Satan's Service,' as have PMRC supporters, do indeed seem to fear monsters. These monsters are capable of entering the minds of unsuspecting adolescents through the medium of rock music."

When you've heard that music leads to—or even causes—violent behavior, it's easy to fear and mistrust those who make it. The media fueled many of these mistaken assumptions. Even the most respectable, well-researched news outlets were not immune; *The Economist* repeated faulty information that Judas Priest's "Eat Me Alive" was about "forced sex at gunpoint," wrote Bruce Friesen in "Powerlessness in Adolescence: Exploiting Heavy Metal Listeners." It was an interpretation they picked up from the PMRC—not by reading the lyrics or consulting the band.

In 1987, *20/20* aired a segment called "The Children of Heavy Metal," interviewing PMRC co-founder Tipper Gore and others. Bruce Dickenson of Iron Maiden was also quoted, saying, "I wish people would get a sense of proportion about what's right and wrong, and who are the real people poisoning people's minds, and why they're doing it," pointing the finger at Gore and her collaborators.

"Many of those who testified in the PMRC senate hearings were representatives of parental interest groups ... fundamentalist ministers, and physician-owners of psychiatric hospitals specializing in the treatment of adolescents," Deena Weinstein wrote in "Expendable Youth." These were people who were not in a good position to sympathize with "deviant" teenagers; instead, they stood to profit from calling more teens "troubled."

News outlets zeroed in on a number of hot-button teen issues, including drug use, violence, and suicide, which then became reduced to a single problem: "juvenile delinquency." This, in turn, was blamed largely on rock and metal music. Instantly, "good folk" were absolved of any responsibility.

"Rock music and performers are exceptionally attractive targets for such righteous indignation. It is certainly intuitively pleasing, even if not empirically accurate, to find fault in an unregulated and highly visible industry that does indeed pander to the fantasies of youth culture. Clearly, these performers who openly flaunt conventional authority as the stereotyped embodiment of parental nightmares of children gone wild, do at least seem to be guilty of something," Markson wrote.

It didn't help that a number of high-profile lawsuits were lodged against heavy-metal artists in the late 1980s and early 1990s, blaming them for suicides or other violent acts. The media was rife with stories linking metal and violence. For example, Richard Ramirez, the serial killer known as the Night Stalker, told investigators that he worshipped Satan—and that he was introduced to Satanism by AC/DC's popular song "Highway to Hell." It's clear that Ramirez's crime spree was motivated by his mental state, not rock and roll or Satanism, but reporters still played the blame game.

When teen metal fans, including Thomas Sullivan, Steve Boucher, and John McCollum, committed suicide while listening to their favorite tunes, plenty of news articles linked the music with ending one's life. Such situations were played up by reporters and read widely by parents and legislators across the country. It wasn't long before heavy metal practically became synonymous with violent or suicidal behavior. Such associations frustrated the metal fans I talked to.

"No matter how heavy the music, or crazy or full of hate [and] death, combined with the fact that everyone in my school made my life hell, I still never once thought about killing them," said a 14-year-old from Northern California who became a metal fan when he was 8.

Despite these sentiments, numerous metal bands have been sued for allegedly causing a teenager's violent behavior or suicide. In each case, the band has been exonerated. In many cases, a band's music or recording techniques were misrepresented by prosecutors in order to secure a win for a grieving family. In fact, the songs they blamed weren't even songs about suicide. Many of them weren't even songs with bummer lyrics.

In 1985, James Vance and his friend Raymond Belknap made a suicide pact. It was the end of a day of drinking and listening to Judas Priest's albums "Stained Class," "Sin After Sin," and "Sad Wings of Destiny." Belknap's suicide—from a 12-gauge shotgun to the chin—was successful. But when Vance took his turn the gun slipped, leaving him alive but extremely disfigured.

In 1990, Vance and Belknap's parents sued Judas Priest, claiming "Better By You, Better Than Me" (a song about a boy who can't bear to tell his girlfriend that he's going off to war) had a backwards subliminal message: "do it." They also claimed the song "White Heat, Red Hot" (about triumphing against difficult odds) contained another backwards message: "Fuck the Lord, fuck all of you." "Stained Class," about being true to yourself in a deteriorating world, allegedly contained a masked message, "Sing my evil spirit." A criminal grand jury rejected the families' claims, and they eventually dropped their lawsuit.

"We dismantled that theory and allegation [of backward messages] in the courtroom and showed the judge very clearly how these strange quirks of sound and mysterious things that go on in recording can make it onto a disc and be misconstrued," Judas Priest singer Rob Halford told Terry Gross in a radio interview. "[We proved] that we had not done this, and that we never would do this, and that there was never intent or any reason on our part to actually do something like this. Why on earth would any band want to kill its fans? These boys were two hard-core Judas Priest fans that came from a very tough family life, there was a history of alcohol abuse, a history of drug abuse, and the boys were finding solace in the music of Priest."

The band was very shaken by the accusation that their music had caused the death and disability of two young men who had loved it. "It was utter shock and disbelief, and dismay that it had come from a country where we'd had so many great times. You can imagine—perhaps you can't—to get off the tour bus and be handed a subpoena by the deputy in Reno," Halford told Gross. "We looked at [the court summons], we were very upset, we thought the allegations were completely ridiculous and without foundation, but the only way we could put our side of the story across and tell everybody the truth was to go to Reno sit in a courthouse for five weeks and deal with each issue as it was presented to us. That was a very upsetting time for all of us to go through."

Despite the experience, Halford said that most of the band's fans have grown up to become successful, healthy adults with families—not the depressed, suicidal, wasted youth described by some of their critics. "Our teenaged fans have grown up now, and they're healthy, stable, balanced family-oriented fans. They bring their children to our shows. If that isn't proof that Judas Priest has stood by nothing other than giving people some escape and great nights out when they see us live, and some very personal enjoyment at home on the headphones or speakers, I don't know what else to say. It kind of puts to sleep that moment in the '80s when not only this band, but individuals like Sheena Easton were attacked by a political agenda that had, in our opinions, some misconceptions."

Despite the grand jury's findings in the Judas Priest trial, the effort to place legal blame on musicians didn't end there. Ozzy Osbourne, the former Black Sabbath frontman and solo artist—practically the father of heavy metal—was sued twice in the 1980s under similar circumstances.

John McCollum's parents pursued a case against Osbourne after their son committed suicide in 1984. McCollum spent his last evening listening to Osbourne's music. "[His parents] claimed that the themes of Osbourne's music were particularly personal and attempted to connect with the listener as a peer who has the same problems and struggles as he does," wrote Cynthia Cooper in *Violence in the Media and its Influence on Criminal Defense*. A California court of appeals rejected the claims, citing Osbourne's First-Amendment right to free speech.

Then the parents of Michael Waller sued Osbourne in 1991 for allegedly inspiring their son's suicide with the song "Suicide Solution." Waller's parents didn't realize that the song laments the alcohol-related death of AC/DC singer Bon Scott, who was a dear friend of Osborne's. Although the jury ultimately sided with Osbourne in the case, "the court chided the musician for his choice of themes," according to Cooper.

"The lyrics do contain the phrase 'suicide solution,' and it's possible to imagine how an adolescent might have dwelled on that phrase to the exclusion of the rest of the lyrics. Nevertheless, defenders of Ozzy are right that it is ludicrous to hold him legally responsible for the boy's suicide," wrote Jeffrey Jensen Arnett in *Metalheads*. "If this were valid, then no one should ever be allowed to publish a story, song, or factual account in which a person commits suicide. The fact is, even adolescent boys are not so easily manipulated. Literally millions of boys have listened to that song, and the fact that one of those boys killed himself shows nothing about the song as a 'cause' of his suicide."

Unfortunately, what stuck with the public was not Osbourne's innocence, but the lawsuits and media reports about these cases, forever linking his music with suicidal behavior.

The fact that Osbourne and his publicity team courted a reputation for bloody theatrics and outlandish behavior—including mistakenly biting the head off a live bat onstage—didn't help. In fact, that reputation for many years masked the fact that Osbourne is a fairly upbeat, fun-loving person.

Even outside of court battles, Black Sabbath and its flamboyant first frontman reveal just how heavy-metal's message can become twisted by outsiders. Almost from the beginning, Osbourne and Black Sabbath were synonymous with dark themes, including black magic. Early press releases claimed, purely for dramatics, that the band was "getting more in tune with the dark arts," and that bassist Geezer Butler knew how to summon demons. The band's debut album, called Black Sabbath, was released on a Friday the 13th in 1970 and featured a black-clad woman on the cover who resembled a witch.

"People like us because they want to listen to our music, not because of any black magic gimmicks. We only do two numbers about black magic in fact, and they are both warnings against it," Butler said.

"To me, Ozzy's never been about creating fear or terror, like the Alice [Cooper] character," shock-rocker Cooper told Lonn Friend in a radio interview. "His songs aren't scary. His show isn't scary. I mean, he's got happy faces tattooed on his knees."

Academic studies of Osbourne's music and appearance tend to agree. "Through a brief biographical sketch, it becomes obvious that Ozzy Osbourne is far from a worshipper of the Dark Lord, but simply a talented iconoclast with a flair for creating controversy, and thus publicity. A comparison can be made between Osbourne and the turn of the century occultist, Aleister Crowley. Crowley too was branded a devil-worshipper, and equally relished the attention that came with the title of 'Most Evil Man in the World.' The connection between the two has been reinforced by Osbourne's song, 'Mr. Crowley,' which has been described by some as an homage to the Great Beast himself. While neither of these men actually worshipped the Devil, their anti-authoritarianism, combined with such vices as drugs and women, made them both suitable straw men against whom conservative moralists might rail," wrote Christopher

Moreman in "Devil Music and the Great Beast."

In later years, Osbourne publicly defeated his alcoholism and starred in a live reality television show featuring his wife, Sharon, and his children, Kelly and Jack. The public saw a different side of the rocker—a family man who struggles with the same issues many parents face when raising teenagers.

"I'm about caring, I'm about people, and I'm about entertaining people. I'm a family man. A husband. A father. I've been a lot of other things over the years, which we don't really want to talk about. I'm always working on trying to better myself, you know? I think that that is an ongoing thing with me. I think I'll do that for the rest of my life. I'm always thinking of what I can do today to better my life," Osbourne told Launch.com in 1998.

He also cautioned people against taking any of his personae too seriously—or deciding they know who he is based on what they know from stage, screen, and media. "I don't even know who Ozzy is. I wake up a new person every day," he told *Rolling Stone* in 1997. "But if you've got a fantasy of Ozzy, who am I to say? I mean, if you think I sleep upside-down in the rafters and fly around at night and bite people's throats out, then that's your thing. But I can tell you now, all I ever wanted was for people to come to my concerts and have a good time. I don't want anyone to harm themselves in any way, shape or form—and my intentions are good whether people want to believe it or not."

Unlike Judas Priest and Ozzy Osbourne, Metallica has never faced a grieving family's lawsuit. But that hasn't kept many parents and leaders from suspecting that the band's music could encourage suicidal thoughts and feelings. In some of Metallica's most famous early songs, such as "Fade to Black" and "(Welcome Home) Sanitarium," the band describes the bleakness and nihilism of depression, as well as lunacy and institutionalization.

"The common interpretation offered by groups such as the PMRC is that these lyrics function to suggest, if not support, suicidal thoughts and tendencies among vulnerable teenagers," Joseph Kotarba wrote in "The Postmodernization of Rock and Roll Music: The Case of Metallica." Fans told Kotarba they associated two of Metallica's songs with suicide: the ballad "Fade to Black" and the rip-roaring "Ride the Lightning," which can also be heard as a song about execution via electric chair.

"[Fans] may use these songs to make sense of friends' suicidal attempts; to make sense of their own thoughts and feelings about suicide; to make sense of their own general feelings of meaninglessness and hopelessness. In my interviews with fans, I rarely heard any mention of music like this suggesting suicide. On the contrary, the kids often talked about the way heavy metal music in general and Metallica in particular serves to prevent suicidal attempts by providing some viable meaning for an otherwise depressing life," Kotarba wrote.

In *Teenage Wasteland,* Donna Gaines explores "Fade to Black" in depth—and finds that it does more than explore suicidal feelings; it also provides a way back out of those feelings. "After almost six minutes of morphine agony, the rescue guitars come in. This song goes to the bottom, but comes back up. It gives you the will to power, to triumph; it's cathartic, it's killer. Of course, the song has been blamed in more than one teenage suicide. Kids just laugh about adult cultural retardation, like how they worry about satanic 'backward masking' of messages in songs, and take the poetics of songs literally."

Metallica frontman James Hetfield was just 18 when he joined the band. Raised in a Christian Scientist household, his father abandoned the family when James was 13. His mother died when he was 16. Hetfield was left frustrated and angry at the loss of his parents and at his childhood religion, which contributed to his mother's death. Making music became his outlet. It was also an antidote to high school and working-class life.

"I wanted [Metallica] to be freedom from school, from work, from the typical music we were hearing. Music was somewhat of an escape for me that turned into a really great gift eventually. But it was a way to get away from my screwed-up family. [Christian Science]—I was alienated from society and from my family. [Metallica was] the soundtrack of our lives. It spoke for us," Hetfield told Terry Gross in a radio interview.

Despite ample evidence to the contrary, news outlets continue to play up links between aggressive music, violence, and suicidal behavior. "People who suspect the songs of being guilty in this respect naturally scrutinize metalheads for evidence that that their suspicions are valid. The media aid them in this process by helpfully pointing out when someone under investigation for a sensational crime is also a fan of heavy metal music," Arnett wrote.

It's easy to blame the music, and the outrageous musicians who perform it, when teens do wrong. It can be much more difficult to navigate the waters of upbringing and environment, as well as thorny issues such as mental illness or substance abuse. This kind of blame-shifting continued in the late 1990s, when journalists converged on Littleton, Colorado to report on one of the most violent teen-perpetrated incidents in modern history.

After Eric Harris and Dylan Klebold went on a shooting rampage at Columbine High School, rumors circulated that they were fans of Marilyn Manson, Rammstein, and KMFDM. Although the first turned out to be false, the other two were true. A new generation of parents began to mistrust loud, aggressive music and the teenagers who listen to it.

In fact, the whole culture was awash with renewed anxieties about teenagers. "In the 1950s, the relatively new concepts of 'teenager' and 'juvenile delinquent' appeared simultaneously on our symbolic landscape. They were often used interchangeably and freely associated in the media," Markson wrote. Little had changed by 1999.

In the weeks and months following the shootings, media and other agencies lashed out at the music industry and at Marilyn Manson in particular. The National School Safety Center issued a checklist of "danger signs" that your teen might be about to bring a gun to school, including mood swings, fondness for violent television or video games, cursing, depression, and antisocial behavior and attitudes—many of which describe most teens from time to time. The checklist was decorated with photos of Marilyn Manson, Adolf Hitler, and teenagers in goth makeup.

Senator Samuel Brownback of Kansas wrote a letter to

Seagram's, the owner of Marilyn Manson's record label, telling them to "Cease and desist profiteering from peddling violence to young people," and told the company to drop the band from its roster.

In response to the media frenzy and controversy, Marilyn Manson canceled most of his tour dates and issued a response in *Rolling Stone* magazine. "When it comes down to who's to blame for the high school murders in Littleton, Colorado, throw a rock and you'll hit someone who's guilty. We're the people who sit back and tolerate children owning guns, and we're the ones who tune in and watch the up-to-the-minute details of what they do with them," he wrote. He called the post-Columbine panic a "witch hunt."

"It was unthinkable that these kids did not have a simple black-and-white reason for their actions. And so a scapegoat was needed," Manson continued. News outlets quoted some of Harris and Klebold's alleged classmates, who claimed that the boys liked the band. In fact, they hated the band.

"Even if they were fans, that gives them no excuse, nor does it mean that music is to blame," Manson wrote. "I think that the National Rifle Association is far too powerful to take on, so most people choose *Doom*, *The Basketball Diaries* or yours truly. This kind of controversy does not help me sell records or tickets, and I wouldn't want it to."

Alice Cooper, whose music and theatrics inspired Marilyn Manson, echoed Manson's sentiments. "We're always looking for societal scapegoats for these bad seeds. We blamed television, we blamed the movies, as soon as Columbine happened everybody blamed the music: Rammstein, Marilyn Manson. That's absolutely insane, because every other kid at that school listens to Rammstein and Manson, every other kid at that school played the same games, every other kid at that school watched the same movies, so why didn't they kill everybody? Why these two guys?"

Reporters didn't seem to learn from the mistakes made in Columbine. They continued to cite metal music every time a young fan became violent. In 2011, when 17-year-old Kyle Smith allegedly murdered his grandparents and then set their house on fire, crime-scene inspectors zeroed in on a CD found in his room: a Slipknot album featuring the band's signature nonagram, or nine-pointed star. Some mistakenly interpreted this as a "demonic" symbol of some sort; others simply suggested that Slipknot's harsh music might have played a role in the crime, without ever saying how.

Likewise, some writers managed to find a link—however tenuous—between Tucson shooter Jared Lee Loughner and heavy metal. Before shooting nearly two dozen people and killing six of them in an Arizona grocery-store parking lot in early 2011, Loughner apparently made a video set to the tune of Drowning Pool's rock-metal song "Bodies," featuring the refrain, "Let the bodies hit the floor." The song celebrates metal's well-known style of dancing, known as moshing, but non-fans often mistakenly assume the lyrics are about death or murder. There was no obvious link between the video and the shootings—or the song and the shootings. But it was clear that some felt Loughner's music choices should be questioned—and so should the music choices of anyone who might prefer loud, aggressive sounds.

After 15-year-old Bobby Gladden opened fire in the lunchroom at Perry Hall High School in Baltimore in 2012, wounding a fellow student, reporters quickly landed on Gladden's Facebook page. There, they discovered he was a fan of Rammstein and Slipknot, and quickly connected those facts to descriptions of the shooting. The *New York Daily News* went so far as to call Gladden a "heavy metal misfit" in one headline. But the day of the shooting, metal didn't really seem to be on his mind. On his Facebook page, where Gladden went by the telling moniker of "SuicidalSmile," he wrote, "First day of school, last day of my life. Fuck the world."

Battle Hymns

Among metalheads, many an hour has been spent debating what's "metal" and what isn't. Metal fans fiercely crave authenticity, so it can become important to verify that the bands they love most are truly part of the genre, branding themselves authentic by association. But if the debate over the boundaries of metal is so heated within the subculture, it's no wonder that the picture might be unclear to outsiders.

Heavy metal sprouted from two very different roots: American blues and European classical music. Born in the late 1960s and early 1970s, metal is marked by loud, distorted electric guitars, massive bass and drums, and, frequently, guitar solos. Heavy-metal singers often shout, howl, shriek, or growl their lyrics. Drummers keep time to a very fast beat, often leading the band through crazy tempo changes. It's ear-splitting, intense stuff.

While heavy metal music is characterized by these sounds, it also often features a certain "look": long or wild hair, leather or denim clothing and jackets, piercings and tattoos, black or dark t-shirts featuring the names and emblems of particular bands, and frequently boots or other "tough"-looking shoes. Although heavy-metal music has transformed and matured since its early days—and especially since its mega-popularity in the 1980s—the look has hung onto many of these elements.

Heavy metal's appearance and sound tell the same story: this is music for rebellion. Sure, it has other purposes, such as boosting energy and providing solace or catharsis. But some teens (and adults) enjoy the music precisely because so many others find it offensive and unlistenable. Parents who are openly bothered by their teen's tendency to blast metal music at home might be making their child that much happier.

Metal emerged from some of the most democratic forms of music, including blues and slave melodies—"oppressed people's music," as filmmaker Sam Dunn phrased it in his film, *Metal: A Headbanger's Journey*. In the beginning, metal was the music of the white poor and working class, making it an underdog among genres. It is especially popular among working-class teens, although its influence has long since spread to middle-class, suburban adolescents as well.

"[Metal is] a negation of the world as it's handed to you. It says, 'This boring-ass high school or this dead-end Dairy Queen job? Just no. This is something that's mine, and that I own, and fuck you, I won't do what you tell me,'" said Rage Against the Machine's Tom Morello, quoting one of his band's own songs.

Gaines described metal as "white suburban soul music." For the kids she studied in *Teenage Wasteland*, "music is the kids' religion; a belief system organized around guitar gods, sacred bands, [and] outspoken rock heroes." Heavy metal is not mere background music for parties and weekends, but something much richer and more emotionally and culturally important.

Metal comes from a long line of music that has irritated and offended parents for a variety of reasons. Some of those reasons are obvious: it's loud, in-your-face music. But many argue that there are more cultural and sociological factors at work. "Rock 'n' roll was the musical expression of delinquent street culture, critics charged, which had to be nipped in the bud. It celebrated the wrong kind of values (and the wrong kind of people) and promoted a hedonistic view of life that mocked the very notion of wholesome adolescence," wrote Grace Palladino in *Teenagers: An American History*.

The fact that metal comes from blue-collar music only made matters worse. Many adults feel that when working-class kids establish popular styles, then teen culture will distract so-called "nice" kids from their most important job: growing up, according to Palladino. Working-class music also offers blue-collar cultures something to call their own, an important role in its own right. Black Sabbath rose out of industrial Birmingham, England, and its music provided a soundtrack for that culture, according to Christopher Moreman in his essay, "Devil Music and the Great Beast: Ozzy Osbourne, Aleister Crowley, and the Christian Right."

"Most people are on a permanent down ... but just aren't aware of it. We're trying to express it for the people," said Black Sabbath drummer Bill Ward. Sabbath's songs were hymns for the powerless, combining gothic horror with pessimism. Their thunderous, massive sound only added to the mood. The band hoped to create music that might scare listeners. At the same time, they also captured the emotions of a largely silent population, according to Moreman. What started as blue-collar rock and roll wound up resonating with a whole generation of teens who felt alienated and powerless growing up in the turbulent late 1960s. "The world today is such a wicked place/Fighting going on between the human race/People got to work just to earn their bread/While people just across the sea are counting their dead," Osbourne sings in "Wicked World," the closing song on Sabbath's 1970 debut album.

Because so many early metalheads came from working-class backgrounds, metal's critics came to believe that the music is what makes kids give up their dreams. "Headbangers (or metalheads) have pushed teenage alienation to new heights. The most extreme romanticize suicide, ridicule education, and rely on drugs to give color to their lives, as if the world holds nothing in store for them but disappointment. Apparently convinced there is nothing they can do to alter their futures, they do not look forward to the 'McJobs' they will inevitably hold ... The idea that college might open doors to a better life does not seem at all realistic ... 'They seem convinced there's no point in trying, that maybe this is all there is,' [one adult said]. 'So they get high, they party on, they tattoo and pierce their bodies in a celebration of the moment. They try one last time to stand out in a crowd,' she adds, 'hoping to be heard once before it's all over,'" Palladino wrote. However, it's not the music that causes these feelings in teens. Quite the opposite; teens already feel this way, and seek out music that mirrors the world they see around them every day.

A core experience of the metal world is live concerts, where it becomes obvious just how physical the music is. Adults who see a metal show for the first time might be confused, particularly by the "mosh pit," a swirl of dancing, body-slamming fans careening in time to the music.

Sitting in your seat and tapping your toe will not do at a Metallica show, wrote Lonn Friend in *Life on Planet Rock*. Friend should know. He's the former editor of *RIP* magazine, one of the most popular heavy-metal magazines of the 1980s and 1990s. "Motion and contact are required to truly feel the power of the songs. And so the mosh pit—a swirling whirlpool of human bodies crashing into one another—spontaneously evolved at metal shows in clubs and theaters and eventually to arenas and stadiums. The zeitgeist of metal in perfect, unchoreographed chaos. The more intense the strains, the faster you moved. Volume and fury inspired bumps and bruises and a hell of a good time."

So, metal is loud, offensive, rebellious, and physical music—much more so than average rock and roll. Fans embrace the fact that metal is quite different from mainstream rock, and they don't see that as a reason to mistrust it. "Metal is just a genre of music. It's louder, more obnoxious than most. But it's good music. There are people who put thought into what they say and have pride in their musicianship. It serves a purpose," said an Arizona resident who started listening to metal when he was 13.

Unfortunately, many adults in power don't see any purpose in it. As heavy metal gained popularity in the late 1970s and 1980s, it earned its share of public detractors, from Larson to the PMRC. During the PMRC hearings, Dr. Joe Stuessy claimed that heavy metal lyrics focused on "extreme rebellion, extreme violence, substance abuse, sexual promiscuity/perversion—including homosexuality, bisexuality, sadomasochism, necrophilia ... and Satanism." However, Stuessy's interpretations were not based on deep understanding of the songs, but rather on a cursory glance at the lyric sheets.

Meanwhile, others pursued more scientific studies of heavy metal and its obsessions. *Hit Parader* magazine analyzed the 100 most popular metal songs of the 1980s, and found that they focused on rather different topics. Of them, 27 described intensity or a longing for intensity; 17 focused on lust; 17 portrayed loneliness, victimization, or self-pity; 14 featured affirmation or loss of love; 8 described anger, rebellion, or madness; and 5 were didactic or critical of culture in some way. Similarly, Bruce Friesen and Warren Helfrich studied the lyrics of 500 metal songs released between 1985 and 1991. Among them, the authors identified 10 predominant topics, including gender, oppression, physical conflict, exploration of the mystical and supernatural, excitement, escape, loss of control, and social justice.

Another popular theme in heavy metal is night, according to author Deena Weinstein. "Night is a time of danger, obscurity, and mystery when the forces of chaos are strongest. But it is also the time for Bacchanalian revelry. Heavy metal's rhetoric and imagery puts forward Dionysian themes and themes of chaos. These themes are related in that both conjure with powers that the adult world wishes to keep at bay and exclude even from symbolic representation. Under the cover of night, everything that is repressed by the respectable world can come forth. What is that respectable world? For heavy metal's youthful audience, that world is the adult world."

Unfortunately, parents heard what the PMRC said because it was on the evening news. Most didn't read *Hit Parader* or Freisen, Helfrich, and Weinstein. That left millions with the impression that heavy-metal music was scary and dangerous for kids. It's true that metal explores and often celebrates concepts of violence and alienation. Its lyrics frequently describe the world as dangerous, corrupt, and ruined —a place where nobody can be trusted and violence is everywhere. The melodies, including the frequent use of minor keys, reinforce these pessimistic words, Arnett wrote.

Metal does go to some dark places. However, few who have studied it feel that the music tells listeners how to feel or what to do. "Heavy metal has consistently evoked negative reactions from the broader public, simultaneously endearing it to the hearts of millions of disaffected youth. It has been blamed for the moral corruption of young people, encouraging drug use, and causing suicides," Friesen and Helfrich wrote. "While examining the content of heavy metal songs, we make no claims ... that the messages promulgated within the music influence those who listen to them in any particular fashion."

Arnett felt similarly. He confirmed that violence is prominent in many heavy metal songs, and that it can be brutal violence at times, but found no sign that listening to the music provoked violent feelings in listeners. In fact, fans told him that listening to heavy metal purged their anger and violent feelings in a safe way.

"A common misconception is that metal music will possess someone to act outrageously. This is not true," said a 20-year-old from Michigan who started listening to the genre when he was 4. "Metal music is just music. Metal is not evil. Music can't be evil. It may be macabre, it may be dark, it may be angry, but it's nothing more than a positive outlet for sometimes bad feelings."

Sun That Never Sets

When Kim Kelly found out her mom was in the hospital, the teen figured it was no big deal—after all, her mom worked as a waitress, and frequently endured cuts and scrapes. But it was a big deal: Kelly's mom had an aneurysm, which led to multiple brain surgeries, a hemorrhage, and a coma. Kim spent a considerable chunk of her 17th year wondering if her mother was going to die.

"Seeing my mother's newly frail body speckled with dried blood, threaded with tubes, and lying in a ICU bed with half her skull sawed off forced me out of the last vestigial moments of childhood, and out into the harsh realities of the adult world," Kim, now a well-known heavy-metal writer and editor, wrote about the experience.

After extensive rehabilitation, Kim's mom survived—but emerged with a personality her daughter didn't recognize.

In those early dark days when nobody knew what was happening to Kim's mom, the teen turned to black metal music, known for its chaotic and whirling sound, low-fi production, and harrowing lyrics. That's what helped most.

"Nothing made sense anymore, except this. The raw, seething hatred, bottomless despair, and chaotic nature of the music itself spoke to me in a way that my friends and family could not. Only this cold, lightness music that celebrated death, destruction, and elitism could articulate the suffocating, bleak feelings that consumed me," Kelly wrote. "Without this crackling, razor-edged hellnoise, all the horrible emotions and thoughts and questions that perpetually swirled through my consciousness would not have had an outlet, and I could easily have succumbed to the pressure. It's almost too cliché to say it, but heavy metal—specifically black metal—saved my life."

Metal may be linked to suicide or violent behavior in court cases and news reports, but there's no real evidence that music can make anyone end his or her life. To many fans, like Kelly, metal serves as a lifeline. "It is quite popular for music censorship advocates to point to the high correlation between rap fandom and gang participation or heavy metal fandom and suicide," according to Nuzum. "While it is true (and well researched) that certain genres of music attract certain types of people, it is important to remember a fundamental truth of social science: correlation does not prove causation."

Often, adults have blamed heavy metal for causing teen depression and misbehavior. This allows them to avoid the more serious—and more complicated—reasons that teens hurt themselves or others. "Music alone certainly does not create depression, alienation, violence or misogyny, and focusing only on music enables us to ignore, for instance, how our society may breed alienation," Sternheimer wrote.

Likewise, Arnett found that listening to metal did not worsen sad feelings. "In spite of the hopeless, even nihilistic quality of the lyrics of most heavy metal songs, not one of the boys—not a single one—said that the songs make him feel hopeless or even sad," he wrote.

In fact, none of the researchers who studied this issue came away with the idea that music—as powerful as it is to teenagers—is powerful enough to drive someone to end his or her life.

"Whatever influence rock music has on the lives of its fans pales when compared to the influence of family, church, community, peers, school and every other very tangible and real institutions in a person's life," Nuzum wrote.

When metal fans turn violent, either toward themselves or others, it's likely that they were mentally unstable already, according to Jeanne Fury, who writes for heavy-metal magazine *Decibel*. Adults point fingers at the music so they can ignore the much more real problems going on. "Then when something does go wrong, they can't comprehend that they themselves are part of the problem," she said. "If they truly cared about their kids, they'd listen to them, not judge them."

"Many parents worry about the images of death in rock 'n' roll music, never noticing that the romance of death is all around us," Kate Williams wrote in *A Parent's Guide for Suicidal and Depressed Teens*.

In fact, death and violence are deeply woven into our

culture, from the colloquialisms we use ("shooting" for "taking pictures," or "taking a stab at it," or saying we "killed it" when we did something exceptionally well) to the news stories we favor. While adults may shrug off these violent references as a part of everyday life, younger people are still struggling to figure out what's important and how it all fits together in the context of their lives. Violent entertainment can help them process violent reality.

"Young adolescents take in these images [of death] and become overwhelmed by them if they have no way to express or release their feelings. And at times they reach out to the images of death in the world because these external images express their inner pain," Williams wrote.

There's evidence that teens who listen heavy metal become adults with bright outlooks. That's what author Natalie Purcell discovered when she undertook an academic study of the death-metal scene, asking adult metalheads about everything from faith to marriage. Overall, metal fans become adults who are thoughtful about religion, optimistic about the future, and generally happy.

Opinions about religion were as varied among death-metal fans as among folks in the general population. "Among the respondents, 14.9 percent felt organized religion is a very positive institution and stated that they themselves are religious; 14.9 percent felt that organized religion is a very positive institution, but stated that they themselves are not religious. Another 17.9 percent felt indifferently toward religion, and the largest percentage, 37.3 percent, stated that organized religion was not a good idea and that they would not become religious. Only 14.9 percent agreed with the statement, 'Religion is stupid, and no one should be religious,'" Purcell wrote.

Many metal bands, including some death-metal bands, actively criticize religion in their music—or explore occult themes. However, Purcell said that it would be a mistake to say that the music caused listeners to abandon religious feelings. "Instead, religious persons will probably not seek entertainment which is considered hostile to their belief systems, whereas the nonreligious will be more open to it,"

Purcell wrote.

Some in the heavy-metal world may appear to be anti-religious when, in fact, religion is an important part of their lives. That's the case with Alice Cooper, one of the most influential metal performers of the past 30 years and a born-again Christian. "I've filled my life with a sincere, divine love of rock n' roll. I will never back down in my rock n' roll attitude because I think rock is great! I'm the first one to turn it up. ... It has also gotten me in trouble with the staunch Christians who believe that in order to be a Christian you have to be on your knees 24 hours day in a closet somewhere. Hey, maybe some people can live like that, but I don't think that's the way God expected us to live."

Interestingly, one researcher discovered that metal fans who were religious were less likely to consider suicide as a way out. This finding further proves that heavy-metal music doesn't cause suicidal feelings in listeners. "[Steven] Stack found ... that suicide acceptability was higher for metal fans than for non-fans, and he wondered at the reasons for this. Stack made a major discovery when he introduced the factor of religiosity into his study. When he controlled for religiosity and church attendance, metal fans showed no greater acceptance of suicide than non-fans. This led him to believe that the relationship between metal fans and suicide was indeed spurious, and that the truly influential factor was religiosity," Purcell wrote.

In other surveys, Purcell found that more than half of death-metal fans supported the idea of marriage, considered themselves reasonably social people, tended to believe they had a good chance of achieving economic success, and tended to feel contented and positive about life. So much for the idea of miserable, antisocial, down-on-their-luck metal fans living in sin. Even if teens turn to metal in the tumult of adolescence, by adulthood they seem to be a generally well-adjusted bunch. Many of them remain fans of heavy metal for life.

"A close examination of the values in the scene reveal that heavy-metal participants do not adhere to values that are contrary to those of society," Markson wrote. "While the symbols used to express such values do indeed deviate from traditionally accepted means of symbolic communication, the implied messages are similar to those espoused in conventional society."

In 2011, UK metal magazine *Metal Hammer* urged readers to list "heavy metal" as their religion on the UK census. Although it was partly in jest, more than 6,000 people complied, making the culture a more prevalent "faith" in in the region than Satanism, Scientology, or Druidry. For some fans, their love of heavy metal is serious stuff—and they may show more faith in it, and more dedication to it, than some who consider them devout followers of other religions. Metal's intensity inspires intense loyalty. It's no wonder so many teens adore it.

Welcome to the Family

The teenage years are an intense, hormone-soaked time. The music teenagers fall in love with during these years is the music that stays with them for the rest of their lives. For many adults, hearing a song from adolescence can bring back memories and emotions like nothing else. How does that work?

Music begins to catch fans' ears when they're 10 or 11, Daniel Levitin wrote in *This is Your Brain on Music*. Music's appeal continues through the teen years, if not beyond, and the music we love during those years becomes "our music." "Part of the reason we remember songs from our teenage years is because those years were times of self-discovery, and as a consequence, they were emotionally charged; in general, we tend to remember things that have an emotional component because our amygdala and neurotransmitters act in concert to 'tag' the memories as something important," Levitin wrote.

Many teens are passionate about music, and they know exactly why. Researchers Barbara Wilson and Nicole Martins asked teens what media they would want if they were stranded on an island. Students in junior and senior high school overwhelmingly chose music over other media, including television. The duo also asked teens why they listened to particular songs or genres of music. Most (81 percent) said they used music to relieve tension or ease their troubles, and 67 percent said they listened to counteract loneliness. Male fans were more likely to say they used music to "get pumped up," and about half of heavy-metal fans said they listened to the music when they are feeling angry about something. Music fans also said tunes relieve boredom, help them establish or maintain a social identity, and help them make friends and connect to social groups.

Other studies found similar responses. When researcher Keith Roe asked teens why they listen to music, they reported three main reasons: to create an atmosphere and to control their mood, to fill the silence and pass boring periods of time, and to listen to the lyrics, according to Peter Christenson.

To some extent, boys and girls listen to music for different reasons. In a piece called "Changing Channels" (excerpted by Christenson), Robert Kubey and Joseph Colletti found that girls tended to prefer ballads and love songs. For girls, music was associated with sadness, depression, and sometimes anger. They used the music to explore and cope with new concerns and worries that accompany adolescence, especially emotions related to budding romance and intimacy. Boys, on the other hand, used music to energize themselves, and also matched music to negative moods.

Music itself is very evocative—even for adults. Robert Zatorre, a neuroscientist at McGill University, asked subjects to listen to their favorite pieces of music, whatever "sent chills down their spine," according to reporter Shankar Vedantam. "He found that music activated very ancient parts of the brain. ... [Zatorre] says, 'We got this very ancient system which is usually involved in biological reward ... What we found in a nutshell is when people experience chills, there was a huge range of activity all over the brain. It lit up like a Christmas tree,'" Vedantam wrote. "Music seems to activate pleasure networks that are typically activated by food, water and sex."

In particular, the sounds that evoked the strongest emotions were non-speech vocalizations—the moans and "oohs" so common in rock music. Harvard neuroscientist Mark Jude Tramo linked this reaction to humans' centers of nonverbal communication, which developed as a survival mechanism throughout the animal world, according to Vedantam. "For social species such as humans, Tramo said music can bind groups together."

Charles Darwin believed that humans began using rhythm and melody in order to attract and charm mates, according to Levitin. In that sense, music may even play a role in natural selection—in other words, being able to play music can feel like a survival instinct. That may explain why so many teenagers long to join bands.

Adults might be able to relate to the idea of their teenager enjoying a pretty pop song. But why would kids adore music with blisteringly loud guitars and a singer who sounds like he's furious or yelping in pain? Everyone has different thresholds for intensity and novelty in music. Levitin compared these differences to the experience of getting into a car with someone who is in full control of the destination: "If the driver takes you out on back roads with no explanation, and you reach a point where you no longer see any landmarks, your sense of safety is sure to be violated. Of course, different people with different personality types react differently to such unanticipated journeys, musical or vehicular. Some react with sheer panic ... and some react with a sense of adventure at the thrill of discovery."

Metal appeals to listeners because it resonates with them emotionally, Fury said. "To say metal fans are somehow weird for liking such aggressive music is all a matter of perspective and personal taste."

Adolescence is a time when hormones are peaking, particularly testosterone. This hormone is linked with aggressive feelings and behavior, but our society does not tolerate those kinds of feelings, let alone destructive activity. At the same time, youths often lack the kind of self-regulation that adults have practiced for years. Teens may look high and low for some way to purge those feelings in a way that's socially acceptable, and by hurting as few people as possible. Some of them find it in heavy metal, finding that this loud, fast music—in a seeming paradox—calms them down.

"Given that the metalheads in this study reported consistently and independently that listening to heavy metal music has the effect of purging their anger and other negative emotions, and given that none of them said that the music incites them to aggressiveness or other antisocial behavior, it is difficult to make a case that the music is harmful to them or harmful to society because of the effects it has on the metalheads. Ironically, it would seem to make more sense to prescribe a steady program of listening to heavy metal music ... so that their aggressive tendencies might be purged harmlessly by the music instead of being taken out in disruptive ways on the people around them," Arnett wrote.

In addition to being aggressive, heavy-metal music can be intensely sexual, from its throbbing bass guitars and drums to its raw vocalizations—not to mention the tight leather and denim clothing popular among many rockers. While this may unsettle some parents, Arnett argues that it provides an outlet for teens, whose bodies become sexually ready while society tells them to wait.

"For adolescents, at an age when sexual maturity has been reached and sexual desire is new and strong but interdicts limit their sexual behavior, anything that invites them to defy the [social] interdicts and enjoy their sexuality is likely to have powerful transgressive appeal," he wrote in "Music at the Edge: The Attraction and Effects of Controversial Music on Young People."

Live metal performances can provide another outlet for teenage aggression. Remember the roiling image of the mosh pit? It's easy to see the pit as a violent place, but for metalheads, it's a space where they can be consensually aggressive, in the same way that young animals and children play roughly together. "I'd rather have kids in the pit working out the stuff they have to go through in their lives then out hurting other people," Slipknot singer Corey Taylor told filmmaker Sam Dunn in *Metal: A Headbanger's Journey*.

Many of the metal fans interviewed for this book said catharsis was one of primary reasons they love metal so much. It both validates and purges negative feelings—those caused by major traumas and those caused by everyday frustrations.

Catharsis is a common goal of music, theater and other performing arts, and it works like this: the audience experiences sadness, fear, or pain along with the characters in the song, film, or play they're watching. As the crisis unfolds and reaches a resolution at the end of the story, those negative feelings are released and purged, wrote Natalie Purcell in *Death Metal Music*. "Metal is a philosophical response, whether conscious or subconscious, to terrifying questions about nebulous human nature. In this way, the fantasy of the metal realm is a response to reality."

My interview subjects said heavy-metal music provided catharsis in a variety of tough times. "Having a fight with my parents made me storm to my room, slam the door, and turn up the music," said a German who started listening to metal when she was 16. Metal also helped her heal after she was raped by her boyfriend at age 17. "That was when songs needed to have lines like, 'Loving you was like loving the dead,' [from Type O Negative's 'Black No. 1'] or about hearts being ripped out, wading in gore, etc."

For many teen metal fans, the music is a profound ally. Not only does it help them work out sexual and aggressive feelings, but it can provide an altered state of consciousness— one that's often healthier than the alternatives. Arnett interviewed one metalhead, named Jack, who said heavy-metal music was a kind of addiction for him. "He said that he had used the music as a substitute for his former drug addiction. 'You can get the same feeling from the music. I mean, I can listen to a song and it can put me in a better mood than smoking a joint or doing some drugs or something. I used to have a pretty bad drug problem, and the music has helped me stay away from it.'"

Finck discovered similar stories among teen metal fans in rehab. While many parents considered the music amoral and destructive, their kids said it was empowering and uplifting. It allowed them a feeling of control in their own lives, Finck wrote in her introduction to Jeff Dess' book *Turn Up the Music*.

"I worked with several kids during the '80s who were into the darkest parts of the genre. Teenagers who were listening to Satanic music came into treatment bringing their Satanic bibles with them. Many of these kids shared experiences that were horrifying, and it was difficult for them to understand what was real and what was drug-induced," Finck wrote.

She found one teenage boy sitting on his bed, quoting Bible passages and making threats against the other kids in rehab. He seemed to be in a trance. When she spoke to him, he told her he was quoting song lyrics. "This was a teenager who was enmeshed in a culture that romanticized death and evil at its core. He was listening to bands I had never heard of, and I felt that if I was going to reach him, I needed to understand what his music was saying. We worked together for about five months, and I learned how the music filled a void in his life. He felt powerless, alone, and out of control, and the music provided him with power and a sense of control."

In the heavy metal world, these kinds of stories are everywhere. Hatebreed singer Jamey Jasta told Fury that if someone can come to one of his concerts, leave their stress at the door and experience some kind of release, then he has done his job. "People have come up to him after shows and thanked him for it. Not to sound trite, but life isn't easy. People carry a lot of weight around. If they can find a way to get rid of some of that stress in a positive way ... then that's excellent," Fury said.

Heavy metal offers respite for teens who are struggling with powerful emotions—or wayward aggression. That doesn't always signify real trouble in an adolescent's life. Most metal listeners said the genre provided solace and comfort from the day-to-day challenges everyone faces at one time or another. "Metal teaches the listener about the darker side of reality, and, as intelligent beings, who would not want to know everything they could about their existence?" asked one teen, an 18-year-old from Ealing, near London, who started listening to metal when he was 11. "Where pop and R&B sing about love, money, drugs, and so many other things which are just barely in reach of the average person, metal talks about death, pain, darkness—things which are far more common, far more prevalent. The experience of listening to metal is cathartic, as one sees that such suffering is inherent to existence, and must be accepted, along with the good, in order to enjoy life more fully."

To adults, it might seem that love and money are more easy to come by—but to the average teen, they can seem unattainable. On the other hand, emotional upheaval can be an everyday occurrence, one that can be soothed by the right music. Adults might hear one thing when they listen to heavy metal, but many teens hear something entirely different.

"If you were to put a pair of headphones on and play messages that represented hopelessness, fear, irrational thinking, violent images, and overall exhaustion on a daily basis, how much love and hope would you have in yourself, your neighbor, and society at large? It would make sense to think that negative and pessimistic information—or exposure to violent sounds and sights on a constant and consistent basis— would put most of us on a downward spiral without much hope of returning," Finck wrote. "Sometimes that same music that adults find negative and pessimistic some adolescents may find uplifting, provocative, and validating."

Metal musicians hear similar sentiments from their fans. "We get letters all the time from these kids that say how much our songs help them and they go home [from our shows] feeling better and they can go back to school. I have a lot of kids say that when they wear their Slipknot t-shirts or gear they feel safe," Slipknot drummer Joey Jordison said in *Metal: A Headbanger's Journey.*

Metal's lyrics play a major role in uplifting listeners. Yes, researchers have found that those lyrics explore lust and loneliness, oppression and political frustration. It would be easy to pigeonhole metal as a genre that focuses on the darker side of life. But its lyrics run the gamut from happy-go-lucky and romantic to sorrowful, angry, rebellious—a wider range than many genres.

"What I like about metal is that it's broad lyrically, it's broad with the emotions it can capture, and its hits you hard," said a fan from Michigan who started listening to heavy metal when he was 4.

Many outsiders to metal are surprised by the lyrics, and by the way musicians and fans interpret them. For instance, when Fresh Air's Terry Gross interviewed Rob Halford, the former lead singer of Judas Priest, she commented on the lyrics for "Hellrider." Judas Priest's music has been derided in the media for its link to a pair of suicides, so Gross was surprised by "Hellrider's" hopefulness and mythic qualities. "The overriding story is of optimism, of defeating anything that stands in your way that prevents you from achieving your goals or your dreams," Halford told Gross. "A lot of the lyrics I write for Priest come from this streak I have inside of me which has always been one of determination, of overcoming the odds." Who wouldn't want their teen listening to a song about achieving one's goals?

Metal songwriters frequently draw inspiration from literature, mythology, and fantasy writing. Such epic lyrics match the bombastic nature of the music. In the process, they often wind up educating listeners about literature and mythology. "The epic-ness of metal appeals to me," said Vincent, whose story opens this chapter. "Metal is filled with darkness, magic, war, history, literature. I feel a deep connection to this music. I want to feel the lightning of the music coursing through my blood." For him, the genre provided songs and lyrics for every emotion. "If I was depressed I'd listen to something slow and dark I could slide into. If I was happy I'd listen to something powerful and upbeat (say from Manowar or Helloween) to enhance my mood."

Many fans connect with metal's tendency to draw on myths and legends. "I don't believe a song that uses lines from 18th century poetry or quotes from famous literary figures as lyrics (occult-related or not) would be anything but educational, because borrowing lines from 'The Raven,' 'The Rime of The Ancient Mariner,' or quoting Nietzsche or Oscar Wilde in the liner notes is a lot more beneficial for a teenager's aptitude for learning than songs about guns, drugs, women, and sex," said a metalhead from Jordan and the United Arab Emirates who started listening when he was 5 or 6. "For me, metal was an education ... an escapist culture, a fantasy land which offered as much information as Wikipedia does now, but in an indirect and artistic form."

In a study of Metallica's music, Joseph Kotarba was struck by how important the band's music and lyrics are to fans. He noted that Metallica had become a primary cultural resource for listeners, one that provided context and meaning for life's problems and possibilities.

As part of his research, Kotarba attended a Monsters of Rock show. When Metallica took the stage and began to perform, "bodies ceased to move and everyone's attention seemed to shift to the *stories* being told. Thousands of 14-, 15- and 16-year-old kids, mostly boys, and all attired in appropriate black T-shirts, did not so much sing along as they *spoke* along. Song after song, the kids moved their lips in sync as they collectively tuned into another reality. This reality was not predicated by drugs, alcohol, or sensuality but by the ability of the narrative to collectively conceptualize individual experiences of growing up."

Although fans shared the experience of knowing and following the lyrics, each listener created his or her own meaning from those same songs, according to Kotarba. For example, "I asked a [a homeless boy] where 'Never Never Land,' as mentioned in ['Enter Sandman'], was. I heard a homeless kid's philosophy of life in his answer: 'It's where you go when you have no place to go.'"

When Gross interviewed Metallica's Hetfield, she asked him about the nature of his lyrics. He told her how angry he was growing up, particularly because he was raised in a Christian Scientist family in which his mother died because seeking medical treatment was forbidden. She asked him whether that anger worked well for him as a musician. He said that it did, particularly during the early years of the band. In later years, that same anger nearly ended the band.

"After getting clean and sober and going back and reading a lot of the lyrics—wow, that's pretty intense," Hetfield reflected. For example, "'Dyer's Eve.' This is a song about my parents and how they kept me in a cocoon, not allowing me to see the world, of what different religions there were, or different kinds of people, learning about other things, they were trying to keep me almost in a cult type of religion. This song talks about now that you're gone, I'm out in the world, and I'm lost, and I blame you. ... It's pretty heavy stuff when I read it now. I realize my parents did the best they could with what they had to work with. I didn't realize the trickle-down effect from their parents. You know, you look at your parents like they're gods in a way. They could never do wrong."

Hetfield has one interpretation of the song—the one that describes his feelings toward his parents. But fans have different relationships to their own parents, so the song will mean something else to them. Still, "Dyer's Eve" touches on the struggle for independence from parents and their influence, an experience most teens can relate to.

Lyrics are interpreted one way by the songwriter, another way by fans, and a third way by people who don't like the music. That's what happened when the PMRC criticized Twisted Sister's lyrics for referring to rape and violence—claims that singer Dee Snider refuted when he appeared before the senate committee. "On the contrary, the words in question [in 'Under the Blade'] are about surgery and the fear that it instills in people. ... As the creator of 'Under the Blade,' I can say categorically that the only sadomasochism, bondage, and rape in this song is in the mind of Ms. [Tipper] Gore," Snider said.

Twisted Sister's biggest hit, "We're Not Gonna Take It," earned a "V" rating from the PMRC for violent content. Snider pointed out, "You will note from the lyrics before you that there is absolutely no violence of any type either sung about or implied anywhere in the song. ... I am very pleased to note that the United Way of America has been granted a request to use portions of our 'We're Not Gonna Take It' video in a program they are producing on the subject of the changing American family. They asked for it because of its 'light-hearted way of talking about communicating with teenagers.'"

Many adult critics focus heavily on metal's lyrics, but not all fans pay attention to them. Some researchers found that many teens don't know the words to their favorite songs. One study, cited by Nancy Dowd in *Handbook of Children, Culture, and Violence,* asked 266 12- to 18-year-olds to name their three favorite songs and then describe the songs in a few sentences. Students in the survey were unable to explain 37 percent of the songs they listed as favorites—meaning they understood them less than two-thirds of the time.

"Many teens reported that they had no idea what their selected song meant but that they liked the rhythm or melody. Although no precise percentages were given, the researchers found that teens frequently misinterpreted the songs they liked. A number of them thought, for example, that the song 'Stairway to Heaven,' by Led Zeppelin, which focuses on a young woman's quest for meaning in life, was about going to heaven on a stairway. The researchers pointed out that students, often unable to grasp complex metaphors, provided very literal interpretations for the songs," Dowd wrote.

Parents who hear metal's intense lyrics may immediately assume their kids are listening just as closely and taking them to heart without questioning their meaning. But that isn't always the case. "One time my dad got ahold of one of the liner sheets and read the lyrics. He started lecturing me on how depressing the lyrics are," said a Denver resident who started listening to metal when he was 16. "I tried to tell him that I didn't care about the lyrics. He said, 'Well, it still gets into your subconscious.' [My step-sister-in-law] tried to convince me that the music I like was too dark and it isn't therapeutic at all. It just throws fuel on the fire and when I get older I'll understand. Well, 15 years later I still listen to dark music. In fact I listen to much darker music than I did then."

Interestingly, Dowd cited another study that suggests metal fans listen more closely to the lyrics than teens who enjoy other genres. In this study, 41 percent of heavy-metal fans knew all the lyrics to their favorite songs—compared to 25 percent of other music fans. Even so, that leaves more than 50 percent of listeners in the dark about the subject matter of their favorite tracks.

Other researchers speculated about the reasons why lyrics are important to some music fans and not others. "Songs are not regarded as 'texts' to be studied and analyzed," wrote Stephen Markson in "Claims-Making, Quasi-Theories and the Social Construction of the Rock 'N' Roll Menace." "They are not cognitively monitored for maximum comprehension as they are used as background noise to provide a setting for other activities in which beat and sound are much more relevant than words and imagery. Furthermore, it is rather difficult, even if it was the lyricist's intention, to tell much of a story in approximately two minutes and 250 words with many of the lyrics garbled and unintelligible in their delivery."

For metal fans, music is less of a background experience. It demands more attention from the listener. On the other hand, many of the lyrics—often sung in high-pitched wails or low, guttural growls, are nearly unintelligible. Some vocalists, such as John Tardy of Obituary, occasionally sing wordless vocalizations rather than actual lyrics. When vocalists obscure the lyrics in this way, their voices become like another instrument in the band, conveying feeling and meaning through tone, rather than through the words they're singing. In many cases, bands deliberately don't print lyrics on their album sleeves or include them with digital downloads. Then there is the problem of meaning: even when you can understand the words, lyrics are often written like poetry, employing literary devices that leave their meaning open to interpretation.

Sometimes, parents catch the words to a heavy metal song, and their discomfort prompts a tense conversation with their metal-loving kids. "My mother did not approve of my choice of music. She feared I was opening myself up to demonic influence," said Vincent, whose story opens this chapter. "One time, when I was outside doing yard work and had music playing loud so I could hear it, my mother asked me if I actually understood what the singer was singing. I said yes and proceeded to quote lyrics. She waved me off in disgust. I understood my mother's fears, but I felt like I knew what I was doing. Lyrics were very important to me. I was very much aware of everything that was entering my ears by way of music."

A Michigan metal fan remembered a similar conversation with his parents. "They asked me why I listened to such angry music. Read me back the lyrics. Asked me if I was angry or if I hated my life ... I responded with 'No.' Tucked my tail between my legs and felt ashamed for a music choice and took the obsession underground and learned to hide my CDs better! Eventually my parents realized that music choice has little effect on actions and stopped taking my CDs."

One fan from South Carolina started listening to metal when he was 13. He grew up in a Pentecostal household, and his mother talked with him extensively about his interest in the genre. "She was very worried about me listening to Satanic stuff. She would ask me to pray that anything actually of the devil would disappear," he said. "I would show her what was in a lot of the lyrics so she could see that it was not about that, that

[Metallica's] 'Master of Puppets' is actually about drug addiction, that 'Creeping Death' is just another view of something she celebrates in church every year. She never actually interfered with my listening, just never shut up about it."

Many listeners found that adults who are uncomfortable with heavy metal's lyrical content feel that way, in part, because they take the words too literally—and out of context.

"A given rock song may carry so much 'expressive ambiguity,' cryptic symbolism, and buried irony that its meaning cannot be clearly deciphered. Adding to the difficulty is the challenge of simply hearing the lyrics ... and even if the lyrics are intelligible, they may convey only one message among several that the 'total package' communicates," according to Quentin Schulze and others in "Dancing in the Dark."

So what about that "total package?" Rock and metal lyrics do not exist in a vacuum; they are meant to be heard against the backdrop of the singer's voice, the melody, and the guitars, drums, and bass performed by the rest of the band.

As with lyrics, rock music (and heavy metal specifically) has been criticized by detractors, some of whom claim it takes no talent whatsoever to play. "There is definitely a distinction between rock and roll and every other type of music that has been written or performed to civilized nations," Larson wrote. "Some will try to equate jazz and rock and roll, but the comparison breaks down at one point. The key ingredient in a jazz performance is improvisation of the melody within an established rhythmic framework. This requires much talent, and unless the performance becomes too 'far out,' the attention of the listener is sharpened. This is not the case with rock and roll."

On the contrary, several of the metal fans I interviewed —and others interviewed by metal scholars—said one of the things they like most about the music is how intricate it is and how much skill it takes to perform. In some cases, metal's musicianship sparked listeners to pick up an instrument or start a band of their own. "[There's a misconception] that metal is just noise and takes no talent to perform," said a 28-year-old metal fan from Denver who started listening at 16. "It takes skill to perform. It can inspire [kids] to play an instrument."

Some metal fans focus predominantly on the music—to the exclusion of the lyrics. "As a person with a musical ear, I was attracted to the rhythms and the melodies," said the metal fan from Jordan and UAE. "Heavy metal was a genuinely musical experience with roots that extended down to blues, rock 'n' roll and even classical music."

Heavy-metal musicians adopted the tritone, a type of chord that was considered dissonant during the Middle Ages but re-emerged in classical and jazz. To this day, it has a reputation for sounding scary, oppressive, or evil. Metal shares this and other roots with classical and baroque music, as Robert Walser found when he compared Deep Purple's "Highway Star" to Antonin Vivaldi's "Violin Concerto in D Minor," or Eddie Van Halen's "Eruption" to Rodolphe Kreutzer's "Caprice Study #2." That classical backing allows metal musicians to dabble in a mindboggling array of styles, a fact that impresses many fans.

"I really like the fact that the music is simply much more creative. A lot of mainstream bands and acts nowadays simply take one little ditty and hash it into the same old verse-chorus-verse-chorus-bridge-chorus structure," said a 17-year-old from Kentucky who began listening to metal when he was 15. "But in a metal song, you never know what's going to happen. The music can go any direction at any time, so that when there is a shift in the music, it is a genuine surprise, or the music actually has to provide the expectations instead of you simply knowing the structure already. ... The virtuosity and technical skill are what I most enjoy. And I don't just refer to blindingly fast playing—I mean finding a way to merge a show of one's mastery of their chosen instrument with an amazing example of skill in musical composition."

In *Running with the Devil,* Walser wrote that the bond between metal and classical music surprises and confounds many people—including people who study music. "The classical influence on heavy metal marks a merger of what are generally regarded as the most and least prestigious musical discourses of our time. The influence thus seems an unlikely one, and we must wonder why metal musicians and fans have found such a discursive fusion useful and compelling."

Walser is quick to add that he's not comparing metal to classical in order to make heavy-metal music seem legit. In fact, he calls metal "in many ways antithetical" to classical music. However, he said it's important to compare the two because so many metal musicians have raided the classical music vault in order to compose their songs. Swedish guitarist Yngvie Malmsteen, recognized as a virtuoso, played metal music clearly inspired heavily by classical forms. His work spawned a mini-genre called "neo-classical," or occasionally, "Bach-n-roll." One band, Stratovarius, crafted its moniker by combining the name of the famous rock guitar, Fender's Stratocaster, with one of the most renowned violin-makers in the world.

Another key component of the heavy-metal "package" is the look. Beyond the black leather and denim, many musicians wear costumes or even adopt different personas when they perform. For some, this is a minor enhancement of their everyday personalities. For others, such as Alice Cooper, there is a strong separation between their on-stage and off-stage appearances and behavior. A few musicians, such as the members of Marilyn Manson or Slipknot, bur the line between performance and day-to-day life.

To fans, these personas can become very important psychologically. "When I listen to the music of a great composer I feel that I am, in some sense, becoming one with him, or letting a part of him inside me," Levitin wrote. "This sense of vulnerability and surrender is no more prevalent than with rock and popular music in the past forty years. This accounts for the fandom that surrounds popular musicians." This can be especially true among metal fans, some of whom resonate with the fictional personas of certain performers. Others look for signs of "authenticity" in the way musicians present themselves to an audience. Fans can find authenticity in a performer whose onstage look is stripped-down and casual, or in a performer whose elaborate makeup and costumes give an outward face to troubling, even ugly internal feelings.

"Many metalheads find a crucial source of meaning in their involvement with heavy metal, not just from the way they resonate to the lyrics of the songs but from their admiration of the performers," Arnett wrote. "To metalheads, heavy metal performers represent a rare authenticity in a corrupt world, and the ideology of alienation gives metalheads a way of making sense of the world. Paradoxically, they find meaning and consolation through sharing in a declaration that the world is meaningless and without consolation."

That authenticity is communicated in a variety of ways, including long hair, tattoos, earrings, dark clothing and other traditional metal garb. Arnett argued that these trappings communicate that musicians "care little for the societal convention of how men should look, and little for the society that convention represents."

When Gross interviewed Hetfield on Fresh Air, she remarked, "What I find interesting the kind of fan that relates to the persona you created, the mythic version of yourself, the onstage version of yourself. They're trying to model themselves on somebody you're not even."

Hetfield responded, "There are parts of me on the stage that are certainly me. There's somewhat of a hat or jacket that you put on to go up and perform. We're performers. But with a real heart, it's really about the music. But when fans come to see you play, they want to see something. You can't just stand there and play. You could. But it's not as entertaining as running around or showing, on your face, the anger of a song, or some of the sadness of a song. It is performing."

While Hetfield presents a relatively straightforward onstage persona—black jeans, black t-shirt, tattoos and guitar—other musicians take their performance much further. Many appear on stage in makeup or face paint, and unusual clothing that is much more akin to a costume. One of the first metal musicians to do this was Alice Cooper, who discussed his onstage and off-stage personas with Lonn Friend on KNAC in 2001.

"Most people have a light side and a dark side. My dark side gets to go on stage. I get paid for playing my dark side," Cooper said. "I know several people, however, who are total split personalities, where one second they're my best friend and the next I don't even wanna be near them. But they don't get the luxury of doing it on stage. The stage is where I purge my demons."

Cooper's look, which includes black clothing, stage blood, snakes, and face paint meant to look like a "tragedy" theater mask, has inspired generations of other metal performers. KISS, who were performing in black-and-white makeup and studded leather at the same time as Cooper, also provided plenty of fodder for future artists. Marilyn Manson's unusual look owes something to Cooper and KISS, as do plenty of modern metal musicians who wear "corpse paint"—artificially whitened faces with black makeup around the eyes—as part of their performance attire. Others, like Blackie Lawless of WASP, used stage blood and wore unusual clothing, such as a codpiece with a sawblade protruding from the front. Musicians use costumes like these as a form of theater, either to convey meaning or for simple shock value, particularly onstage. "People like to dress up," Darkthrone drummer Gylve "Fenriz" Nagell said in *Until the Light Takes Us*, a documentary on the Norwegian black-metal scene.

Other bands, particularly Slipknot, wear masks onstage instead of makeup. Slipknot's masks look like something out of monster movies; they're outrageous and unsettling. The musicians pair them with jumpsuits featuring bar codes printed on the back, and claim they wear these disguises to force fans to focus on the music. However, fans wind up identifying with the way the masks look. Similarly, GWAR has made a career out of wearing elaborate onstage costumes and masks inspired by science fiction and horror films. Although their live performances are often raunchy and obscene, they're also intended as humorous commentary on ideas considered politically or morally taboo.

This suggests what psychologist Carl Jung described as the shadow, or dark side, of the psyche. He warned people not to ignore their shadow. If ignored, the shadow would cause trouble subconsciously. Instead, he urged people to acknowledge the shadow, but not allow it to overpower the "light" part of the self. "To confront a person with his shadow is to show him his own light. Once one has experienced a few times what it is like to stand judgingly between the opposites, one begins to understand what is meant by the self. Anyone who perceives his shadow and his light simultaneously sees himself from two sides and thus gets in the middle," he wrote in "Good and Evil in Analytical Psychology."

When musicians take on these wild onstage personas, they are giving their shadow selves a little fresh air, and letting the audience do the same in a safe and protected way. This certainly fits with the themes of purging and catharsis that are so important in heavy metal. When you're a teenager and you feel like you don't exist, or that the world is a cruel and unpleasant place, it can be comforting to see faces that reflect that. Some teens even wear masks or corpsepaint themselves. This lets them feel closer to the musicians who inspire them, and creates a kind of tribe unified by alienation and turmoil.

That said, even the most shocking onstage persona or scene is intended to be interpreted as fiction or metaphor, rather than something to be taken literally. "Even when the notorious black metal band Mayhem regrouped for a tour ... and came on stage with pigs' heads on sticks, corpsepaint and pig's blood, and black cloaks, people saw it for what it was— theatrics," Fury said.

At the same time heavy metal helps listeners connect with their most private internal feelings, it also helps them connect with one another. Some teens form tight friendships— at school, at concerts, at the local record store—based on their shared love of metal. Others celebrate live shows especially because they know each person in the room adores that band. Because the music often appeals to teens who feel alone, or like they don't fit in, this ready-made social group can feel like an enormous gift.

"One of the biggest things about heavy metal, and perhaps the least understood aspect by outsiders, is the fraternity of it all," said a 17-year-old from Kentucky who started listening to metal when he was 15. "All metalheads, all over the world, share a sort of brotherhood. We are a tribe, a group of likeminded individuals. It's hard to explain, but I feel accepted and loved when I am with my brothers and sisters in metal."

A 16-year-old from England discovered that brotherhood when his family uprooted and moved to Finland in his early teens: "In Finland, there are pretty much 20 metalheads for every square meter, so it really helped me make some friends at school."

"My experience with people into metal, goth or any other genre that kind of creates a romanticized version of the world are that they were people who felt pushed from childhood into adolescence," said a Missouri resident who has been listening to metal since he was 15. "They feel like outsiders with their peers. These types of music usually have subcultures that surround them that don't require someone to be the smartest, prettiest or most athletic to be accepted. They just have to enjoy the music."

Levitin found that music's ability to create social bonds is one of the reasons it is so popular and important. "Collective music-making may encourage social cohesions. Humans are social animals, and music may have historically served to promote feelings of group togetherness and synchrony, and may have been an exercise for other social acts such as turn-taking behaviors. Singing around the ancient campfire might have been a way to stay awake, to ward off predators, and to develop social coordination and social cooperation within the group," he wrote.

For those seeking a deeper sense of what metal means to its fans and musicians, the Middle East and North Africa offer some particularly potent examples. In these regions, musicians and fans literally risk their lives to play and listen to the music that means the most to them.

Baghdad teens Faisal Talal, Tony Aziz, Firas Al-Lateef, and Marwan Riyadh formed thrash-metal band Acrassicauda in 2001. They were longtime metal fans who wanted to perform the music they loved. Metal called to these boys for the same reason it calls to many teens: it's a comfort and escape from daily stress. "In my family there was a lot of tension and arguments that I witnessed and I hated everything about it, but I had to repress it and I couldn't really live my teenage years," Marwan said. "We were growing up so fast, so it was the anger in metal music that I identified with. I remember literally banging my head against the wall with my friends to the song 'Roots Bloody Roots' and when the song was finished I felt pacified."

THE COLUMBINE EFFECT

At first, Acrassicauda played covers of other popular heavy-metal songs, but soon began to write their own music. The band also wrote a pro-Saddam Hussein song, "Youth of Iraq," to appease the political powers-that-be and ensure that it would be safe for Acrassicauda to perform live.

When the United States and Britain launched air strikes against Iraq in 2003, the situation became more dangerous for Acrassicauda. They often dressed like Western metal fans, in black clothing and band t-shirts. "No one minded me dressing like that," Faisal said. "You used to be able to wear whatever. ... All that has changed now—since the U.S. invasion, it has become harder to dress freely. Now it's dangerous. After the occupation you could get killed for it. People would think you were devil worshippers or Americanized."

In 2004, *Vice* magazine published a piece on Acrassicauda and its struggle to make music in the fundamentalist country. The documentary *Heavy Metal in Baghdad* followed, earning the band worldwide attention—and death threats at home. It wasn't safe for them to stay in Iraq. Slowly, they were able to achieve refugee status. Bandmates moved to Syria, then Turkey, and eventually to the United States.

Vice sponsored the band's final show before they left Baghdad. Despite being held in a dangerous part of the city, dozens of fans turned up, proving just how important this music was to them. "I didn't think many would," Marwan said. "I was teary eyed—these people were really risking their lives to come and see us. Especially in such a place, it was too dangerous. So we did the concert, for like two hours, and it was a real rush. ... During that time we forgot about everything: the killing, the civil war, the bombs, and mortars. The music made us feel safe and relieved."

Baghdad isn't the only Arab city where heavy-metal fans have faced reprisals. In 1997, the government of Cairo arrested more than 80 metal fans, accusing them of Satanism—a crime punishable by death. All of the fans were released from jail 10 weeks later when prosecutors could find no evidence against them. However, the arrests forced metal music underground for many years, leaving bands and fans afraid they would run afoul of authorities again.

In 2003, 14 teen metal fans were arrested in Rabat, Morocco for such offenses as "possession of objects contrary to good morals." Their black T-shirts may have been part of the problem: "Normal people go to a concert in a shirt and tie," said the judge in the case. Some 500 people protested outside the Rabat parliament building. During an appeal of their case, 11 of the 14 were acquitted, but three were prosecuted for devil worship.

A U.S. anthropologist, Ted Swedenburg, studied the Cairo situation and the ways in which journalists following the arrests fostered a moral panic. Rather than questioning the imprisonment of fans, reporters "seemed to fan the flames of the panic," according to Swedenburg. "They offered tips on how to recognize Satan worshippers (black clothing, long hair on men); identified places where Satan worship was likely to occur (nightclubs, furnished flats); and described a variety of Satanic rituals (chanting, black candles, sexual depravity)." Not only did these details have nothing to do with the arrests, they're not even necessarily accurate depictions of Satanism.

These articles heightened Cairo's cultural anxieties about the broader social freedoms enjoyed by Egyptian youth and the influence of Western, particularly American, culture on those youth, according to Swedenburg. Raising the specter of Satanism heightened those anxieties. "The allegation of Satanism was serious enough," he said. "But the situation was exacerbated by religious doctrine. In Islamic law, it's a serious crime to abandon your faith. That's the main reason the government got involved." Kids were forced to cut their hair. Parents confiscated and destroyed heavy-metal CDs. Concerts were not permitted within the city.

However, as police controls eased, fans began gathering discreetly again—first in the outskirts of Cairo, and then towards the city center again. By 2006, heavy metal was enjoying a true resurgence in central Egypt. "The first step is always the hard one," said one metal musician named Noor. "People cannot get over all the negativities that happened in the past. We are Arab Muslims. We respect our religion. But we only love this music."

Cries in the Night

Though it may seem like undifferentiated noise to nonfans, metal is astonishingly diverse. It includes laid-back rock reminiscent of the 1970s and music that sounds, as *Rolling Stone* critic Robert Cherry described Slipknot, "a threshing machine devouring a military drum corps." Metal can be upbeat and poppy or extremely discordant. Looking at album covers and t-shirts won't necessarily tell you what a band will sound like.

Many qualities unite the genre: electric guitars, usually fed through some kind of distortion device; loud, often fast, drums and bass; powerful vocals. But bands take those sounds in many different directions. Saying you're a metal fan isn't enough to describe what you actually like.

Metalheads love to argue about the origins of metal. Some believe that the bands that inspired metal—including Deep Purple, Led Zeppelin and Black Sabbath—should be considered part of the gang. Others feel that these bands were merely prototypes, and that the genre really kicked off with Judas Priest, the Scorpions, Iron Maiden, and Dio, part of what's known as the New Wave of British Heavy Metal. They took the heavy 1970s sound and ran with it. They pushed their guitars to the limit, shredding louder, harder, and faster. In some cases, they added a second lead guitar for more bombast.

These bands have been around so long that you've probably heard of them, even if you haven't heard them. While younger generations listen to the original metal bands, just as teens in the '80s rocked out to Led Zeppelin, the Beatles, and the Doors, plenty of new bands are putting their own stamp on the traditional-metal sound, including Wolfmother, Manilla Road, Holy Grail and Witchcraft.

Classic metal songs follow a pretty universal template: verse, chorus, verse, chorus, guitar solo chorus. They're usually in 4/4 time and feature catchy guitar riffs, fast drumming, and soaring vocals. Many contemporary bands take this template and mess with it in at least one way. Maybe the song is in 7/4 time, or the drumming changes every few bars, or the singer growls instead. Each change creates a completely different sound, and yet it's all considered metal.

Glam metal is like classic metal's flashy younger brother. It has the same intense chords, strong drums and bass, and guitar solos, but takes those sounds to a more flamboyant place. The term "glam" refers more to the look than the sound, but the music's often glitzier, too.

Arguably the first glam-metal band was Van Halen, with its day-glo spandex pants, fringed shirts, and makeup. The glam scene exploded in the 1980s, particularly on Los Angeles' Sunset Strip, where Poison, Cinderella, Twisted Sister, Mötley Crüe, and Ratt stormed the stages. Many of these bands hit heavy rotation on MTV during metal's most popular years. Guns N' Roses became the most successful glam-metal act, though they soon left their glam roots behind, opting for a bluesier sound.

Glam metal suffered a serious blow in the early 1990s, when pop music fans rejected the glossy, outrageous style and embraced a new genre they felt was more "authentic": grunge. Nirvana, Pearl Jam, Alice in Chains, and Soundgarden wore thrift-store clothes and played sludgy, low-fi music that came off as democratic and accessible. But glam didn't die. Originals like Mötley Crüe reformed in the late 1990s. Modern bands, including The Darkness, Steel Panther, and Andrew W.K., incorporate glam-metal style into their sound, although Steel Panther is more of a satirical sendup of the early glam days.

Progressive metal, often called prog metal, tinkers with rhythm, meter, and arrangement. Often, these cues come from jazz and classical music—though they sound pretty different funneled through electric guitars. Prog-metal fans tend to get off on the genre's musicality and skill. Progressive metal can provide a deep sensory experience, but it's often appreciated on more of an intellectual level.

Rush and King Crimson were among the earliest prog influences, though neither would be considered a metal band. In the 1980s, metal outfits such as Queensrÿche and Dream Theater made prog their own—particularly Dream Theater, whose albums have gotten more and more complex and experimental with time. Tool also explored progressive elements in later albums, and even toured with King Crimson as a tribute to the band's influence.

Unlike glam, progressive metal has survived well beyond the 1970s and 1980s. Plenty of modern bands wear their prog influence proudly, including Opeth, Mastodon, Baroness, Ludicra, Cynic, and Coheed & Cambria.

If you take classic metal and step on the gas pedal, you'll get speed metal. It's played extremely fast, demanding heaps of skill and endurance. And if you think classic metal sounds aggressive, you wouldn't want to meet speed metal in a dark alley. Speed-metal fans are fond of its extreme intensity, as well as the talent it takes to perform.

Motörhead arguably kicked off the speed-metal movement in 1975, after bassist Lemmy Kilmeister left Hawkwind for something edgier. The genre quickly spawned dozens of bands, including Accept, Helloween, Overkill, and Nuclear Assault. Some bands also borrow from prog metal, boosting speed metal's reputation for virtuosity. Paul Gilbert of Racer X is known for his nimble-fingered guitar solos that blend high-speed riffs and unusual chord progressions, earning him a reputation as a guitarist's guitarist.

Lyrical topics run the gamut, but speed metal is one of the more political subgenres of metal, frequently focusing on war, pollution, nuclear fears, and capitalist greed. Though speed metal is one of the most influential genres, it has barely survived in its pure form. Some of speed metal's founders, such as Blind Guardian and Motörhead, still make music today. A handful of others, including Agent Steel, Primal Fear, and Gamma Ray emerged in later years to continue the speed-metal tradition.

If speed metal takes classic metal on a Le Mans course, thrash metal is more like a demolition derby. Original thrash bands Metallica, Slayer, Anthrax and Megadeth made it their mission to play faster, more aggressively, and more discordantly than what had come before. They even competed against each other to prove who could thrash hardest. Speed metal, though fast, can be elegant and pretty; thrash is choppy, angry, even ugly. Thrash bands frequently use that sound to relay political, oppositional messages in their songs.

"Emotionally and intellectually provocative, thrash was a harsh, healthy combination of social outrage and personal remorse. By exposing, lyrically and musically, how society ate people up alive, thrash ultimately brought people together from traditionally oppositional class cultures," Gaines wrote. "It illuminated as it relieved, accomplishing this across traditional aesthetic categories. Thrash is so fast it actually calms you down."

Founding thrashers continued to influence later bands, such as Suicidal Tendencies, Vio-lence, and Sadus, into the late 1980s. At the same time, the original bands mellowed as they matured, playing more straight-ahead rock and metal. Metallica's music, in particular, became more melodic and accessible, a move that left many fans feeling betrayed. Megadeth's later albums are more approachable, and more obviously based on blues and classical elements.

Plenty of bands still carry the thrash-metal torch, such as Lazarus A.D. and Municipal Waste. Meanwhile, the originals are still going strong; Slayer, Megadeth, Death Angel, and Metallica all released albums in recent years, while thrash's original "big four" toured together in 2010 and 2011.

Death metal is one offshoot of thrash metal that's not for the faint-hearted. The name alone is enough to make people uneasy, and that's part of the point. Death metal cranks up the distortion, while singers growl menacingly over complicated melodies with prog-style tempo changes. Death-metal drummers are known for "blast beats"—extremely fast rhythms played across different parts of the drum kit—that sound like an explosion of rhythm.

Death-metal singers perform in a so-called "Cookie Monster" style, a tongue-in-cheek jab that references the popular Muppet's gruff, gravelly voice. As it turns out, a deathly bellow is a great way to deliver songs about violence, including slasher-style horror violence; occult and anti-religious themes; social commentary and philosophy, which are death metal's mainstays. Sociologist Keith Kahn-Harris has speculated that the celebration of violence in death-metal music could be due to humans' fascination with the human body, part disgust and part desire.

THE COLUMBINE EFFECT

The term "death metal" was coined by Chuck Schuldiner of the band Death, one of the first in the genre. Bands such as Sepultura, Cannibal Corpse, Napalm Death, Deicide, Kreator, Celtic Frost, Obituary, and Morbid Angel helped cement death metal in the mid-1980s. By the late 1980s, dozens of bands had joined the death-metal ranks, though its extreme sound and subject matter kept it predominantly underground. It also spawned plenty of offshoots, including black metal.

You may have heard of black metal, if only because a tiny cluster of musicians have made this one of the most notorious metal genres, more for their antics than for the music. Some black-metal musicians fancy themselves modern-day Vikings who want to revive ancient pagan practices. A few have gone so far as to burn Scandinavia's historic churches, particularly in Norway, in rejection of Christianity's influence over the region.

Infighting within the Norwegian black metal scene led Burzum frontman Varg Vikernes to murder one of his rivals, Mayhem guitarist Øystein "Euronymous" Aarseth. Vikernes was additionally found guilty of burning three Norwegian churches. He served 16 years in prison for his crimes and was paroled in 2009. He has also supported National Socialist (Nazi) ideologies, something he shares with a smattering of other black-metal musicians.

These controversial aspects of early black-metal culture have spawned books and documentaries that study the scene in depth. But none has really been able to explain why this branch of the heavy-metal tree is so marked by violent and criminal behavior. To be fair, only a handful of musicians—all of whom knew Aarseth personally, either through his band or his black-metal record store in Oslo, called Helvete—committed these crimes. Others may have sanctioned them, but did not participate. While the music they made reflects their personal philosophies, the music did not make anyone commit arson or murder.

The majority of black-metal musicians stay out of trouble and focus on performing the music, one of the most extreme forms of metal. Black metal takes the fast, ballistic speed and blast-beat drumming of death metal and adds high, shrieking vocals. Many black-metal bands celebrate low production values, especially because early albums were produced on low-cost equipment in bands' basements or garages. Some intentionally sought out the worst equipment they could find. This low-fi sound was intended as a rejection of the glossy production values used by the rest of the music industry.

If you're getting the sense that black metal serves as a rejection of the mainstream (even of mainstream metal), you're on the right track. Its lyrics sometimes focus on misanthropy and anti-Christian sentiment, appealing to listeners who feel like outcasts even among outcasts.

Some fans may be drawn to black metal because they've read about these notorious musicians. But they usually stick around because they appreciate the music for its own sake. Some like what the lyrics say. Others may not understand them —black-metal singing is fairly difficult to decipher. Still others see the bleak, nihilistic songs as metaphors for darkness in their own lives.

Some well-known early black-metal bands include Bathory, Hellhammer, Sodom, Ancient Rites, and Venom. Their influence led to a second wave of bands such as Gorgoroth, Emperor, Satyricon, Darkthrone, and Carpathian Forest. Black metal is one of the most active subgenres today, although bands have begun to blur the lines between black metal and industrial, ambient, and even shoegaze.

Black-metal music can be challenging even for fans who love other kinds of heavy metal. But for some, it can become just as satisfying. A 16-year-old from Florida told me that he was a devout Christian when he downloaded all of Gorgoroth's albums and began listening to them. "This music scared the living crap out of me. And that is the reason I kept coming back. It scared me. I was scared of it, and I couldn't tell myself to turn it off when it started playing," he said. "Over time, it grew on me and didn't scare me as much as the first couple of times listening to it, but nonetheless it helped me venture further in my quest for the heavy metal underground."

Although black metal has remained mostly an underground phenomenon, its notoriety has earned it plenty of scrutiny in the mainstream press. In response to the anti-Christian themes of black metal, some musicians created unblack metal, also known as Christian black metal.

"For most kids, black metal is fun, entertainment, culture; much of their imagery is appropriated from movies and comics to begin with," according to Gaines. "While most kids view this stuff [black metal etc.] like carnival amusement, as art, as a means of expressing profound anxiety and the frustrations of living, adults take it seriously, undermining whatever confidence kids would have had in their abilities to make sense of an overwhelming world."

Not all black metal—in fact, not all heavy metal—is Satanic, but there are plenty of bands who play up the Satanism angle, either symbolically or for theatrics. Slayer's music, for example, might be infused with references to the Devil, but the musicians themselves aren't practicing Satanists. Slayer frontman Tom Araya is a Catholic who recognizes the stark line between song lyrics and religious beliefs: "People have these heavy issues and ask, 'Isn't this a problem for you?' and no. I'm well-rounded, I have a really strong belief system and these are just words and they'll never interfere with what I believe and how I feel," he told the *Edmonton Sun*. "People are not in good shape to where they have to question their own belief system because of a book or a story somebody wrote, or a Slayer song."

With other bands, the line is blurred, if it exists at all. Black-metal band Watain goes to great lengths to convince listeners that it is bringing Satanic religious rites to the rock stage, complete with "sacrifices" and dark lyrics. "The dark nature within us—we have a genuine affection for it, and we need to express that. We need to put that into music," frontman Erik Danielsson said in an interview with *Invisible Oranges*. One recent metal band, Ancient VVisdom, take the acoustic-metal sound popularized by Guns N' Roses, Days of the New and Godsmack, but sing heartfelt odes to the Devil, arguably making them more akin to Christian-rock acts whose music is predominantly devotional.

And then there's Ghost BC, the Sweden-based metal act whose musicians are cloaked in black robes while their frontman, Papa Emeritus, wears a cardinal's hat and skeleton makeup. Their infectious songs, influenced by Blue Oyster Cult and the Beach Boys, get you humming along before you realize they're all about how wonderful Satan is. The band's flair for theatrics makes it tough to tell whether they're serious—or whether it's all in fun. Either way, they're poised to become the most mainstream Satanism-inspired band Satanism in history.

Metal has a reputation for flirting with pagan ideas. But it also has a reputation for rebellion, and some bands rebel against the metal mainstream by championing Christian ideas. Christian metal, sometimes known as white metal, is defined by its philosophy rather than its sound. Christian-metal bands run the gamut from polished, melodic pop-metal to deep, growly sludge.

Christian metal emerged in the 1970s but didn't become widely known until Styper hit it big. Stryper adopted the glam-metal look (down to the colorful spandex pants) and released albums with titles such as "To Hell with the Devil" and "In God We Trust." Few Christian metal bands have achieved Stryper's commercial success, but fans had plenty like-minded groups to choose from, including Whitecross, Guardian, Warrior, and Bride.

The genre even spawned its own magazine, *Heaven's Metal,* which launched in 1985 and is still going. Christian metal hit the mainstream again in the 2000s when POD, rooted in grunge, blues, and nu metal, outsold Stryper to become the most successful act in the genre.

Between the "cookie monster" vocals, the shrieking, the distortion, and the blast beats, you may be wondering whether metal offers anything you'd enjoy hearing. If your teen likes power metal, you're in luck. Power metal features classical-inspired, epic music with clean, soaring vocals. It's a little faster than traditional heavy metal, but lacks the frantic pace and aggression of speed and thrash.

Many power-metal songs sound like anthems worthy of cheering, waving flags, and pumping your fists. They're often inspired by fantasy, myth, and literature—suitable subjects for such sweeping, epic music. For example, Blind Guardian's *Nightfall in Middle-Earth* is inspired by J.R.R. Tolkein's books, while Iced Earth's *Horror Show* is based on horror stories, including Bram Stoker's *Dracula.* Jag Panzer's *Thane to the Throne* is a power-metal rendition of Shakespeare's *Macbeth.* In power metal, fans get a literature lesson along with their rock 'n' roll.

Take the epic, symphonic bombast of power metal and add operatic vocals, keyboards, and violins, and what do you get? Symphonic metal. It's still metal—with plenty of electric guitars, heavy bass, and drums. But if any branch of the heavy-metal tree proves the genre borrows heavily from classical, it's this one. Symphonic metal has as much in common with Beethoven's Ninth as it does with "Smoke on the Water."

Its lyrics tend to focus on myth and fantasy. In many cases, bands will produce "concept" albums or epic pieces based on these subjects.

Symphonic metal was inspired by early gothic, death, and progressive metal. It came into its own in the mid-1990s with debut albums from Nightwish, Within Temptation, and others. Epica and Therion borrow symphonic-metal elements without belonging wholeheartedly to the genre. Symphonic metal has recently splintered, spawning symphonic gothic metal, symphonic black metal, symphonic power metal, and others.

Folk music seems like it would go as well with heavy metal as spots go with plaid. But many bands combine the two in a way that melds the warm, acoustic feel of folk instruments and the bombast of electric guitars. Folk metal features the same elements as other metal genres but adds a host of old-time instruments, including fiddle, flute, hurdy-gurdy, and many others. Although some folk-metal bands keep the tempo mellow, others play at blistering tempos, making it clear that this is still heavy-metal music. Their lyrics often explore myth, fantasy, nature, history, and paganism.

England's Skyclad became one of the first folk-metal acts when they married thrash-metal guitars, drums and bass with fiddle. Meanwhile, Finland's Amorphis combined Scandinavia-infused metal with acoustic elements, often drawing lyrical inspiration from Finland's rich mythic tradition.

From there, the genre branched out into medieval metal, inspired by Western European music and instruments of the Middle Ages; Celtic metal, featuring the themes and instruments of Celtic folk music; and Oriental metal, informed by musical traditions of the Middle East and Far East.

Folk metal is a relative latecomer to the metal scene, but has exploded in the 21st Century with bands such as Finland's Korpiklaani, the Faroe Islands' Tyr, Latvia's Skyforger, Italy's Elvenking, Switzerland's Eluveitie, and Brazil's Tuatha de Danaan—a Celtic-metal outfit. Folk metal has already sparked one subgenre: pirate metal, popularized by a Scottish band called Alestorm.

Even parents who balk at the idea of a genre called "stoner metal" probably listened to some of its ancestors, particularly the blues rock and psychedelic rock of the 1960s and 1970s. Sometimes called stoner rock, this genre also takes cues from classic and doom metal. It's more downtempo than typical heavy metal, and features a sludgy, loose guitar style with prominent bass. In a nod to stoner metal's roots, the psychedelic-tinged music is often recorded in a low-fidelity style. Despite the name, songs do not typically focus on marijuana usage, although many fans tend to be pot smokers. Some say stoner metal's laid-back tempos are a good accompaniment to getting high.

Stoner metal was inspired by a host of classic bands, including Black Sabbath's heavy riffs, Blue Oyster Cult's melodic sound, and Hawkwind's psychedelia. Some have suggested that Soundgarden—one of the predominant grunge bands to emerge from Seattle in the late 1980s—was one of the first stoner-metal acts. Kyuss was another. Today, stoner metal runs the gamut from very sludgy, impenetrable metal played by Sleep and High on Fire to melodic and almost pop-hued rock from acts like Queens of the Stone Age.

After grunge and hip-hop surpassed metal took over the airwaves in the early 1990s, metal took some time to regroup. The new wave of metal embraced its usurpers, birthing nu metal, a hybrid of metal, rap, and grunge elements. The music is loud and aggressive, but often melodic and quite listenable. Lyrics borrow from the introspection of grunge-rock, focusing on personal struggles, angst, and alienation.

Nu metal rejected the virtuosity of earlier metal acts,

avoiding flashy composition; even guitar solos are rare. Nu metal's roots are especially broad, taking cues from metal-fusion acts like the Red Hot Chili Peppers and Faith No More, as well as hip hop (particularly the Beastie Boys) and grunge (Nirvana). Nu metal's superstars including Slipknot, Soulfly, Korn, and Limp Bizkit.

After black metal, industrial metal is one of metal's most notorious siblings, mostly through no fault of its own. This music has been the favorite of violent teens and young adults, including Columbine High School shooters Eric Harris and Dylan Klebold.

It's also one of metal's most hybridized genres, borrowing from industrial music, thrash and heavy metal, and electronic music. Industrial metal embraces both electric guitars and electronic instruments (keyboards and computers), which most metal bands avoid on the grounds that they're not "authentic." "Industrial" earned its name because many of the sounds resemble noises you would hear in a factory or other machine-based environment. Groundbreaking industrial bands, including Ministry, Nine Inch Nails, and Godflesh, incorporated electric guitars into their sample-based music in the 1990s, accidentally giving birth to industrial metal.

A number of very big-name—and sometimes controversial—acts have followed, including White Zombie (and singer Rob Zombie), Marilyn Manson, Rammstein, and KMFDM. Some of their lyrics explore drugs and violence, while White Zombie and Marilyn Manson both adopted horror-themed makeup and costumes. KMFDM and Rammstein were among Harris and Klebold's top bands. Rammstein has occasionally used Nazi imagery in its videos and album artwork, even though the German-based band is vehemently anti-racist.

As intense and extreme as metal can be, there are many kids who begin listening to it precisely because they crave that intensity. Either it's part of their temperament, or life is stressful and difficult enough that they crave music that resonates with their experience. Other times, teens just aim straight for the noisiest, most offensive music they can find in order to put distance between themselves and their peers, or even between themselves and their parents. Either way, they know exactly why they like metal and what purpose it serves in their lives.

Teens also know when the music is too much. Some indeed pick the harshest of the harsh, but plenty of others don't. "A lot of bands and albums were too intense for me, including speed metal and death metal," said a German mom who became a metal fan when she was 16.

"A lot of the speed and death bands I couldn't hang with," said a Phoenix, Arizona, resident who started listening to metal when he was 13. "Slayer, I felt, was out of my league."

"I got bored quickly with the slash-and-gore lyrics of Cannibal Corpse and other death metal bands," said a fan from Arizona who became a metal fan at age 12. "There was no real substance to that kind of music."

"Some of the Satanic stuff got a little over the top. Deicide, Slayer, Cannibal Corpse, stuff like that. Sometimes I wasn't into listening to some low-Earth-rumbling 'singing' about spilling God's blood," said a San Francisco Bay Area fan who started listening to metal when he was 11.

Sometimes, a fan's religious beliefs will prevent him or her from listening to certain genres of metal. "There are band that are way too aggressive or Anti-Christ, like Slayer, Dimmu Borgir, Gorgoroth, etc.," said Dian, a 16-year-old in the Netherlands who started listening to metal when she was 12. "I'm a Christian, so I don't listen to that."

Others just find some themes distasteful. "I relish intensity, though I still find some lyrical themes are a bit too much for me, like with Torsofuck and other gore-grind/cybergore bands," said Chris, a 16-year-old living near London who became a metal fan when he was 14—and now runs his own black-metal record label. "I'm not keen on the whole 'You just got raped by elephants' lyrical theme, nor that of having sex with a body you just dug up from the ground. I know it's only for show, but it's not all that palatable for me."

Yes, some metal lyrics do go that far. But so do the "oddly enough" news stories floating around the Internet, horror novels, even comic books. And most teens will react the same way most adults do: with a mixture of, "Ew, that's horrible" and, "Why would anyone write that?" A few keep listening, out of fascination or a need to shock people. But teens aren't the unblinking sponges we often take them for. Every metal fan finds his or her own intensity level—or most of them do, anyway. When fans were asked whether any particular band, album, or genre was too much for them, one 20-year-old responded, "Never. There have been a lot of albums that weren't intense enough, though."

Whatever their tastes, metal fans universally found that the genre helped them get in touch with themselves, comfort themselves, and find confidence in a frequently disheartening world.

"I used to get bullied a lot on the way home from school. It would make me upset and angry, so I went home and blasted some metal through the speakers, and it helped me calm down a lot and made me stand up to them eventually," said Neal, a 16-year-old Scottish fan who started listening to metal when he was 6. After listening to heavy metal, "I was a better person. I was more true to myself about who I was inside."

One Portugese teen said his mom approached him and asked whether he wanted to see a psychologist because of his musical interests. "That didn't make me think different about my music. I just felt well listening to metal," he said. "When I started to listen to metal, I became a little more sociable, I don't know why. I also became calmer, because I used to be very aggressive and slightly anti-social."

But another mom—and metal fan—said she looks forward to the time when her young son discovers rebellious music. "I hope he will have a phase in his teenaged years where he wears his hair down to his ass and listens to horrible music that will have me banging against his door, shouting at him," she said. "If not, what else will he do to piss off his parents? What or who will he turn to find a 'mirror' for the feelings and thoughts inside him? Where will he turn to to battle that anguish, insecurity, pain that growing up puts inside him?"

Appendix
Teens and Mental Health

Tony[*] was a bright, outgoing, and very social teenager. He attended tons of parties and girls loved him; he seemed to have a new girlfriend every few weeks. He excelled at languages and athletics, including badminton and archery. He was rebellious at times, sneaking cigarettes and taking his parents' car without asking. He slept late on weekends and thought going on vacation with his family was lame. Toward the end of his teenage years he became interested in photography and art, and after he graduated high school, went away to art school to develop his skills.

When he came home for Christmas break, the difference was dramatic. He had lost weight. He kept to his room and didn't talk much. In addition, his artwork had changed. Originally, it was experimental, but now it was much darker, his sister Kamali[*] recalls. "It was more provocative with violent undertones: images of bodies half skeletal, in sexual poses, that sort of thing. My family assumed he was trying to be shocking, because of being at art school. We thought it was like a late adolescent [phase]."

As it turns out, Tony's return home came just weeks after he began experiencing symptoms of schizophrenia, including frequent visual and auditory hallucinations. He hid the condition from his family, predominantly because he was afraid they would institutionalize him. He went unmedicated for 11 years, fighting off the hallucinations that were much

---

[*]   Not their real names.

worse during periods of stress. He is now being treated, though the symptoms haven't gone away.

"Even on medication he has many hallucinations a day," Kamali says. "He'll be sitting on the couch watching TV and a car will seem to drive through the room. Or he'll be in a lecture and someone will talk to him (always a male voice) or a dead body will roll over." In nearly two decades, the longest he's gone without hallucinations is five days.

Kamali stumbled upon her brother's mental illness when she urged him to see a doctor for an unrelated medical issue. When he came back, he told her that the doctor had prescribed Abilify, which she discovered was for his schizophrenia. Her whole family was surprised; they do not have a history of mental disorders, she says.

Even with treatment, Tony is still very different from the outgoing teen he once was. He's more reserved and doesn't like to talk as much. He has a much harder time trusting people, and no longer makes friends easily. He currently lives with his domestic partner—whom he says is more helpful in keeping him stable. "Not the meds, the shrink, or the therapists, but having someone really check in with him every day about how he is doing," Kamali says.

Looking for the Signs

After Adam Lanza went on his shooting rampage in Newtown, Conn., Liza Long, the mother of a violent teen, wrote an essay that circulated on The Blue Review, Huffington Post, and others. In it, Liza wrote, "I love my son. But he terrifies me. A few weeks ago, Michael pulled a knife and threatened to kill me and then himself after I asked him to return his overdue library books. His 7 and 9 year old siblings knew the safety plan —they ran to the car and locked the doors before I even asked them to. I managed to get the knife from Michael, then methodically collected all the sharp objects in the house into a single Tupperware container that now travels with me. Through it all, he continued to scream insults at me and threaten to kill or hurt me."

Liza also explained that her son doesn't have a definitive

diagnosis, something her family and doctors can identify and treat. Even if they did know exactly what's wrong, they have struggled to obtain support—both from the healthcare world and from law enforcement. She objected to the closure of long-term care facilities for the severely mentally ill, violent or no. And she criticized the existing system for sending violently ill boys and men like her son to jail for short periods, rather than giving them the medical treatment they—and their families—need.

When an adolescent develops such violent tendencies early, they're easier to identify for what they are—even if they're not so easy to resolve. But when a teen seemingly transforms overnight, as Kamali's brother did, it's tougher to pin down the cause. Is it just a hormonal phase? Could it be the angry music he suddenly likes, or the violent video games she's been playing? Adolescence is full of emotional and behavioral turmoil. How do you know when it's "just part of growing up," and when it's something more serious?

In some cases, like Tony's, a mental-health diagnosis can come as a surprise. Tony was able to successfully hide his condition for years, and his family assumed that the change in his demeanor and artwork was the product of a semester at art school. It is common for families not to recognize the signs of mental illness, which is one reason they are so likely to look at other factors—such as personal interests—when a child commits suicide.

If a family doesn't have any history of depression, bipolar disorder, schizophrenia, or other mental-health problems, family members may not be aware of the symptoms. On the other hand, families with a tendency toward mental illness also may not see it in their kids right away. This can happen particularly when parents are already coping with their own mental-health issues or when they're hoping their kids won't develop the same problems.

Some people may be surprised at how many different kinds of people are touched by mental illness, particularly depression, the most common form. Straight-A students, star athletes, good-looking people, and popular people are just as susceptible to depression as others. Some folks can appear to have a lot of good things happening, but they're miserable inside. In many cases, though, there are clues that something is amiss beneath the surface.

In our culture, mental illness still carries plenty of stigma. Often, people who are depressed or riding the manic-depressive rollercoaster may feel like it's somehow their fault. Some think it's a sign of weakness or a personality flaw. Or they may feel like if they can just think the right way about their situation, they'll be able to overcome their illness without treatment. But most mental illnesses are like chronic physical illnesses—they often do not improve or go away without proper treatment. Feeling ashamed is understandable, but don't let that get in the way of getting help.

Undiagnosed mental illness can get worse, particularly if it also goes untreated. Teenagers who are already struggling with typical hormonal woes will find life even more difficult to navigate when they're also depressed, suffering manic episodes, or experiencing psychotic thinking. Academic and social development can suffer. And, in the worst cases, kids seriously consider harming themselves or others.

Substance Abuse

Many teens try out a variety of drugs during their adolescence, and a small percentage of them become heavy users or even addicts. The most popular drug among teens is alcohol. Roughly 42 percent of high-school students used alcohol in 2009, according to the Centers for Disease Control. That same year, 24 percent of high schoolers said they had occasionally drunk heavily or binged on alcohol.

Meanwhile, marijuana is the most popular illicit drug. In 2009, 21 percent of high schoolers said they had used pot. Three percent said they'd used cocaine, 7 percent said they'd used ecstasy, 12 percent had used inhalants, 4 percent had used methamphetamines (speed), 2 percent had used heroin and 8 percent had used hallucinogens. When it comes to prescription drugs, 20 percent of high-school students had taken one or more, including oxycontin, percocet, vicodin, adderall, ritalin, and others.

Drugs fall into a few main categories: stimulants or "uppers," depressants or "downers," psychedelics, and inhalants. Uppers include anything that stimulates the nervous system, causing the heart to beat faster, boosting blood pressure, and creating a sense of confidence in the user. Cocaine, speed, caffeine, nicotine, and ritalin are all uppers. Downers slow down the heart and relax the body, lower inhibitions and subdue anxiety. Alcohol, heroin, anti-anxiety medicines, muscle relaxants, and painkillers are all downers. Psychedelics create an altered state of reality, often including delusions or hallucinations, as with LSD, "magic" mushrooms, ecstasy, peyote, marijuana, hash, and herbs such as belladonna, jimson weed, datura, salvia, and even nutmeg. Inhalants such as glue, gasoline, metallic paints, and household sprays cause dizziness, drowsiness, and stupor.

Not every teen who tries these drugs becomes addicted. Some never use drugs and some experiment once in a while because they're curious, but it never goes beyond that. Some teens only use drugs socially—among friends, after school or particularly at parties. Once in a while, a teen begins using a drug regularly, such as smoking pot or drinking every weekend. A few get to the point where they continue using a drug regularly, even though its effects aren't as strong as they were before, the side effects are causing problems, or drug use is interfering with day-to-day life. And, in some cases, a teen will become physically or psychologically dependent on a drug. Many drugs are addictive, but the most addictive are nicotine and heroin.

Adolescents try drugs for a variety of reasons: to get high, to boost their confidence or energy levels, to find relief from physical or psychological pain, to impress their friends, or simply because they're bored and looking for something to do. Kids who have been bullied or abused, who live in poverty, who have mental or emotional disturbances, who lack self-esteem, who have friends that use drugs, or who have permissive families are more likely to use drugs.

It's hard to say exactly how many teens are addicted to drugs. A 2001 study from the National Center on Addiction and Substance Abuse at Columbia University found that 85.7

percent of teens who had tried smoking kept at it, and that 83.3 percent of teens who had been drunk were continuing to get drunk regularly. Among those who had tried pot, 76.4 percent were still smoking it.

Drugs can lead to more serious consequences. Teens who smoked pot weekly said they were six times more likely to skip classes. Because teens are inexperienced with drinking and drugs, they may overdo it, running a greater risk of overdose or alcohol poisoning. And, since so many teens think they are invincible, they may think they're not going to overdose or become addicted. Drugs may delay some aspects of physical, mental, and psychological development, in part because they distract the user from learning through their real-world experiences.

It can be very important to get treatment for teens who are abusing or addicted to drugs. With many drugs, it can be difficult and even physically harmful to go "cold turkey" without medical supervision. Recovery takes time, structure, and support to be effective, particularly because so many drug users do not want to quit.

Depression

Depression is one of the most common mental-health challenges for teenagers as well as adults, and it can be particularly difficult to recognize in teens because so many of its symptoms can be mistaken for run-of-the-mill teenage angst and rebellion.

Often, the symptoms of depression are more persistent and more gripping. They include sadness that doesn't go away, loss of interest in favorite activities, discouragement, and a loss of self-worth. Teens may hide their sadness and tears from their parents, but depression can manifest in other ways— particularly as persistent irritability. In boys especially, depression can mimic anger or defiant behavior beyond what's typical for teenagers.

Depression is frequently, but not always, linked to a serious event in a teenager's life, such as the breakup of an important romance or friendship, a death, social problems or bullying at school, academic challenges, or turmoil at home. It can also be brought on by chemical imbalances in the brain, making the sufferer feel sad or disinterested, and sometimes as though life isn't worth living. In the latter case, schoolwork, family ties, and friendships can suffer as the teen spirals deeper into depression.

Teens who have survived childhood abuse or who have a history of chronic illness, poor social skills, unstable home life, stressful life events, or depression in the family are at risk for developing serious depression.

If a teen exhibits one or more of the following behaviors for two weeks or longer, he or she may need help: missing curfews or other unusual defiance; increase or decrease in appetite; sudden weight gain or loss; criminal behavior; depressed or irritable mood; difficulty concentrating or making decisions; forgetfulness; sleeping too much or not enough; fatigue; excessive guilty feelings; relationships with family and friends falling apart; a drop in school performance; feelings of worthlessness; decreased interest in favorite activities; substance abuse; bad temper; increased isolation from peers; or thoughts about suicide or plans to commit suicide.

Some depression can manifest with psychotic symptoms, causing the person to lose touch with reality and even hallucinate. They may hear voices criticizing them, telling them they're not good enough, or even telling them to commit suicide.

A family doctor can begin to investigate these symptoms, and perform tests to rule out any physical causes for these symptoms. From there, a qualified mental-health practitioner (such as a psychiatrist or psychologist) should also evaluate the teen to determine whether there are any other mental issues at work, such as bipolar disorder or schizophrenia.

Treatment may include medication, psychotherapy, and/or regular visits with your family doctor. Therapy for the whole family may also be a good idea, particularly when the teen's depression is triggered by family tensions or when it's causing tension within the family.

Mania

In mental health, mania is often considered the opposite of depression. Manic phases are marked by agitation, irritation, increased energy or even hyperactivity, poor impulse control, racing thoughts, inflated self-esteem, little need for sleep, overcommitment to activities, and reckless behavior such as binge eating, sexual promiscuity, and spending sprees. People who are in a manic period may also be easily distracted and prone to temper flare-ups.

Mania is often seen in people who have bipolar disorder, sometimes known as manic-depression because it involves weeks or months of depression followed by similar phases of mania. There are several kinds of bipolar disorder, and they describe people who experience manic and depressive phases with different levels of severity. These conditionsß are caused by disturbances in the parts of the brain that regulate mood.

It's important to know that people with bipolar disorder are at a heightened risk of suicidal feelings, and getting treatment is essential. A family doctor can begin the process of diagnosis, but at some point it's a good idea to see a psychiatrist for a thorough work-up.

The doctor may prescribe antipsychotic medications, mood stabilizers, and/or lithium to help moderate the symptoms. Antipsychotic drugs can be particularly helpful for someone whose illness has progressed to the point where he or she has lost touch with reality. Anti-anxiety drugs may also help, depending on the circumstances, and some psychiatrists will prescribe electroconvulsive therapy, which is one of the most effective treatments for depression that doesn't go away with other medications.

Teens can be particularly susceptible to bipolar disorder, as it usually emerges between the ages of 15 and 25. People with this illness often need help remembering to take their medication, and to get enough sleep, which can help stabilize moods in bipolar folks. Psychotherapy can also help, particularly during depressive phases and with ensuring compliance with medication.

Psychotic Thinking

Some teens experience auditory or visual hallucinations, which can make it difficult to tell the difference between reality and the images or sounds produced by the mind. While the most common cause of psychotic thinking is schizophrenia, it's also occasionally seen among teens with severe depression or bipolar disorder.

Psychotic thinking can really be a challenge, particularly for teens. The constant barrage of auditory and visual fictions disrupt day-to-day thoughts and activities, emotions, and the ability to function at work and among friends and family. Although doctors don't know what causes hallucinations, some factors, including a family history of them, or psychological and social stresses, may be involved.

From the outside, hallucinations can be difficult to recognize, especially at first. However, there are some hallmarks, including strange physical behavior; false beliefs or delusions that do not relate to reality; signs that the person is seeing or hearing things that are not there; and disordered thinking, in which the person's thoughts seem to jump between unrelated topics. Teens with schizophrenia may also display "flat affect"—in which they appear to have no mood at all.

There are five types of schizophrenia, each with its own set of symptoms. Some schizophrenics show agitation, a reduced sensitivity to pain, negative feelings, motor problems or rigid muscles, stupor, and may become unable to take care of themselves. In other cases, the person becomes unusually angry, anxious, argumentative, and experiences delusions that they are being followed or persecuted, or that they are better and more successful than they actually are. Still others may experience child-like behavior, delusions or hallucinations, little or no mood, or repetitive behaviors. They may also laugh at inappropriate times, become incoherent, or withdraw from social situations. Some will have symptoms of more than one type.

There is no formal test for schizophrenia. A doctor will interview the patient and his or her family for a history of symptoms, as well as to gather some family history and find out whether the symptoms have responded to any forms of treatment. There are a number of medications, including antipsychotics, which can help treat schizophrenia—but many of them have side effects, from sleepiness and weight gain to restlessness. Therapy can also help, particularly with the social setbacks many schizophrenics experience.

People with schizophrenia often need a lifetime of support to help them remain on medication, in housing, and in the work world. If they abandon treatment, their symptoms can return and worsen.

Anxiety

Almost everyone worries, but for some people, anxiety can become extreme and constant, even debilitating. Some teens have a lot of trouble controlling their worries and fears. As a result, they may have trouble concentrating on other aspects of life, from friends to homework. Their worries are typically out of proportion with the situation they are worrying about. They often experience fatigue, irritability, muscle tension, restlessness and feeling "on edge," and may have trouble falling asleep or staying asleep.

Teens whose anxieties become severe can develop other mental conditions, such as panic disorder or depression, so it's important to seek treatment. Treatment can include psychotherapy, especially cognitive behavioral therapy, which trains patients to change their thoughts and behavior patterns to avoid problematic ones.

Defiance

Most teens are a little bit rebellious. However, for some teens this conduct can develop into a pattern of hostile, defiant, and disobedient behavior toward authority figures. It can include arguing with adults, being in frequent trouble at school, being angry and resenting others, blaming others for their own mistakes, frequent loss of temper, being touchy or annoyed easily, or often seeking revenge on others.

Although many children resist authority to some extent,

these behaviors are marked by their difference from the behavior of peers the same age. If it begins to significantly interfere with school or social life, a teen may have something called oppositional defiant disorder. It's diagnosed in roughly 20 percent of school-age children, though that figure may be skewed because of racial, cultural, and gender biases. The behavior usually begins by the age of 8.

Children with signs of this disorder should be evaluated by a psychiatrist or psychologist, who may also examine whether the subject has attention deficit hyperactivity disorder. Treatment can include therapy, management by parents, and/or medication, depending on the specific diagnosis and causes of behavior. It's important to treat, as many children with oppositional defiant disorder become adults with conduct disorder, which is similar—and can lead to incarceration.

Violent and Criminal Behavior

In rare cases, a teen develops a pattern of manipulating and violating the rights of others, often criminally. They may break the law repeatedly, as though the rules don't apply to them; they lie, steal, and fight frequently, they disregard their own safety and the safety of others, and they show little or no guilt. They may be arrogant and unjustifiably angry, and may abuse drugs. At the same time, they are often able to act witty and charming, using flattery and manipulation to cover up their behavior. They also tend to think highly of themselves and their ability to get away with their behavior.

Although the causes of this behavior are unknown, it's seemingly more prevalent among males, and is thought to be linked to childhood abuse, genetic factors, or both. Younger children who set fires and harm animals may move on to manipulative criminal activity in their teens. This behavior is often called antisocial personality disorder, psychopathy, or sociopathy.

Symptoms tend to peak during the teenage years, though the condition often goes undiagnosed until adulthood. Dave Cullen, the author of *Columbine*, uncovered evidence that Columbine High School shooter Eric Harris was a sociopath by age 17. It's unknown how many other school shooters have the disorder. Many adult serial killers also fit the profile.

Treating this condition is difficult, predominantly because people who have it often refuse treatment until they are court-ordered to get help.

Self-Harm

Self-harm is the term for many types of behavior in which a person is injuring him- or herself deliberately. It is often done to provide temporary relief from emotional pain, and in many cases is found in people who are suffering from depression, schizophrenia, borderline personality disorder, or anxiety disorders. Most self-harm takes the form of making superficial cuts into the skin, though burning, self-poisoning, and alcohol and drug overdose also fall into this category. Most self-inflicted wounds are found on parts of the body that aren't regularly exposed; this allows the person to hide what's happening and avoid scrutiny or creating worry in others.

Many who engage in self-harming behavior say they do it to help themselves disassociate from other issues, particularly emotional pain and agitation. In part, this may happen because the injury can release endorphins, which provide natural pain relief and a calm, relaxed feeling. One recent study, reported in *Scientific American*, found that self-harm does create a moment of intense pain, followed by a long period of relief as that pain fades away. This can alleviate any other discomfort the self-harming person is feeling at the time, including emotional pain.

"Imagine that one morning you visit the doctor for a routine check-up, and later that afternoon the doctor's office calls to inform you that you're in the advanced stages of cancer and have weeks to live. ... Now imagine that the doctor's office calls back five minutes later and tells you that they mixed up your lab work with someone else's—you're actually in good health. You would not immediately go back to how you felt before the first phone call; rather, you would feel extreme relief, lasting for hours or even days. Note that it was not a reward (e.g., winning the lottery) that made you feel better, only the introduction and removal of something unpleasant," Joseph Franklin wrote in *Scientific American*.

Although self-harm is found in people of all ages, it's most common in people under the age of 25. Self-harm is not considered suicidal behavior. However, sometimes the injury is so severe that it can be life-threatening. In addition, this pattern is common among people who may develop suicidal feelings.

Suicidal Thoughts and Behavior

Although no single mental condition will necessarily lead someone to consider or commit suicide, roughly 90 percent of all suicides are related to mental illness or mood disorders. Teens, in particular, are vulnerable to suicide, which in 2007 was the third leading cause of death for people ages 15 to 24. Granted, that's in part because teens enjoy a lower natural-mortality rate than many other age groups. However, among teens age 15 to 19, there were nearly 7 deaths by suicide per 100,000. Some experts estimate that 500,000 teens attempt suicide every year, and 6,000 succeed. That's 18 every day.

In part, adolescents are likely to try to take their lives because they believe there's nothing that can help them, they don't want to tell anyone that they're having problems, they think it's weak to seek help, or they don't know where to go for help. Teens who are considering suicide may feel that they are doing their friends and family a favor by removing themselves from the world. They may feel as though they are nothing but trouble, or a burden, for their loved ones. Some teens may not realize just how permanent suicide is. Other times, they make a suicidal gesture because it's the only way they can think of to communicate their pain—but sometimes these gestures go too far, and wind up being fatal.

Early signs that someone is thinking of ending his or her life include periods of depression, impulsive or nervous behavior, saying or showing that they feel guilty, or marked anxiety and tension. They may also begin giving away their belongings or sorting out their affairs. Sudden changes in behavior, such as calm after a period of anxiety, can also be a warning sign. In teens, other actions can provide red flags, such as a loss of interest in favorite activities, worsening school performance, dramatic shifts in sleeping or eating patterns, withdrawal from friends and social activities, and extreme irritability. As their suicidal feelings worsen, they may actually attempt or threaten to kill themselves.

"Suicide is the end result of a complex mix of pathology, character, and circumstance that produces severe emotional distress," wrote Susan Klebold, mother of Columbine killer Dylan Klebold, who committed suicide at the end of the massacre. "This distress is so great that it impairs one's ability to think and act rationally. From the writings Dylan left behind, criminal psychologists have concluded that he was depressed and suicidal. When I first saw copied pages of these writings, they broke my heart. I'd had no inkling of the battle Dylan was waging in his mind."

Even though some teens who mention suicide may simply be longing for more attention and care, such threats—as well as attempts—should be taken seriously. Roughly a third of people who attempt suicide will repeat the attempt within a year, and 10 percent who make suicide threats and attempts ultimately end their lives. Mental-health care is important in such circumstances and should be located right away.

As this book is written, the media is paying increasing attention to a spate of suicides among gay teenage boys, many of whom were bullied, and among young women who were sexually assaulted and later taunted about their assaults. Many teens are vulnerable to bullying for a variety of reasons—many of which add up to the idea that they're different from their peers in some way. Although school officials and other adults are beginning to learn how to end bullying, it will be a while before the behavior goes away. And, unfortunately, some kids who are bullied will be pushed so far that they end their lives.

People who are feeling suicidal need to hear that others have survived suicidal feelings and have recovered from them—and were thankful that they did. Teens who are feeling suicidal may simply not realize that there are resources available to help them, or other ways of coping. They're looking for relief from pain, and there are other ways to get relief. In addition, wanting to kill yourself, in and of itself, can be a traumatic experience—and that's important to keep in mind if you want to help someone get through it. But what's most powerful is helping that person realize that they want to live.

"It came down to this: should I kill myself or should I make myself a life worth living?" asks Kate Bornstein in *Hello, Cruel World*. "And it wasn't so much the question that kept me alive or even my answer. What kept me alive was the notion that it was me who was asking the question. Somewhere inside me there was a me that wanted to stay alive, whether I knew that me yet or not."

Bornstein's book, subtitled *101 Alternatives to Suicide for Teens, Freaks, & Other Outlaws*, offers a variety of alternatives for someone who is feeling deeply suicidal. Her recommendations range from short-term distractions ("do your homework instead," "play a game you like to play," "get a makeover") to long-term, transformative acts ("choose your battles wisely," "make your peace with Death," "try to keep someone else alive").

If that's not enough, a suicide hotline can be a crucial next step. Adolescents are more likely to be willing to talk to a stranger or peer about their feelings before they're ready to approach their parents or other adults. After that, professional help is especially important. In many cases, regular and intensive visits with a psychotherapist can be enough to turn things around.

A Few Other Ideas

This book was written because so many parents, faced with the unthinkable loss of their child to suicide or violence, began looking for a cause. Something to explain—or even to blame. In many cases, it seemed like the child's lifestyle—black clothing, Slayer albums, books describing how to become a wizard and navigate a dungeon—was the obvious culprit. However, the real causes are often more serious, and often more difficult to pin down. Sometimes a teen is hiding out in his room because he's an introvert and needs lots of time alone to recharge; other times it's because she's hearing voices and doesn't want to admit it. It's crucial to find the true cause—not the one that makes life easiest for everyone else but the teen.

Overcoming a teen's mental illness or suicidal feelings is real work for everyone involved. It takes time and resources. It may require adults to be involved in a teen's life in a way that they haven't been since he or she was very young. This comes at a time when teens are fighting hard to gain their independence, and for that reason—or due to mental illness—they may fight others' attempts to help.

"Many [adults] look back at adolescence as a carefree time—somehow forgetting the difficult struggles the teen years held," according to psychiatry professor Elizabeth McCauley. "Some idealize this period as the 'best years of your life,' while others minimize adolescent concerns with a 'what do *you* have to worry about?' attitude. ... It's important for parents of teens to try to understand what it's like to walk in their shoes."

For Further Reading

There are many, many other and better resources out there for parents of teens who are feeling suicidal, who are suffering a mental illness or disorder, or both. This book isn't intended to be one of them, but here are some places to learn more:

www.metanoia.org: A Web site with detailed advice on what to do if you're feeling suicidal, and how to choose a competent counselor. It also features links to deeper descriptions of many of the mental-health conditions described in this chapter.

www.suicidehotlines.com: A list of national suicide crisis call centers, as well as local ones, broken down by state. This site also includes a "what to expect when you call" section. Remember, people who are worried about a suicidal loved one can also call these hotlines for help and advice.

www.oregonyouthline.org: Based in Oregon, Youthline provides a toll-free hotline where teens can discuss suicidal feelings and mental-health concerns with fellow teens, many of whom have been there. Their number is 877-YOUTH-911.

www.teendepression.org: Although this site is littered with ads, it also has good information about adolescents and depression. Includes an advice section for parents on how to approach and aid their depressed teen.

www.bpkids.org: An extensive site with deeper descriptions of bipolar disorder, diagnosis, and treatment, specifically for kids and adolescents.

www.itgetsbetter.org: The It Gets Better Project was created specifically to provide hope and perspective for gay teens who are considering suicide, but many of the videos are inspirational to a broader audience. Even if your teen isn't suicidal for reasons related to his or her sexual orientation, hearing stories about misfit people who survived suicidal feelings (and adolescence) can really help.

www.thetrevorproject.org: If, on the other hand, your teen IS coming to terms with his or her sexual orientation, the folks at the Trevor Project provide round-the-clock crisis counseling as well as online forums so teens can find ways to feel more supported and less alone.

www.livingmatters.com: A site for parents of depressed teens, written by Bev Cobain, a nurse who has survived the suicides of several family members, including her cousin, Nirvana singer Kurt Cobain. Cobain offers advice and resources related to depression and suicidal feelings. She has also written two books, including *When Nothing Matters Anymore: A Survival Guide for Depressed Teens*.

www.familyaware.org: Families for Depression Awareness' Web site provides support for parents and families whose kids are suffering depression.

www.safeyouth.gov: STRYVE, or Striving to Reduce Youth Violence Everywhere, studies the causes of youth violence (including suicide) and is working on prevention strategies. Parents will find lots of helpful information in the resources section of STRYVE's Web site.

Acknowledgments

The Columbine Effect has been in the works for many years and owes its existence to a number of incredible people. Not least are the hundreds of folks who responded to my surveys, answering questions about how they came into video games, heavy metal or paganism and the occult during their teen years. Their voices are the backbone of this book.

Thanks, also, to those who contributed interviews, including Margot Adler, Leland Yee, Steven Leyba, Angelina Fabbro, Abel Gomez, Jeanne Fury, Lonn Friend, Don Daglow, Morgan Jaffit, Tim and Zach Berglund, Evan Jones, Chris and Cisco Piazzo, Corey Scott, Scott Graham, S. Kelley Harrell and Frater Lux Ad Mundi at the Ordo Templi Orientis.

This book has had many helpers behind the scenes who edited, assisted or made key suggestions. My endless appreciation goes to Bonnie Eslinger, Jeff Johnson, Michelle Maitre, Michael Hammond, Sara Gaiser, Nagasiva and Catherine Yronwode, Eric Colon, Mike Aldax, Barry King, Rebecca Murray-Metzger, Alee Karim, Tyler Winegarner, Jaan Uhelszki, Gerard Jones, Ann Powers, Dave Cullen, Melissa and David Andre, Angyl Bender, Hans Anderson, Ted Samson, Jamie Wesson, Peter Davidson, Nadyne Mielke, Saul Sugarman, Arielle Eckstut and David Henry Sterry.

A number of blogs and writers highlighted or published my work as it developed, and their support for what I'm doing often kept me from throwing in the towel, including Ian S. Port, Chris Kohler, Laura Houghton McClure, Whitney Matheson, Mallary Tenore, Alan Scherstuhl, Nico Mara-McKay, Vanessa Van Petten, Jenna Lane, Lenore Skenazy at *Free Range Kids*, Cosmo Lee at *Invisible Oranges*, Darci and Andrew Groves at *Giant Fire Breathing Robot*, Jason Pitzl-Waters at *The Wild*

Hunt, Natalie Zina Walschots at *Canada Arts Connect*, Nathan Thornburgh at *DadWagon* and the folks behind *Musical Warfare* and *City of Devils*.

Thanks most of all to my partner, Devin, and my daughter, Laurel, whose patience while I researched, wrote and published the book was endless. And to our nanny, Mya, who provided many of the hours in which *The Columbine Effect* was created.

Bibliography

Aites, Adrian and Audrey Ewell. *Until the Light Takes Us.* Variance Films, August 12, 2010.

Anderson, Craig A. and Christine R. Murphy. "Violent Video Games and Aggressive Behavior in Young Women." *Aggressive Behavior* Vol 29 (2003), 423-429.

Anderson, Craig A., Nicholas L. Carnagey and Janie Eubanks. "Exposure to Violent Media: The Effects of Songs with Violent Lyrics on Aggressive Thoughts and Feelings." *Journal of Personality and Social Psychology* Vol. 84, No. 5 (2003), 960-97.

Arnett, Jeffrey Jensen. *Metalheads: Heavy Metal Music and Adolescent Alienation.* Boulder, Colorado: WestView Press, 1996.

Arnett, Jeffrey Jensen. "Music at the Edge: The Attraction and Effects of Controversial Music on Young People." In *Kid Stuff: Marketing Sex and Violence to America's Children*, edited by Diane Ravitch and Joseph P. Viteritti. Baltimore, Maryland: The Johns Hopkins University Press, 2003.

Astinus. "The History of Role-Playing, Part IV." *Places to Go, People to Be.* Web. 1998. Accessed Oct. 21, 2010.

Barrowcliffe, Mark. *The Elfish Gene: Dungeons, Dragons and Growing Up Strange.* New York: Soho Press, Inc., 2008.

Bartholomew, Bruce D., and Craig A. Anderson. "Effects of Violent Video Games on Aggressive Behavior: Potential Sex Differences." *Journal of Experimental Social Psychology* 38 (2002), 283-290.

BBC.com. "Two men jailed after violent tram attack in Greater Manchester." July 9, 2012.

Bernstein, Dr. Neil I. *How To Keep Your Teenager Out of Trouble and What to Do If You Can't.* New York: Workman Publishing Company, Inc., 2001.

Bissell, Tom. *Extra Lives: Why Video Games Matter.* New York: Random House, Inc., 2010.

Blabbermouth.net. "Report: SLIPKNOT CD, 'Demonic Drawing' Seized During Search Of Homicide Scene." March 31, 2011.

Bornstein, Kate. *Hello, Cruel World: 101 Alternatives to Suicide for Teens, Freaks, & Other Outlaws.* New York: Seven Stories Press. 2006.

Bowman, Sarah Lynne. *The Functions of Role-Playing Games: How Participants Create Community, Solve Problems and Explore Identity.* Jefferson, North Carolina: McFarland & Company Inc. Publishers, 2010.

Bratton, Anna Jo. "Mall Gunman Was Satanic, Suicidal." *Associated Press*, Dec. 27, 2007.

Bronson, Po, and Ashley Merryman. *NurtureShock: New Thinking About Children.* New York: Twelve/Hachette Book Group, 2009.

Burtenshaw, Madeline. "An Open Letter To The Church of England." *Quoth The Raven* (personal blog), July 5, 2012.

Caldwell, Simon. "Exorcist warns parents of rise in 'demonic' websites." *Catholic Herald,* February 2, 2011.

Capper, Andy and Gabi Safire. *Heavy Metal in Baghdad: The Story of Acrassicauda.* New York: MTV Books, 2009.

Carpenter, Deborah. *The Everything Parent's Guide to Dealing with Bullies.* Avon, Massachusetts: F+W Media, Inc. 2009.

Centers for Disease Control. "Healthy Youth! Health Topics: Alcohol & Drug Use." http://www.cdc.gov/HealthyYouth/alcoholdrug/index.htm.

Chonin, Neva. "Bay Area Goths Say Media Has It Wrong: Many teens offended by snap association of subculture and suspects." *San Francisco Chronicle,* April 22, 1999.

Christenson, Peter G. "Equipment for Living: How Popular Music Fits in the Lives of Youth." In *Kid Stuff: Marketing Sex and Violence to America's Children,* edited by Diane Ravitch and Joseph P. Viteritti. Baltimore, Maryland: The Johns Hopkins University Press, 2003.

Cobain, Bev. *When Nothing Matters Anymore: A survival guide for depressed teens.* Minneapolis, MN: Free Spirit Publishing, 1998.

Cobb, Nancy. *Adolescence: Continuity, Change and Diversity (Fifth Edition).* New York: McGraw-Hill, 2004.

Cooper, Cynthia A. *Violence in the Media and Its Influence on Criminal Defense.* Jefferson, North Carolina: McFarland & Company, Inc., 2007.

"Colo. Church shooting victims identified." *Denver Post,* December 12, 2007.

Costikyan, Greg. "The Problem of Video Game Violence is Exaggerated." In *Is Media Violence a Problem?,* edited by James D. Torr. San Diego, California: Greenhaven Press, 2002.

Cullen, Dave. *Columbine*. New York: Twelve/Hachette Book Group, 2009.

Cutler, Maggie. "Research on the Effects of Media Violence is Inconclusive." In *Is Media Violence a Problem?*, edited by James D. Torr. San Diego, California: Greenhaven Press, 2002.

Dess, Jeff. *Turn Up The Music: Prevention Strategies to Help Parents Through the Rap, Rock and Metal Years for Parents, Educators and Other Adults Who Care About Kids.* New York: iUniverse, Inc., 2004.

Wilson, Barbara J. and Nicole Martins, "The Impact of Violent Music on Youth." In *The Handbook of Children, Culture and Violence*, edited by Nancy E. Dowd, Dorothy G. Singer and Robin Fretwell Wilson. Thousand Oaks, California: Sage Publications, Inc., 2006.

Dugan, Ellen. *Elements of Witchcraft: Natural Magick for Teens.* St. Paul, Minnesota: Llewellyn Publications, 2004.

Echols, Damien. *Almost Home: My Life Story Vol. 1.* New York: iUniverse, 2005.

Edwards, Emily D. *Metaphysical Media: The Occult Experience in Popular Culture.* Carbondale, Illinois: Southern Illinois University Press, 2005.

Entertainment Software Association. "Industry Facts." http://www.theesa.com.

Entertainment Software Rating Board. "Game Ratings & Descriptor Guide." http://www.esrb.org.

Feniak, Jenny. "Slayer Likes Bad-Boy Image." *Edmonton Sun,* July 9, 2006. http://jam.canoe.ca/Music/2006/07/09/1675185.html

Franklin, Joseph C. "How Pain Can Make You Feel Better: Scientists find a strange connection between physical pain and positive emotions." *Scientific American,* November 16, 2010.

Freedman, Jonathan L. *Media Violence and its Effect on Aggression: Assessing the Scientific Evidence.* Toronto, Canada: University of Toronto Press, 2002.

Freedom du Lac, J. "Jared Loughner's music choice, Drowning Pool's 'Bodies,' strikes chilling chord." *The Washington Post,* January 10, 2011.

Friesen, Bruce K. and Warren Helfrich. "Social Justice and Sexism for Adolescents: A Content Analysis of Lyrical Themes and Gender Presentations in Canadian Heavy Metal Music, 1985-1991." In *Youth Culture: Identity in a Postmodern World,* edited by Jonathon S. Epstein. Malden, Massachusetts: Blackwell Publishers, 1998.

Friesen, Bruce K. "Powerlessness in Adolescence: Exploiting Heavy Metal Listeners." In *Marginal Conventions: Popular Culture, Mass Media and Social Deviance,* edited by Clinton R. Sanders. Bowling Green, Ohio: Bowling Green State University Popular Press, 1990.

Fuller, Robert. *Naming the Antichrist: The History of an American Obsession.* New York: Oxford University Press, 1995.

Gaines, Donna. *Teenage Wasteland: Suburbia's Dead-end Kids.* Chicago: University of Chicago Press, 1990.

Garbarino, James. *Lost Boys: Why Our Sons Turn Violent and How We Can Save Them.* New York: The Free Press, 1999.

Gentile, Douglas A., Hyekyung Choo, Albert Liau, Timothy Sim, Dongdong Li, Daniel Fung, and Angeline Khoo. "Pathological Video Game Use Among Youths: A Two-Year Longitudinal Study." *Pediatrics,* January 17, 2011.

Gilsdorf, Ethan. "How Dungeons & Dragons Changed My Life." *Salon.com*, March 8, 2011.

Goodlad, Lauren M.E. and Michael Bibby, introduction to *Goth: Undead Subculture,* edited by Lauren M.E. Goodlad and Michael Bibby. Durham, North Carolina: Duke University Press, 2007.

Google Health. "Suicide and Suicidal Behavior." Publish date unknown. Accessed November 11, 2010.　　https://health .google.com/health/ref/Suicide+and+suicidal+behavior.

Gore, Tipper. *Raising PG Kids in an X-Rated Society: What Parents Can Do to Protect their Children From Sex and Violence in the Media.* Nashville, Tennessee: Abingdon Press, 1987.

Greenfield, Patricia Marks. *Mind and Media: The Effects of Television, Video Games and Computers.* Cambridge, Massachusetts: Harvard University Press, 1984.

Halford, Rob. Interview with Terri Gross, *Fresh Air.* National Public Radio, June 21, 2005.

Harshbarger, Jeff, with Liz Harshbarger. *From Darkness to Light: How to Rescue Someone You Love From the Occult.* Gainesville, Florida: Bridge-Logos, 2004.

Hasan, Heba. "The Hunger Games Trilogy Climbs on List of Most-Challenged Books." *TIME*, April 10, 2012.

Hayward, Andrew. "Tekken 6." *Gamepro.* October 26, 2009. *Time Newsfeed.* April 10, 2012.

Healy, Jack. "Threats and Killings Striking Fear Among Young Iraqis, Including Gays." *The New York Times*, March 11, 2012.

Henderson, Barney. "Mass Shooter Adam Lanza 'Spent Hours Playing Call Of Duty." *Business Insider,* December 18, 2012. http://www.businessinsider.com/adam-lanza-played-call-of-duty-2012-12.

Hetfield, James. Interview with Terri Gross, *Fresh Air*. National Public Radio, November 9, 2004.

Hicks, Robert D. *In Pursuit of Satan: The Police and the Occult*. Buffalo, New York: Prometheus Books, 1991.

Hodkinson, Paul. *Goth: Identity, Style, and Subculture*. Oxford, United Kingdom: Berg, 2002.

Inaba, Darryl S. and William E. Cohen. *Uppers, Downers, All Arounders: Physical and Mental Effects of Psychoactive Drugs (Fifth Edition)*. Medford, Oregon: CNS Publications, Inc. 2004.

Johnson, Steven. *Everything Bad is Good for You: How Today's Popular Culture is Actually Making Us Smarter*. New York: Riverhead Books, 2005.

Jones, Gerard. *Killing Monsters: Why Children Need Fantasy, Super Heroes and Make-Believe Violence*. New York: Basic Books, 2002.

Jung, Carl: "Good and Evil in Analytical Psychology." In *Civilization in Transition*, 2d ed., vol. 10, June 18, 2005.

Kail, Tony M. *A Cop's Guide to Occult Investigations: Understanding Satanism, Santeria, Wicca and Other Alternative Religions*. Boulder, Colorado: Paladin Press, 2003.

Kain, Erik. "Ralph Nader Calls Violent Video Games 'Electronic Child Molesters.'" *Forbes.com*, January 21, 2013. http://www.forbes.com/sites/erikkain/2013/01/21/ralph-nader-calls-violent-video-games-electronic-child-molesters/

Katz, John. "Voices from the Hellmouth." *Slashdot*, April 26, 1999.

Katz, John. "Report from Hell High." *Brill's Content*,

July/August 1999.

Kelleher, Michael J. *When Good Kids Kill.* Westport, Connecticut: Praeger Publishers, 1998.

Kelly, Kim. "How Black Metal Saved My Life—Or, At Least, My Sanity." *XOJane*, January 31, 2013.

Kinnaman, David and Gabe Lyons. *UnChristian: What a New Generation Thinks Really Thinks About Christianity and Why it Matters.* Grand Rapids, Michigan: Baker Books, 2007.

Klebold, Susan. "I Will Never Know Why." *O, The Oprah Magazine.* October 13, 2009.

Kondlon, Dan, and Michael Thompson. *Raising Cain: Protecting the Emotional Life of Boys.* New York: Ballantine Books, 1999.

Kosmin, Barry A. and Ariela Keysar (principal investigators). *American Religious Identification Survey 2008.* Sponsored by Trinity College, Hartford, Connecticut.

Kotarba, Joseph A. "The Postmodernization of Rock and Roll Music: The Case of Metallica." In *Adolescents and their Music: If It's Too Loud, You're Too Old,* edited by Jonathan Epstein. New York: Garland Publishing, Inc., 1994.

Kuchera, Ben. "Harder for Kids to Buy an M-Rated Video Game Than See an R-Rated Movie. *Ars Technica,* September 16, 2010.

Kuchera, Ben. "*How Games Saved My Life* offers stories of hope from gamers." *Ars Technica,* September 14, 2011.

L., N. "Why World of Warcraft is Good for You."*The Economist,* September 13, 2010.

Larson, Bob. *Rock & Roll: The Devil's Diversion.* McCook,

Nebraska: Self-published, 1967.

Larson, Bob. *Larson's Book of Rock: For Those Who Listen To The Words and Don't Like What They Hear*. Wheaton, Illinois: Tyndale House, 1980.

Lee, Cosmo. "Interview: Watain." *Invisible Oranges*, June 9, 2010. http://www.invisibleoranges.com/2010/06/interview-watain/

Leveritt, Mara: *Devil's Knot: The True Story of the West Memphis Three*. New York: Atria Books, 2002.

Levitin, Daniel J. *This is Your Brain On Music: The Science of a Human Obsession*. New York: Penguin Group, 2006.

Livescience staff. "Risk-Glorifying Video Games Linked to Reckless Driving." *Livescience.com*, September 11, 2012. http://www.livescience.com/23104-video-games-teen-reckless-driving.html#.

The Local. "Video games 'don't make kids violent': study." December 6, 2011. http://www.thelocal.se/37756/20111206/#.UXLSxSvEog9.

Long, Liza. "I am Adam Lanza's Mother: It's time to talk about mental illness." *The Blue Review*, December 15, 2012. http://thebluereview.org/i-am-adam-lanzas-mother/.

Manson, Marilyn. "Columbine: Whose Fault Is It?" *Rolling Stone*, June 24, 1999.

Marcus, David L. *What it Takes to Pull Me Through: Why Teenagers Get in Trouble and How Four of Them Got Out*. New York: Houghton Mifflin Company, 2005.

Markson, Stephen L. "Claims-Making, Quasi-Theories and the Social Construction of the Rock 'N' Roll Menace." In *Marginal Conventions: Popular Culture, Mass Media and Social*

Deviance, edited by Clinton R. Sanders. Bowling Green, Ohio: Bowling Green State University Popular Press, 1990.

Mayko, Michael P. "Adam Lanza's online gaming history probed." *SFGate*, December 24, 2012. http://www.sfgate .com/crime/article/Adam-Lanza-s-online-gaming-history-probed-4141582.php.

Merlin. "It's Official: Heavy Metal Is A Bigger Religion In The UK Than Scientology, Druidism And... Um... Shamanism." *Metalhammer.co.uk*, December 11, 2012.

Metanoia. "If You Are Thinking About Suicide ... Read This First." Accessed November 11, 2010. http://www.metanoia.org/ suicide/.

Meyer, Jeremy P., David Migoya and Christopher N. Osher. "YOUR Columbine: Gunman wrote of rejection as reason for revenge." *The Denver Post*, December 12, 2007.

Molina, Brett. "Believe the hype on *Call of Duty: Modern Warfare 2*." *USA Today*, November 10, 2009.

Moore, Michael. *Bowling for Columbine*. United Artists, October 11, 2002.

Moorey, Teresa. *Spellbound: The Teenage Witch's Handbook*. Berkeley, California: Ulysses Press, 2002.

Moreman, Christopher M. "Devil Music and the Great Beast: Ozzy Osbourne, Aleister Crowley, and the Christian Right." In *Journal of Religion and Popular Culture* Vol. 5, Fall 2003.

MSNBC staff. "Sketchy reports emerge on alleged high school gunman." *MSNBC.com*, February 27, 2012.

National Institutes of Mental Health. "Suicide in the U.S.: Statistics and Prevention." Publish date unknown. Accessed November 11, 2010. http://www.nimh.nih.gov/health/

publications/suicide-in-the-us-statistics-and-prevention/index.shtml.

Novak, Jennie, and Luis Levy. *Play the Game: A Parent's Guide to Video Games*. Boston, Massachusetts: Thompson Course Technology, 2007.

Nuzum, Eric. *Parental Advisory: Music Censorship in America*. New York: HarperCollins, 2001.

"Ohio Teen Accused of E-mailing Satanic Leader with Threat to Kill his Own Grandparents," *Associated Press*, December 16, 2007.

Olepeder. "LARPs can change the world." *Imagonem*, March 27, 2012.

Palladino, Grace. *Teenagers: An American History*. New York: BasicBooks, 1996.

Parks, Sharon. *The Critical Years: The Young Adult Search for a Faith to Live By*. San Francisco: Harper & Row, 1986.

Parrott, Les. *Helping Your Struggling Teenager: A Parenting Handbook on Thirty-Six Common Problems*. Grand Rapids, Michigan: Zondervan Publishing House, 1993.

Parry, Wynne. "Battling the Boys: Educators Grapple with Violent Play." *LiveScience.com*, August 29, 2010.

Poplak, Richard. "Heavy Metal Cairo." *The Daily Maverick*. February 8, 2011.

Pow, Helen. "CSI student, 17, who 'murdered and dismembered Jessica Ridgeway was a Goth, wore black and was infatuated with death.'" *The Daily Mail*, October 25, 2012.

Provenzo, Eugene F. "Violence in Video Games is a Serious Problem." In *Is Media Violence a Problem?*, edited by James D.

Torr. San Diego, California: Greenhaven Press, 2002.

Pulling, Pat, with Kathy Cawthon. *The Devil's Web: Who is Stalking Your Children for Satan?* Lafayette, Louisiana: Huntington House, 1989.

Purcell, Natalie J. *Death Metal Music: The Passion and Politics of a Subculture.* New York: McFarland & Company, Inc., 2003.

Rossignol, Jim. *This Gaming Life: Travels in Three Cities.* Michigan: Digital Culture Books, University of Michigan Press, 2009.

Pollack, William S., with Todd Shuster. *Real Boys' Voices.* New York: Penguin Books, 2001.

Rivera, Geraldo. "Devil Worship: Exposing Satan's Underground." *The Geraldo Rivera Show.* October 22, 1988.

Ryerson University press release. "Gamers may not be desensitized by violent video games: Ryerson study." February 15, 2011.

Sanders, Clinton R. "A Lot of People Like It: The Relationship Between Deviance and Popular Culture." In *Marginal Conventions: Popular Culture, Mass Media and Social Deviance* edited by Clinton R. Sanders. Bowling Green, Onio: Bowling Green State University Popular Press, 1990.

San Francisco Chronicle staff and wire reports. "Classmates Describe Shooters As Obsessed With Goth World: 'Trench Coat Mafia' members treated as social outcasts." *San Francisco Chronicle*, April 21, 1999.

Scotsman.com. "Teenage yobs batter mum for being 'goth.'" March 27, 2012.

Sattin, Samuel. "Dungeons and Dragons: My dorky literary muse." *Salon.com,* December 8, 2012.

Scelfo, Julie. "In Their Backyard." *Brill's Content,* July/August 1999.

Schoebelen, William. "Straight Talk on Dungeons & Dragons." 1984. Accessed on Oct. 17, 2010. http://www.chick.com/articles/dnd.asp.

Shamoo, Tonia K. and Philip G. Patros. *Helping Your Child Cope with Depression and Suicidal Thoughts.* San Francisco, California: Josey-Bass Inc. Publishers, 1990.

Shelton, Charles M. *Adolescent Spirituality: Pastoral Ministry for High School and College Youth.* New York: Crossroad Publishing Company, 1989.

Schulze, Quentin J., Roy M. Anker, James D. Bratt, William D. Romanowski, John W. Worst and Lambert Zuidervaart. *Dancing in the Dark: Youth, Popular Culture and the Electronic Media.* Grand Rapids, Michigan: Wm. B. Erdmans Publishing Co., 1991.

Seigel, Jessica. "Hugging the Spotlight." *Brill's Content,* July/August 1999.

Shea, Christopher. "Video Games Inoculate Against Nightmares." *Wall Street Journal Blogs,* January 13, 2012.

Siemaszko, Corky. "Teenager who allegedly opened fire in Baltimore area high school was heavy metal misfit obsessed with Rammstein and Manson Family." *New York Daily News,* August 28, 2012.

Sinan, Omar. "In Egypt, Heavy-Metal Music is Making a Comeback. *Daily News Egypt.* August 18, 2006.

Smith, Timothy. *The Seven Cries of Today's Teens.* Brentwood, Tennessee: Integrity Publishers, 2003.

Sommers, Christina Hoff. *The War Against Boys: How Misguided Feminism is Harming Our Young Men.* New York: Simon & Schuster, 2000.

Stackpole, Michael. "The Pulling Report." 1990. Accessed October 21, 2010. http://www.rpgstudies.net/stackpole/pulling_report.html.

Sternheimer, Karen. *It's Not The Media: The Truth About Pop Culture's Influence on Children.* Boulder, Colorado: Westview Press/Perseus Books Group, 2003.

Stewart, David J. "Goth will Destroy Your Child!" Publish date unknown. Accessed March 30, 2008. http://www.jesus-is-savior.com/Evils%20in%20America/goth.htm.

Swedenburg, Ted. "UA Anthropologist Studies 'Moral Panic' in Egypt." Press release. December 11, 2000.

Taylor, Alastair. "Family lay floral tributes for Casey." *The Sun,* February 18, 2012.

Teti, John. *"Tom Clancy's Splinter Cell Conviction."* *The Onion: A.V. Club,* April 19, 2010.

The D20. *Podcast #9.* May 3, 2008. http://thed2o.net/media/podcast9_interview_rough.mp3.

Thierer, Adam. "Fact and Fiction in the Debate Over Video Game Regulation." *Progress On Point: Periodic Commentaries on the Policy Debate,* issue 13.7, March 2006.

Thornburgh, Nathan. "Magic Kingdom: Why Live-Action Role Playing is one of Denmark's Most Popular Pastimes." *Time.com,* July 20, 2012.

Vedantam, Shankar. "Same Old Song, But With a Different Meaning." *Washington Post,* January 22, 2008.

Ward, Michael R., Scott Cunningham and Benjamin Engelstätter. "Understanding the Effects of Violent Video Games on Violent Crime." April 9, 2011.

Watson, Justin. *The Martyrs of Columbine: Faith and the Politics of Tragedy.* New York: Palgrave MacMillan, 2002.

Weinstein, Deena. "Rock: Youth and its Music." In *Adolescents and their Music: If It's Too Loud, You're Too Old,* edited by Jonathan Epstein. New York: Garland Publishing, Inc., 1994.

Weinstein, Deena. "Expendable Youth: The Rise and Fall of Youth Subculture." In *Adolescents and their Music: If It's Too Loud, You're Too Old,* edited by Jonathan Epstein. New York: Garland Publishing, Inc., 1994.

Wills, Thomas Ashby and Jody A. Resko, "Social Support and Behavior Toward Others: Some Paradoxes and Some Directions." In *The Social Psychology of Good and Evil*, edited by Arthur G. Miller. New York: Guilford Press, 2004.

Williams, Christopher. "MPs call for violent video game ban after Breivik claims that he 'trained' on Call of Duty: Modern Warfare." *The Telegraph*, May 17, 2012. http://www.telegraph.co.uk/technology/video-games/9272774/MPs-call-for-violent-video-game-ban-after-Breivik-claims-that-he-trained-on-Call-of-Duty-Modern-Warfare.html#.

Williams, J. Patrick, Sean Q. Hendricks and W. Keith Winkler. *Gaming as Culture: Essays on Reality, Identity and Experience in Fantasy Games.* Jefferson, North Carolina: McFarland & Company, Inc. Publishers, 2006.

Williams, Kate. *A Parent's Guide for Suicidal and Depressed Teens.* Center City, Minnesota: Hazelden Foundation, 1995.

Wooden, Cindy. "Vatican newspaper says Harry Potter film champions values." *Catholic News Service*, July 12, 2011.

WorldNetDaily. "Gunman boasted of following 'wickedest man in the world.' Email to ministry: 'I have studied, practiced teachings' of occultists.'" March 30, 2008. http://www.wnd.com/?pageId=45061.

Yong, Ed. "12-year-old uses Dungeons and Dragons to help scientist dad with his research." *Discover Magazine Blogs.* October 30, 2012.

About the Author

Beth Winegarner is a longtime journalist whose work has appeared in the *New Yorker, Mother Jones, USA Today, Wired, Ars Technica,* the *San Francisco Chronicle,* the *San Francisco Examiner, San Francisco Magazine, SF Weekly, PopMatters* and many others. She is the author of several books, including *Read the Music: Essays on Sound* and a novel, *Beloved.* She holds as degree in sociology from the University of California at Berkeley. A native of northern California, she lives in San Francisco with her family. For more, visit www.bethwinegarner.com. For her blog on topics included in *The Columbine Effect*, visit http://backwardmessages. wordpress.com.

Lightning Source UK Ltd.
Milton Keynes UK
UKOW01f0728291216
290947UK00001BA/390/P